HANGD(

Shoulder to Sl

Book One of the Hangdog Trilogy

By: Tylie Vaughan Eaves

Vertū Publishing, 2018

A Component of Vertū Marketing, LLC

VERTŪ PUBLISHING
A Component of Vertū Marketing LLC
www.vertu-marketing.com

Ordering Information:
Quantity sales. Special discounts are available on quantity purchases by corporations, associations, and others. For details, contact the publisher at the address above.
Orders by U.S. trade bookstores and wholesalers.
Please contact: Tel: (866) 779-0795.

Printed in the United States of America
ISBN 9780692149300

ACKNOWLEDGEMENTS

Firstly, all my thanks and praise be to God – for everything.

I would also like to thank my husband, Wade Eaves, who is my chief advice giver, confidant, consultant and genuine hero – Thank you for your service as a husband, father and Airman, but especially, as a man of God. Special thanks to my children, for sacrificing their time and general volume levels so I can write in relative peace – I love you all, with an indescribable fierceness. Massive thanks to Deborah Vaughan, who is my editor extraordinaire and the woman who gave me life – It, quite literally, pays to be born to a professional wordsmith. And finally, thanks to John Dozier and Roy Fanning, for stepping in as my pundits for all things related to the United States Marine Corps and, of course, for their service and sacrifice.

Hangdog – Shoulder to Shoulder

PART ONE

CHAPTER ONE

"Susan … Leigh … McCarter."

The voice echoed over the school auditorium sound system.

"Donald … James … McKie."

Cheers and applause followed each name, but the voice at the microphone never wavered. It was monotonous. Formal. It was the same this year as it had been last year, and the year before that, and, frankly, about as far back as anyone could remember. Assistant Principal Harriet Reid had held the job long enough to read out the names of graduates who were children of graduates. But not for a single one would she ever intone an air of excitement. For all the enthusiasm she put into the job, she could have been a clerk calling names at the DMV instead of announcing the end of a high school career.

"Heather … Catherine … McKenzie."

The crowd, on the other hand, was boisterous. There were cheers, screams and an occasional air-horn blast. The room was packed to the brim with parents, grandparents, friends, cousins, teachers and students. Every graduate was celebrated, with little pockets of family and friends popping up from the sea of faces to show special interest in their particular hero. Facebook was plastered with photos and well-wishes for new graduates and at least one-in-four selfies were cap-and-gown clad.

As unenthusiastic as she was, even Harriet Reid halted a moment before reading the next name. It was only the briefest of pauses, but she knew the next name on her list would signal a volcanic eruption of noise.

"Jonathan … Beau … McKnight."

It wasn't the first time Beau McKnight had heard that kind of noise. He had played football well enough to earn a college scholarship. The records he'd set as a tight end would stand for years. He'd also been the hard-blocking, slam-dunking center for the school's basketball team and was, by all accounts, a local household name.

Without a doubt, Beau was the most dominating student personality at Jackson High, and he bounced up the stairs toward Principal Eric Raven with ever-typical enthusiasm. Raven was a man of medium build, and his dark suit and conservative tie were perfectly made for the formal occasion. Then again, his crisp dress shirts and small-knotted neckties were a staple scene at the school. It was hard to imagine him relaxing. You'd almost expect the man to don his nice shirt and tie if the Raven family spent a week at the beach.

The principal extended his hand toward Jonathan Beau McKnight. He'd already shaken the hands of half the senior class. Now, he used every ounce of his body language to signal to the huge man-child coming toward him that *this* was a moment for decorum.

Beau ignored the handshake. No amount of body language could shake his excitement or his intent.

He grabbed the principal around the waist, bear-hugged him until his feet left the floor, and grinned from ear to ear. Making it to the finish line of high school had been easy on the football field — but tough in the classroom. Beau was squeezing every moment out of the celebration, and it happened to be Raven who could solve his need to squeeze. He shook the man just for a moment, and then took him back to the floor.

While the principal straightened his glasses, Beau turned to the adoring crowd and threw his arms into the air. In the midst of the whoops and hollers and just before exiting the stage, he put the finishing touch on his public display of enthusiasm by lowering himself into a deep bow.

Harriett Reid held on to the podium, terrified that Beau might have a bear hug for her. But instead, he gallantly tipped his graduation cap as he passed her and then left the stage. Order was briefly restored.

"Samuel … Eli … McKnight."

In some ways, the celebration was as identical for Eli McKnight as it had been for his identical twin brother. But though they looked like mirror images, Eli was a far cry from Beau. Eli strolled across the stage and shook Principal Raven's hand with all the decorum the man could desire and politely accepted his diploma. Because it was time for another name, only Eli's family saw what came next.

~

It was only for a moment, just a brief pause. But Eli bowed his head, closed his eyes and silently gave thanks. Then he slipped off the stage into the waiting arms of his brother. The bear-hug on the auditorium floor looked a little like a battle between two giants. But it was no fight. There had been plenty of those over the years, yes. But this time, it was a pure brother-on-brother celebration. Eli threw an arm over his brother's shoulder, and the two of them walked back to their seats and cheered through the parade of the remainder of their senior class. Had it not been for the honors collar over his graduation gown, a stranger might not have been able to tell Eli from Beau.

It was no wonder the pair stood out.

Tall, well-muscled, with straight-backed posture, they had broad shoulders and bright eyes. Their faces were clean-shaven, and their hair was cut short. Each had a strong, set jaw and appeared to be the kind of kid who never suffered from acne. They had gone through braces together as sophomores, and now had wide, perfectly-aligned, All-American smiles set between picture-perfect dimples. To say their features were chiseled would be an understatement. In the high school food chain, the McKnight brothers were standing proudly at the top.

In time, the list of graduates came down to a final name.

"Ivy ... Catherine ... Zellway."

The crowd cheered and the sea of students stirred restlessly in their seats upon hearing the familiar syllables of the final name on Raven's list, the same final name that had been called at many of their corporate school functions for more than a decade. Eli watched in silence. She had taken his breath away a long time ago, long before this day, and she still held him speechless in every way a teenage giant could be held. For Eli, time slowed down as Ivy crossed the stage. She was petite and poised, like the lead character in some fantasy novel about fairies and elves. She politely shook Principal Raven's hand, and, as she walked away, she reached for the tassel that dangled from her Dijon mustard-hued cap, stopped at center stage and turned to face her classmates.

Meanwhile, Beau readied himself for a much less refined moment. Even as Ivy was awarded the last diploma of the ceremony, he'd been reaching beneath his seat to grab the two rolls of cheap toilet paper he'd swiped from the boys' restroom when he and his band of football brothers first arrived at the auditorium for the commencement-rehearsal walkthrough.

Principal Raven signaled for the group to stand together.

On Ivy's perfectly executed cue, the entire graduating class simultaneously moved the tassels, dangling in anticipation, from right to left across their Dijon-colored mortarboards. Principal Raven leaned into the microphone and, as unenthused albeit as crisply as ever, announced, "Congratulations, class of 2011. You are now graduates."

As if under electrical power, Dijon caps flew through the air in all directions. Silly string arched across the room from all angles, creating a multi-colored cargo net of pure, semi-solid, joy. Beau loosed his toilet paper rolls in high arcs, with all the finesse one would expect from a star athlete. And almost as if on his cue, several of his testosterone-riddled fellow graduates launched their own toilet paper assault on the room full of celebrating families and friends.

Ivy found her way off stage and made an elegant bee-line toward Eli. Her long, soft brown hair blew slightly behind her as she walked, and, as she moved, she struggled fruitlessly with her graduation cap. "I couldn't get my cap off!" she said to Eli, almost singing with laughter. "Lisa put enough bobby pins in my hair that I could probably wear this thing for the rest of my life if I wanted to."

Eli reached up and worked his giant fingers against the grips of what felt like a nest of bobby pins, "Seriously?" he asked. "I'm the last person in this room who needs to be doing this." Together, the two of them worked her free of the nest of bobby pins and the confines of her cap. Ivy rolled with laughter as Eli mocked his own ability to perform delicate tasks with his massive hands. "Let me just work this piece out, and you'll be looking fierce," he spoke in a high-pitched voice and laid on a heavy lisp. "Girl, you have got it go-ing-on." He put his hand on his hip and snapped his fingers in a Z formation. He kept a straight face throughout his performance, which succeeded in catapulting Ivy into a fit of laughter so deep no sound came from her body and tears filled her almond-shaped eyes. Finally, her goofy hero released her from her hair-accessory prison and she began smoothing her hair with her hands. If Ivy was going to throw her cap in the air now, she'd have to go on a solo flight.

Standing next to the tower known as Eli, Ivy looked especially tiny. Something about her, though, made her appear larger than her physical size. She possessed true beauty — something that a pretty face and graceful physique alone could never create. Classic, elegant and truly magnetic, it was easy for anyone to see why Eli had been mesmerized for most of his high school career. The couple had attended the school's Christmas Dance two years prior and had been an item ever since. She cheered him through everything he did, and he reciprocated; they were the "Brad and Angelina" of Jackson High, and everyone, from every clique, knew it. To no one's surprise but their own, the yearbook had recently revealed that the pair had been chosen "Cutest Couple."

Eli lifted one of his big arms and placed it ever so gently around her. He leaned in, pointing gallantly to his perfectly-dimpled cheek. Ivy gave him one quick peck, and he watched as her eyes darted cautiously around the room. She made a sharp “tsk” sound when she spotted Valerie McKnight, and then she said to her suitor, “I knew it. Your mom is right there."

"Are you kidding me?" Eli scoffed, laughing and feigning a wounded heart over the ever-so-brief peck on his cheek. “This is one of the biggest days of our lives, and that’s all I get?” He laughed to himself as Ivy gave him a girlish jab to the ribs. Eli waved to his parents and a crowd of other relatives who were carefully making their way down from the bleachers to the silly-string laden gym floor. Beau spotted their descent and pulled himself away from the toilet paper battle, hurling one final bomb before he ran his massive frame over to stand with his brother and Ivy. Together, they watched the group moving down the bleachers, in anticipation of the impending hug-fest once the family reached their chosen piece of real estate on the gym floor.

"Ivy, Honey … you can do better than that!"

Valerie’s accent dripped with sweet tea and buttered biscuits and every word rang on twice as long as it needed to. The way she approached every situation was so endearing that it was almost impossible to imagine she’d ever been angry in her life. She gave Ivy a wink after she spoke, making it obvious that she was referring to the ever so brief micro-kiss she’d witnessed moments before. She spread her slender arms wide and wiggled her perfectly manicured fingers in a not-so-subtle signal to her sons — hugs were now a mandate.

Ivy felt her cheeks get slightly hot, but her minor embarrassment dissolved as quickly as it started when Eli chuckled and squeezed her hand. Valerie McKnight had no daughters, and Ivy Zellway had been practically adopted by the woman ever since she'd been allowed to help pick her corsage for the Christmas Dance two years earlier. Ivy knew it, and Valerie didn't hide it. Valerie turned her widespread arms to Beau and grabbed him around his big bear neck in an embrace reserved only for mothers and sons.

"You're choking the life out of me, Mom!" Beau gurgled.

Valerie let go of Beau's neck and cupped his chiseled chin in her dainty, but oddly strong fingers, squeezing his cheeks together so his lips looked slightly fishlike. Her shoulder-length blonde hair bounced as she spouted playfully, "You're never too big to get that tail whooped, you know!" Beau grabbed her around her deceptively delicate-looking waist and lifted her into the air for a moment. She squealed, "That's more like it boy!" Because of her statuesque height and the heels that made her even taller, her trip back to the floor was brief. But as soon as her stilettos were back on solid ground, she turned toward Ivy and squealed again.

Eli took advantage of the interchange between the two to greet his father. His mother's hugs were legendary for their choke-hold strength. He knew he'd soon get his turn. But for the moment, he was eye-to-eye with his father, whose expression made it clearly evident he had no intentions of trying to contain his pride or his enthusiasm.

Joseph McKnight, better known as Joe, shared his sons' wide, perfect grins. And at this moment, Eli thought for sure every single one of the man's thirty-two teeth were visible. Joe had never been stoic. He had always been forthright with his feelings, and his sons never wondered for a moment if there was love between them. He threw one of his large, calloused hands onto Eli's shoulder. The other was outstretched, awaiting his son's mirroring palm. Eli saw his dad's eyes welling up with tears. "Don't you do it old man." They both laughed. Well, Joe laughed and cried at the same time, as their masculine handshake melded into a Colossus like embrace between a father and his son.

The moment ended when Valerie decided she'd waited long enough to strangle her other baby boy. The two parents swapped sons as seamlessly as they had for the last eighteen years. It was the perfect display of parental teamwork, which had become second nature over time.

"Move it or lose it, Val. It's my turn," Joe boomed, still in the midst of a laugh-cry.

Valerie lunged for Eli, who braced himself for a momentous, legendary, Valerie McKnight hug. He certainly wasn't disappointed. She planted a good twenty to thirty mom-kisses on his smooth skin in short succession and squealed out her pride and adoration without fail.

A few steps away, Beau had managed to turn his own embrace with his father into a miniature wrestling match and had actually succeeded in lifting his equally-weighted elder off the floor a few inches. Joe grunted as the air expelled rapidly from his lungs, and Beau laughingly released him.

"I'm so, so proud of you both," their beaming father said, loudly enough to be heard by the entire family tribe, as he stretched his arms out wide to place a hand on the shoulder of each son. "Today is a good day!"

The remaining members of the family buzzed around the boys like bees around a flowering bush. Nana McKnight left lipstick prints on every family member in sight, Aunt Kay cried… because Aunt Kay was a crier. Uncle Pete, known affectionately as "Sweet Pete" to friends and family, shocked no one with his ever-typical combination of inappropriate comments and lovability. Valerie's little brother put his foot in his mouth so often, most people had simply come to expect it as the man's daily modus operandi. Today's auspicious occasion proved to be no exception. He was the only adult in the auditorium who was still shouting and whoo-wheeing at the top of his lungs, drawing glances from strangers all across the auditorium.

The group threw hugs as if it had been years since they'd seen one another, kisses as though they were tossing beads from a float at Mardi Gras, and the male majority engaged in the occasional fist bump or slap on the back in the moments when the deep levels of affection threatened their masculinity.

CHAPTER TWO

The jovial banter had been in full effect for around five minutes when Ivy turned to Eli and said, “I’d better go meet Mom and Dad. They’ve finally made it down to the main floor.”

Valerie saw the Zellways from across the room and sensed the forthcoming parting of ways for the young couple. She raised her hand and waved across the gym to Ivy’s parents. She then glided over to the young couple as quickly and as gracefully as she could on four-inch heels.

“Are you joining us for dinner, Honey?”

“No ma’am, my parents have something planned at the house. Eli is going to pick me up later tonight.” Ivy smiled a sweet smile, the same sweet smile she had used in declining invitations her entire life, sincere and disarming in a way that made the inviter all the more sorry that she wouldn’t be there.

"Well, poop. But I can't say I blame them. They must be busting at the seams with pride! We'll miss you. Tell your mama and daddy that Joe and I said 'Hello.'"

"Yes ma'am."

Valerie leaned in for one last hug and, in typical Valerie fashion, she stole a moment to tuck the girl's hair behind her ears before she walked away. "Earrings like those are meant to be seen, Darlin'." She smiled and patted her son's shoulder, giving him a quick wink, before she began her stiletto-clad semi-glide back toward her still-buzzing family.

"You like them, don't you?" Eli passive-aggressively sought Ivy's approval of his graduation gift to her. Shortly before the mustard mob of the senior class had lined up for the big march, Eli had presented Ivy with a professionally wrapped, robin-egg blue box containing a pair of earrings that were the product of two months' worth of Saturdays spent doing yard work in his neighborhood.

"I adore them!" She reached for his hand. "They are so pretty; you outdid yourself, I promise." Ivy instinctively knew he had spent more than what was considered practical for an eighteen year old boy, but she had come to learn over the last two years that even though Eli McKnight was the most level-headed and intelligent boy she'd ever met, when it came to her, he was anything but practical. Day-to-day, she managed to protest his gallantry with a modicum of believability, at least to his face; but inside, she secretly reveled in his over-the-top affection for her.

Ivy winked at Eli. “I’ll see *you* later.” She laid on a thick southern accent and smiled her typical sweet smile, but this time that mother-approved sweet smile carried an air of innocent seduction behind it. As far as Eli was concerned, her smile, the looks she gave him, the way she held his hand, all of it seemed seductive. She didn’t even realize it was happening, and she was even less aware of the stunning beauty she had become as the last two years had transformed her from a lovely girl to a gorgeous nearly-woman.

Eli was aware, though, acutely aware. When the word “you” rolled off her tongue, it was flirtatious, sparkling and promising, and altogether tantalizing. Eli was spellbound by her, as always. He wiped his palms on his gown. She’d succeeded in transforming him into a stuttering love-sick idiot too many times to count. He had stopped being embarrassed by his stuttering, spell-bound stares the moment she had returned his mesmerized gaze with a kiss — a real kiss. Because, he figured, if being a stuttering idiot around her meant she kept kissing him like that, he was content to oblige her.

He thought of them as “old-movie moments.” He had often told Ivy that she reminded him of an old Hollywood movie star — she had all the allure of those classic, sophisticated beauties who had been part of the Marilyn Monroe era, and, at the same time, she possessed the brains and tenacity of the most successful women of Generation Y. Eli snapped out of his trance when he realized his body temperature was rising. He smiled, and, after wiping the I-can't-control-my-hormones moisture from his palms, he reached out and squeezed her hand in his.

"Tell your parent's 'Hi' for me, too." He leaned in, hoping for more than a cheek peck, but Ivy ignored his lippy cues and kissed his cheek.

"I'll see you soon," she whispered in his ear.

"Not soon enough." For her benefit, he shook his head a little and forced out a deep breath through an o-shaped mouth. She smiled. His overt internal battle to maintain the self-control his faith dictated stirred feelings of both pride and guilt inside Ivy. She silently enjoyed knowing his gentlemanly conduct on a day-to-day basis took effort and that she was, in fact, his most obvious source of temptation. At the same time, she felt a certain level of guilt because, though she too practiced restraint, she knowingly pushed his buttons, at every opportunity — she couldn't seem to help herself. She had somehow become a master in the art of flirtation, and she aimed every ounce of her skill right at Eli McKnight.

Ivy smiled again and turned to walk away. Eli watched her until she disappeared into the Dijon-colored crowd. Even wearing that shapeless yellow gown, it was obvious she was "well put together," as Val would say. He tried not to notice, but he noticed.

~

Uncle Pete shattered what had been a private moment with a hard, loud slap to Eli's backside. Eli cried out, "Ghaaa!" His audible sense of discomfort came not from pain, but from the shock of his interrupted staring, thanks to an assault on an area of his body that usually remained undisturbed. He turned quickly on his heels, holding his right butt cheek with his hand, to learn that his shock was the result of a typical "Uncle Pete moment." Eli chuckled to himself, "I could crush you, Paw-Paw Pete."

Pete responded to Eli's verbal jab with an expletive, and then said, "You've done pretty dang well for yourself with that one my boy. She's a doll. She got an older sister?" Pete laid the comedic-toned country-bumpkin character on pretty thickly most of the time. He acted the part so often that most people believed he actually *was* a bumpkin. Pete made a "whoo-wee" sound and began poking at his nephew's ribs with his brawny, calloused fingers.

"Don't get any ideas there, gramps. Ivy's only sister is headed into her junior year. I'm pretty sure that's illegal, and I hope it's out of the question — even for you, you sicko!" Pete laughed out loud from way down deep in his belly, as was his custom. He never held back his laugh, ever, and everyone loved him for it. Eli laughed too, but his laughter was motivated more by Pete's laughter, which had always been infectious, than it was by his own statement. Pete managed to grab his towering nephew in a short-lived headlock and forced in one quick noogie at record speed before Eli, who need not try too hard, broke free of his chubby-fisted grasp.

Joe McKnight was moving toward the doors of the auditorium with a herd of other people who all likely had similar plans. "Reservations people, let's roll out!" he yelled. "Getting out of this parking lot is going to be a nightmare." Joe hated traffic. He was never bothered by much, except traffic, his Kryptonite. His unfiltered hatred for traffic was one of the only things about him that irritated his doting wife, whose genteel spirit made it seem as though nothing ever got under her skin, though everyone in her family knew otherwise. She and Joe were laid back, yes, but even they had their moments. As a unit, the entire McKnight clan began moving, engaging in little pockets of private conversation as they shuffled like impatient, yet resigned, sheep toward the exit. Joe led the pack, eager to extinguish his road rage before it started.

As the herd shuffled along, one of the assistant football coaches jogged over to the group.

"There you are! Before y'all head out, Coach B. wants to see his seniors." He made his announcement as matter-of-factly as one might expect from a man who was used to giving orders. His tone left no room for doubt or debate that the boys would do exactly as he requested. He nodded once toward the McKnight family and jogged away, heading toward the small, messy circle of young men who had already assembled. The McKnight boys looked in their father's direction in unison.

“Okay, you two go on. But we ain’t waitin’ around, we’ll meet you at the restaurant. Hurry up, but drive safely, this traffic is going to be murder. Absolute murder,” he grumbled. Val shot her husband a look that signaled her displeasure with his traffic-related impatience. The herd continued shuffling toward the door as Joe put his arm around Val’s waist.

“Bye, my babies, be careful!” Val sang over her shoulder as she blew mom-style air kisses toward her sons.

“Coach beckons, little brother;” he feigned a sniff and pretended to wipe a tear, “one last time.” Beau slapped Eli on the back and smiled.

“Aw, don’t get all teary on me. Your makeup will run.” Eli smirked at his own statement. Beau shoulder-shoved his *little* brother with all his weight and then turned smoothly around on his heel, in a dance-like fashion and proceeded to enact his best hip-hop strut as he sang something that sounded marginally like “Movin’ on up, to the east side…,” but Eli was certain he’d sang the wrong words. They both moved toward the corner of the gym where their teammates were congregating, a strutting Beau now several paces ahead of his brother.

Beau had been born a mere two minutes before Eli, and he had used those two minutes to exert his seniority in as many ways as he possibly could over the course of the last eighteen years. Eli rolled his eyes and smirked. He unzipped his graduation gown, stuffed his hands into his pockets, and continued following his peacock of a brother across the auditorium floor.

The crowd had finally thinned out. As Beau and Eli reached the congregate of football players, Coach Breyers began to speak. "Listen up, ladies. As you know, in an unprecedented season, three members of our senior class were offered football scholarships to our beloved Texas State," he pulled open a cardboard box and started tossing gray balls of fabric to the individual players within the group. "Three, men! Three! And, just so we're clear, I'll be taking credit for that fact as long as they let me coach." He laughed lightly at his own joke, "Two of those three men will go on to play for State in the fall. For that reason, I am mandating that, regardless of your destination, we will *all* be State fans for the duration of their time there — hence these freakin' awesome T-shirts." The boys began unfolding their gray bundles and holding up their gray and maroon colored shirts one-by-one. On the front of each shirt was the Texas State logo, alongside the locally infamous Texas State Bobcat. On the right sleeve, their graduating year had been printed. "I have also decided that rooting for State will be a mandatory requirement to play football at this school for, at minimum, the next four years." Breyers had always been able to keep a straight face. No one ever knew whether or not he was joking or serious. The small band of brothers chuckled awkwardly before collectively deciding that their stoic coach had to be joking, leading the way to genuine laughter.

The coach continued, "Beau, Darrell, come and stand by me." The team began to slow-clap, but Coach Breyers gestured with his hand to silence the group. "And it is with a sincerely-broken and heavy heart that I announce," he paused and looked seriously from face to face and then began to speak again using the vernacular of an old-time, southern, evangelical pastor, "that third member of our graduating seniors has opted to forego his divinely appointed and supernatural opportunity to play the great game of football at Texas State. And, though it pains me to say so, has instead chosen to become a Bobcat in a way most of us can't begin to understand — the academic way."

The coach smiled as he looked toward Eli, as the mob of boys around him began to jeer. Breyers pulled a tightly-wound ball of cloth from the box of gray T-shirts he had been distributing. "I've got a little something special for you, son, signifying your new role in the world of football." He tossed the tightly-wound ball of cloth in Eli's direction. Eli caught it and removed a wide rubber band; he opened it up to reveal a full Texas State cheerleading uniform, complete with a skirt and spankies.

The testosterone-laden group of young men erupted into a thunder clap of laughter, whistles, taunts and mocking. Eli shot Breyers an ominous, yet good-humored look, crookedly pursing his lips and nodding his head slightly, as the man-children around him fell all over themselves laughing. The coach broke his own straight-face rule and laughed out loud heartily. He walked over to where Eli stood, and, as he wrapped an arm around him, he turned to the rest of the group, "In all seriousness, I respect this young man… and all of you young men… as much as a man can respect anyone. Whether you ever play another down of football or not, I encourage you to give this life your all. Nothing is worth doing unless it's done right, and, for most of us, giving one hundred percent effort is as right as we'll ever be. Be careful this summer, and don't do anything I wouldn't do. I expect greatness to come in each of your futures." The crowd of boys fell oddly quiet as each, in his own way, came to the conclusion that this could be the last time many of them would see each other, ever.

"Don't do anything you wouldn't do? That means we won't be able to do anything this whole summer except sit around on our front porches, drink flavored, chick coffee and read the paper in our boxer shorts," Eric Smith, lovingly nicknamed Smitty, blurted out from the midst of the pack, starkly reversing the somber tone of the unfolding "goodbye." Smitty had always been the biggest "smart mouth" in the group, having mastered the art of sarcasm as a toddler. He never missed an opportunity to exercise his wit. Usurping the heavy moment and seizing it as an opportunity to take one final jab at the head football coach earned him rave reviews from the rest of his cohorts, none of whom wanted to admit they possessed the ability to experience any emotions beyond enthusiasm, rage and lust. And, once again, the group was laughing.

CHAPTER THREE

For the two famished behemoths, the drive to the restaurant felt like the longest drive in the history of their eighteen years. The pair's apparent low blood sugar and the excitement of the evening had combined to create a mood that ensured childishness would triumph heavily over maturity. They exhibited a long-standing affection for bathroom humor, and they giggled like eight year olds with nearly every breath. They discussed memories from elementary school, like the time Beau had pushed Eli into the girl's bathroom and then held the door shut with the help of a few friends. There hadn't been any girls in the bathroom at the time, but the experience alone had been enough to make Eli the butt of jokes for an entire semester. It was during this time that Beau began calling him "Eliza," a moniker he'd yet to shake.

As the minutes ticked by, the conversation once again turned to the forthcoming events of the evening. Beau's phone had been dinging in the cup holder every thirty seconds since they left the school. Eli was certain, though his phone was on silent in his pocket, he had his fair share of missed messages as well. As uninhibited as he was, one thing Beau didn't do was text and drive. No Twitter, no Facebook, no nothing. That was a choice both boys, along with many of their friends, had made freshman year when an older classmate, P.J. Hickman, hit a tree head-on because he wouldn't put down his iPhone. His body had been so badly mangled that his family opted for a closed casket. The event made quite an impact on the entire school, the entire town really, and, since the accident, P.J.'s sister and brother had become activists against phone use while driving. His parents even paid for a billboard near where the accident happened, depicting a picture of his shattered phone screen beside a yearbook photo of P.J., above a caption reading *Learn that it can wait, before it's too late.* Beau turned to Eli, "By the way, I need your cover tonight, Eliza. When I asked Mom about lifting my curfew, she gave me that 'over my dead body' look."

"If you'd just come with us to Kevin's, you could stay as long as you want. No curfew." Eli made an attempt at duck lips, an effort that would easily be considered pitiful by anyone looking on, as he shamelessly rubbed his privilege in his brother's face.

"Of course you're curfew free, because why would anyone want to put a limit on all that gee-whiz, nifty, Jesus and ginger ale?" Beau had been in church nearly every Sunday since he was six weeks old, but he'd never been all in and had never understood how his identical twin brother could be so into something that, to Beau, seemed like nothing more than a fun-sucking list of things a person shouldn't do.

"Fine," Eli sighed, "against my better judgment, I'll cover for you. But know it's in protest and subject to change." For years, Eli had been covering for Beau. For years, he'd been keeping his "big brother" out of trouble by finishing the school work he'd neglected when he'd chosen Xbox over reason. He'd artfully omitted facts about Beau's whereabouts where his parents were concerned, even though, deep down, he expected his parents knew the truth each and every time. Eli had even come to the rescue as the getaway driver from a couple of parties that had gone south, once when the police showed up and found obscene numbers of underage drinkers on the premises and another time when the host's parents had come home early. Somehow, Beau managed to get away clean every time. In fact, he managed to avoid trouble most of the time, despite the fact that he seemed carelessly phlegmatic about the circumstances associated with getting caught. And though Eli was always the voice of reason, he too found himself flirting with danger every time he aided and abetted his brother's narrow escapes from justice. He never said no, though. His loyalty to his twin easily overrode his sense of self-preservation.

"You know you love it. Covering for me is as exciting as your life gets, Eliza." Beau gave Eli a shove from the driver's seat.

“One day I’m going to let you get caught. Then we’ll see who’s excited.”

“Touché,” Beau conceded, all the while knowing that his brother would never allow him to be caught if it were within his power to stop it.

“Besides, when we’re old, I'll be the one in good shape, and you’re going to beg me to push your old, snuffed out, partied down and broken up, wrinkly body around in a wheelchair. And I'll probably be the only person alive who’s willing to donate stem cells to help repair your shriveled up, pickled organs." Eli had a knack for straight-faced humor, and though Beau tried to repress his reaction, he failed to hide his reluctant laughter.

Amused by his reaction and already laughing at his own forthcoming statement, Beau responded, “I’ll only agree to move in with you if you promise to change my diapers too.”

"I have to draw the line somewhere. Wiping up your fermented droppings is definitely across that line. I would say maybe your wife will take that job, but there’s not a woman in her right mind who would want to be saddled with you for the rest of her life, so we’ll probably end up having to pay a nurse. You better not party all your money away, private nurses are expensive.”

“Did you really just say ‘fermented droppings’?” Beau was highly amused by his brother’s choice of words. “I have to remember that.”

The incessant banter continued until Beau made the left-hand turn into the steakhouse parking lot and immediately encountered another soon-to-be patron, who had apparently decided to wait on another patron-turned-exiting-driver to back out of a parking spot. The rear of Beau's truck was barely out of oncoming traffic, and when it came to road rage, Beau was definitely his father's son. The white two-door Cadillac ahead of them was dead center in the driving space, turn signal flashing, staking claim to what would eventually be an empty spot as soon as the sloth-like party of four backed out. Beau gripped the steering wheel and let out an impatient growl. Eli was used to his brother's road rage and sat silently with his left arm on the armrest and his right fist covering in-turned lips. He, too, was frustrated with the situation, especially considering the amount of traffic and the starvation they'd battled on the ride from the school, but his ability to maintain decorum was second-to-none, especially for a teenage boy.

Beau glanced into his left-side mirror to see that several cars were in the turn lane behind him, waiting for him to move so they, too, could stampede the restaurant. "Go!" Beau yelled out his window before laying on his very masculine and very un-friendly horn. The lady in the Cadillac nearly jumped out of her own sunroof. "Serves her right," Beau exclaimed as he mocked her reaction. Eli immediately felt waves of shame roll through him, but couldn't deny that Beau's reenactment of her reaction had been solid.

"I wish you'd learn to control yourself. We look exactly the same, so I can't lie and say I don't know you."

The driver of the Cadillac, obviously shaken, pulled forward and made the left turn to circle back, probably searching for another spot.

"Park on the other side of the building, moron. Maybe she won't see us go in."

Beau laughed, "Okay, Eliza, don't get your panties in a bunch." Beau pulled around to the opposite side of the building and found an end spot under a light pole. "Sweet!"

Beau and Eli got out of the truck and made their way toward the door. Eli breathed a silent prayer that they'd beat the harassed lady into the building. Thankfully, there were enough people moving about in front of the restaurant that it would be impossible for him to recognize which woman might have been his brother's victim anyway, and vice versa.

"McKnight, please," Eli said to the hostess. She barely looked up, but grabbed two menus and politely ushered the pair down a paisley-carpeted hallway toward a private room where the McKnight party waited. As they walked, Beau grabbed his brother's arm and attempted to manually force his palm onto the hostess' ample derriere. Eli responded with a Herculean effort to shake his would-be attacker from his wrist. The pair engaged in a whisper-laden battle of wills as they made their way down the hall.

In a final defensive maneuver, Eli put one shoulder into his brother's chest and used his body weight to force him against the exposed brick wall as they walked. The hostess, who was in her early twenties and very attractive, made a valiant effort to ignore the display of testosterone behind her, but when Beau grabbed his scraped arm and cursed with pain under his breath, the hushed snickering coming from behind her caused her to glance back toward them. Neither of them looked up at her, but she felt self-conscious anyway.

They soon arrived at a set of double glass doors that were already open into the room, creating a glass mini-hall for patrons to pass through before reaching the table area. The hostess didn't even speak, she simply held out her arm to gesture to Beau and Eli’s entry point. As she did, she finally got a better look at the source of the debauchery behind her in the hallway, and she was taken aback by the double-dose of striking good looks that stood before her. She reflexively raised her eyebrows in a hostess-like manner and smiled. Beau took the opportunity to raise his eyebrows in return before saying, “thank you Mel-an-ie” as he feigned a closer inspection of her name tag in a thinly veiled attempt to inspect not her nametag, but the area of her body that lived under her nametag. The hostess smirked and appeared unfazed by his behavior. But, she hurriedly left the room while still holding onto the two menus she’d meant for Beau and Eli. Beau watched her leave with something of a smirk on his face and Eli whispered, “You’re unbelievable.”

“Unbelievable is the fact that she got all that ham into those pants.” Beau responded as he turned back toward the room on his heel, hands in his pockets. Since he was old enough to appreciate the female form, Beau had referred to a woman's backside as "ham." Nobody knew why, nor from whence it came, but it did allow him to speak in a moderate form of code on occasion, and, since Val abhorred the other three-letter word he'd occasionally used when referring to the female derriere and, if she heard it, handed down some unpleasant consequences, "ham" had become the lesser of two evils, though he'd finally learned to mind his surroundings before using that word, as well.

Eli shot a disgusted look in his brother's direction, but didn't have time to respond verbally. No sooner than they cleared the glass mini-hall, family members began to applaud and the volume in the room escalated quickly. Two seats were left open at the head of the table, one on either side, near the wall of windows that created a silhouette of the adoring group that was visible from the open door. The waiter was already taking orders.

"It's about freakin' time!" Pete called out from the other end of the table, as family members began passing graduation gifts toward the brothers.

"First things first!" Beau motioned for the waiter. It had taken all of five seconds for him and Eli to decide which featured side of beef they'd be devouring for dinner. Red meat had been a weekly must-have in the McKnight household since the boys were old enough to hold a fork and Val had long ago learned that food consumption was non-negotiable to a McKnight man.

Jokes, laughter and gratitude radiated into space as the boys stuffed their faces and unwrapped all manner of colorful packages, ranging from new laptops from their parents to a pair of reading glasses with photorealistic eyes on the inside of each lens from Uncle Pete.

"Pete has informed me that those specs were designed to allow for sleeping in class, while leaving the professor none the wiser." Uncle James, Valerie's other brother, pushed his own narrow specs up onto the bridge of his nose. He and Pete could not have been more different. James had a wiry frame, a slender build like Val's and the kind of face that begged for glasses. He also had the IQ and fashion sense to go with it. Eli had always admired his Uncle James, who had used his brains to launch a startup in college and was quite comfortable financially by the time he'd turned twenty-five. Now the startup was a source of substantial income for James and his family and employed around fifteen people. He was always trying new things and seemed to enjoy "making life better" for as many people as he could. Eli thought, maybe, he too would join the team someday.

"Dad always told us that in college, they don't even care if you show up, much less sleep or whatever — so, where were these things four years ago Uncle Pete? I could have used these for all my English classes." Beau slid the glasses onto his face and turned his head as if he were looking around; everyone at the table began to laugh.

"And math classes and science classes and history classes…" Eli continued. The laughter of the entire table elevated in volume and the tones the boys associated with what they referred to as a "sick burn." The tone and vibrato of their laughter made it very obvious that most of the attendees were related by blood. Anyone within ear shot would have easily pegged the group as a family.

"That comment about college was meant to instill a sense of personal responsibility and a strong work ethic, Beau. Apparently, that little nugget of wisdom was lost on you, son." Joe, who sat next to Beau, leaned over to playfully smack him on the back of the head.

For just over an hour, Eli, Beau and their family members laughed and relived memories, shared jokes at each other's expense and ate offensive quantities of food, celebrating the rite of passage known as high school graduation. Eventually though, the goodbyes were said and the hugs were doled out. Beau and Eli were simultaneously gearing up for the evening's events, each preparing to go his separate way, when Joe reached into his pocket and pulled out Eli's keys.

"I didn't think you'd want to ride home with us after dinner only to turn right around and go get Ivy, so I drove your truck. I parked over by that brick fountain thing." Joe tossed his son the keys.

"Oh man, thanks Dad! You're awesome!" Eli smiled a broad McKnight grin.

"Yeah, well, maybe you'd be so kind as to remind your mother of that fact." Joe smiled that broad McKnight grin right back at him.

Valerie and Sweet Pete walked toward them, chatting between themselves inaudibly. Valerie grabbed one hand of each son in her slim yet herculean grip. She had always had weirdly strong hands and gave equally strong hugs. "Have fun, but don't stay out too late," she cast a mom-gaze in their direction as she spoke, rightly turning her mom-gaze more fiercely upon Beau.

"Why would you look at me and say that?" Beau pretended to be offended.

"Late, shmate — stay out all night and don't even call!" Pete interjected with over the top enthusiasm before Val could speak. Valerie smacked him on the chest and he mouthed the word "ow" before rubbing the targeted spot with his sausage-like fingers.

Beau laughed before snapping into an *attention stance* and saluting, "Yes, sir! That I can do!"

"You both know better. Pete, you know better too. I'm gonna mash your mouth." Valerie retorted. "You're lucky I'm not carrying my wooden spoon!" Valerie McKnight had carried a wooden spoon in her bag since Beau and Eli were old enough to walk.

"You're not?" Eli's tone signified his legitimate shock. "So, wait, does this mean…?"

"That's right," Valerie nodded reluctantly, "I've graduated the spoon because you've graduated the school. You're officially "men," though it turns my stomach to say so." The circle of family laughed as Beau and Eli mocked their mother with feigned heart attacks and punctuated their antics with a brotherly fist bump. Valerie started to tear up a little before exclaiming, "My babies! I can't do this. Puberty was bad enough, and now this!"

Joe put his arm around her, "Oh dear Lord, you boys better run away while you still have the chance. Once she starts crying, it's out of my hands." He shook his head mockingly, patted her shoulder and chuckled. Val smiled, blinking back the maternal tears in her eyes, and whispered, "Shut it, Joe."

All the members of the immediate McKnight family were laughing and loving as they left the restaurant. Beau and Eli each hugged their parents with the enthusiasm one would expect on such an occasion, and given the fact that Valerie was involved, bones were cracked and spines were torqued. Their extended family got in on the action as well, and the boys spent about sixty seconds in an MMA-style pseudo-spar with Uncle Pete before they disbanded. "See you soon, Mom," Eli shouted over his shoulder. Valerie waved, and Beau returned her wave by turning on his heels and blowing her large and dramatic air kisses. Joe shook his head and watched as his two sons disappeared into the sea of vehicles. He blinked furiously against the welling of emotion in his eyes and wiped them quickly with the thumb and index fingers of his right hand, hoping none would be the wiser.

"Are you sure you won't change your mind and come with me, Bro?" Beau pantomimed a rodeo rider and let out a yeehaw-esque sound as he headed toward his truck. "There's gonna be fillies all over that pasture and I'm just the cowboy ta' break 'em!" His cadence was thick with mockery as he waved his left arm in the air over his head and pretended to turn a lasso.

"Oh my…" Eli stopped short and shook his head, "Never ever do that again," he returned, as he raised one eyebrow and cast a disapproving expression in Beau's direction. His dry humor rolled smoothly out of his perfectly shaped, slightly-open mouth. "I'll see you at home later, Ivy's waiting on me."

"Alright then, but you'll regret it one day, you'd like all the different flavors of ham if you only tried it. I mean, not that I would mind sampling some of your ham, but…"

"I will kill you," Eli cut him off.

"Ooh, so sensitive." Beau had given Eli a hard time about Ivy since the first time he'd seen them together. Though he downplayed the pair's relationship and pretended his brother's love for Ivy was trivial, he knew it was the real thing, and, if he was honest with himself, he'd admit that his mockery stemmed from jealousy alone.

In truth, Eli knew this as well. Beau had only become a wanna-be womanizer because of Julia Snyder. She and Beau had been the king and queen of middle school love for all of the sixth, seventh and eighth grades. Only Eli knew that Beau had been obsessed with Julia since the second grade. When her father was transferred the summer between eighth and ninth grade, they had vowed to stay together despite the distance. Neither of them had cellphones at the time, so they wrote letters and talked on the weekends, but two months into their freshman year, Julia wrote to Beau and broke it off.

She told him she knew it would be for the best because, though she missed him terribly, they both had lives to lead and the distance was just too much. It wasn't long after that when Beau learned from Julia's cousin that she was going to a dance at her new school with an older boy named Blake and that Blake had asked her out a full two weeks before she wrote to him and broke it off. Beau didn't react to the experience the way everyone expected. Instead, he pretended to be unbothered and decided that all girls who weren't his mother were, as he put it, "cold-hearted female dogs." He wasn't allowed to say *the* b-word, but he didn't get into trouble for implying the use of the word that week. Joe and Val had believed the attitude would run its course, but once Beau became officially *available* and learned that he had a talent for wooing the opposite sex, girls became like chum in shark-infested waters and *ham* quickly became one of his favorite things.

"Later, Eliza." Beau shoved his hands in his pockets as he turned and began walking the final feet to his truck.

"Later," Eli called back. He became the mirror image of his brother as he turned toward the fountain.

CHAPTER FOUR

Eli topped the hill in front of Ivy's parent's house and made the right-hand turn onto the long, tree-lined driveway that marked the path to the place he knew he'd find her waiting. The up-lighting on every tree had taken Ivy's dad months to perfect two years prior, the summer after Eli and Ivy began dating, but it turned out to be worth the effort. The view was impressive, and Eli was struck by it every time he saw it, even after all this time.

Eli knew that, at the end of that beautifully landscaped isle, Ivy was waiting. In his mind's eye, he could see her sitting on the porch swing bathed in the soft glow of the setting sun and yet more landscape lighting. As soon as Ivy saw Eli's truck turn into the driveway, she jumped up. She threw her leather bag over her shoulder and darted toward the front door, sticking her head inside for just a moment, she called out, "Eli's here! We're headed to Kevin's! Love you!" She was already bouncing down the porch steps when her mother called out behind her to return her affections and remind her to call if she was going to be too late.

Eli left his truck running but jumped out and trotted around to open the passenger door. Joe had taught both boys the importance and value of chivalry — calling it a dying art, but more importantly, emphasizing the swoon-worthy reactions their female passengers would have if they opened doors and offered arms. This tidbit of masculine wisdom had proved beneficial for both boys, as they'd both taken it to heart, if for no other reason than the girl-factor. After two years of driving, both Beau and Eli had learned just how right their dad had been about chivalry overall — that door-opening move had never failed to impress the ladies. Though lately, their motivations for being chivalrous couldn't have been more different.

"Wow, you look beautiful," Eli said as he opened the door.

Ivy smiled, "I look exactly the same as I did two hours ago when you saw me, but thank you."

"I know, but still." Eli grinned back at her.

Eli ran back to the driver's side and jumped in. He buckled his seatbelt and put his charcoal gray truck into reverse, "I know there's going to be food, but I'm totally stuffed. I'll be lucky to even eat one whole pan of brownies." The long driveway made a three-point turn a necessity for getting back out to the road. Backing out would have been possible, but not smart.

"Just one pan?" Ivy sarcastically feigned shock, "I guess you did eat a lot at dinner." Ivy slid over into the center seat and pulled the lap belt across her petite frame. She didn't do this often, ever the lady, but Eli loved it when she did. He immediately put his arm around her.

"Well, well, Ms. Zellway, what's gotten into you?"

"Special night, special guy — why?" She smiled a coy smile over her left shoulder. Eli felt his guts stir.

The picture-perfect couple chatted casually as they drove down the winding back roads toward Kevin Hinkley's house. Ivy held her hands in her lap while Eli kept one hand on the wheel and one arm around the girl. At one point, after Eli cracked a joke, Ivy laughed and put her hand on his leg. And though it wasn't the first time she'd accidentally taken his mind away from the present, for some reason, this time, he had more difficulty controlling his thoughts than usual. It had been almost four years since Eli committed himself to purity for the sake of his faith. The commitment had made life simpler somehow, because sticking to a standard eliminated the possibility of entertaining other options and left room for relationships to grow from the inside out, instead of the other way around. They'd both eliminated sex as a possibility from day one, and, because this choice had become part of who they were, the relationship was simple. There was no confusing love and lust and there was never pressure to push beyond the line they'd set for themselves where physical contact was concerned. But, the self-sustained standard didn't stop Eli from thinking about it, a lot.

Eli told Ivy all about the family dinner, the glasses, the gifts — even the hostess experience. Expectedly, Ivy wasn't thrilled with that part of the story, but she rightly placed the blame on Beau and his devil-may-care personality. She laughed it off and told Eli about her night's events, and, in what seemed like a short while, they had arrived at their destination.

Kevin Hinkley's father had been the youth director at their church for longer than either of them could remember. As such, it seemed almost fitting that nearly every youth function they'd ever attended took place at the Hinkley home. It also seemed fitting that every member of the youth group felt like they belonged at the Hinkley house. It was home away from home for at least a dozen kids, always stocked with food. Every one of the *adopted* crew knew where the hide-a-key was kept and had their own alarm code. The Hinkley family believed there was never an excuse to get into trouble when you've been handed a way out, and they were that way out. They also worked hard to make sure every kid felt valued and wanted. The whole family was born for the life they led and teens all over town had benefitted from their efforts.

When Eli turned in, there were already about twelve or thirteen cars and pickup trucks parked on either side of the short, wide driveway. Cars were parked on the lawn, in the street, and even in the neighbor's driveway!

"Wow, are we that late?" He looked at Ivy. She formed a pinched face and made big "uh-oh" eyes back at him.

Eli wedged his truck into a not-exactly-big-enough spot near the road and hopped out to open the door for Ivy. She had learned to just stay put and let him do it. Once, she opened the door for herself and he made her close it back so he could do it, telling her she was going to throw him off his game. Every time she thought about it, it made her giggle. As Eli darted around the front of the truck, he suddenly disappeared from view. Ivy immediately sat up straight and leaned forward just in time to see Eli's head pop up again.

"I'm up!" He shouted. When he opened the door, he knew by the look on her face that he needed to explain his sudden disappearance. "I hit my leg on that stupid bumper bar. I told Beau I didn't need that thing — maybe if I ran people off the road regularly…"

"Are you okay?" Ivy inquired with a humored voice, "Because if you are, you have to know that was hilarious."

Ivy grabbed her purse as she slid out of the cab. Eli extended his arm in an escort-like fashion and the pair walked arm in arm through the maze of cars toward the large two-story Cape Cod.

"It's hard to believe we won't be considered kids anymore at church. You know they're going to expect us to start doing grown-up stuff. I mean, you're like one month out from heading up the Women's Committee and you don't even know it yet," Eli looked at Ivy with faux concern in his eyes and then nodded, as if to affirm his own assertion.

Ivy rolled her eyes, "I can't believe my parents agreed to let me go to the same school as you. They must think I'm super desperate." She shot Eli a half-smirk.

Eli laughed and extended his finger to ring the doorbell, but before he could push the button, the door swung open and on the other side stood the tall, wiry, dark-haired Kevin. Kevin was a goofball, but he was also one of the sweetest people Ivy and Eli had ever met. In fact, he was one of the sweetest guys anyone had ever met. He would literally give the shirt off his back to help someone — anyone — in need. He was so loving, he had found himself in more than one fight over the years, because he couldn’t stand to see anyone being bullied. But alas, sticking up for the underdog definitely hadn’t improved his ability to take a punch, so instead he bragged about being a fast healer.

Thankfully, early in his junior year, Kevin had hit a growth spurt. The boy who had always been of average height and very long-limbed quickly became above average in height, but remained just as gangly. The growth spurt hadn’t made him any better in a fight, but it had extended his reach and served to, at least initially, intimidate his opponents. Somehow, despite the fights he’d suffered as a result of his tender heart, he never got in trouble for them. Even the school administration knew his heart.

"Well, if it isn't my favorite couple!" Kevin had an amazingly deep and smooth voice that didn’t match his body type at all. He put on his best butler impression, "Ladies and gentlemen, announcing the arrival of Mr. McKnight and Ms. Zellway," he called into the house.

"Hi, Kev!” Ivy sang. She hugged his neck.

"Hey, man.” Eli extended his hand, but instead of shaking it like a normal person, Kevin slapped it in a sideways five, and then punched it down in an unreciprocated fist bump. Eli chuckled, “What was th…”

"Everybody is down in the basement,” Kevin interrupted. “My mom made that cheesecake you love Eli."

"Anything chocolate down there? You know how I feel about chocolate." Ivy asked with raised brows as she headed toward the stairs.

“You and, like, every other girl I know,” Kevin scoffed. “My mom’s desserts have been the only way I can get a girl into the house since, like, my whole life.”

Eli laughed again and smacked Kevin’s shoulder as he walked by. Though Kevin had been joking, Eli knew for a fact that he’d never had much luck with girls. Ivy had set up double dates for him in the past, but every girl had responded the same way — he was great friend material, but that’s it.

“Curse the friend-zone!” Kevin shook his fist and screamed down the stairs in his buttery baritone as the two headed into the basement.

Eli made a face as if to stifle a laugh, but, when Ivy turned to him and said, “Well, maybe if he didn’t use phrases like ‘curse the friend-zone’ I could do something to help him,” he stopped trying to stifle it and let the laugh out with free abandon.

In his laughter, Eli responded, “That’s why I love you, always willing to go the extra mile.” As soon as it was off his tongue, he covered his mouth with his hand.

“What?” Ivy asked.

“What?” Eli responded awkwardly, obviously awkwardly. He knew exactly what she was referring to, and he couldn’t believe he’d said it out loud. He’d never said it out loud before, ever. He barely felt confident enough to feel it, let alone admit it. He was worried she might not feel the same way. What if she didn’t? His dad always told him that love wasn’t a word to use lightly, that love was God’s idea and when it came to the opposite sex, you only say it to someone you’re willing to die for because that’s how He designed it to be. Not even Beau threw the “L” word around lightly.

“You know exactly what. Do you… I mean, do you think you do? Because, I, well, I know I do… I have for a long time.” Ivy stammered in a whisper with her right hand on her chest. Eli’s stomach churned, his heart pounded, his hands got sweaty. He immediately pulled her off to the side. This was a private moment, or at least it *should* be private.

“You do? Because, I definitely do. No doubts. Don’t say you do unless you do. I mean, I never said anything before because it seemed so, I dunno… huge. And because I thought you might not. And I didn't want to freak you out and I don't even know if I'm allowed to because..." Eli's breathing was staggered. Is it really possible to be in love, really in love, at eighteen? For Eli, love meant a forever commitment. For him, the discussion alone might as well have been a marriage proposal. During a time when the word *love* gets applied to everything and everybody, the McKnights revered it as a word that mattered. At that moment, he remembered that his parents had met in high school, married at twenty, and had been happily married ever since — but they were the exception among his peer group. It seemed like most of the kids in his class had divorced parents, and he knew that going all-in at eighteen meant criticism would soon follow.

"I do too." Ivy took a deep breath, "I mean, I… love you. I have loved you for almost two years."

"What? Why didn't you say anything?"

"I was embarrassed. I didn't want to freak *you* out either. Plus, there's that stigma that girls fall in love too easily and then there's, you know, that whole "puppy love" drama. But I'm positive this isn't that." Her hand was still on her chest, her dainty fingers fumbling with the pendant on her necklace.

"I love you too." Eli was freaking out on the inside. He was excited, but a little embarrassed at his own reaction. "Wow!" he said. Then, "Wow!" again. He leaned in toward her and put his forehead against hers. "Epic," he whispered.

Ivy's eyes glistened with tears. She hugged him once, sharply, quickly, and then darted away and found her seat. Eli composed himself and headed toward the dessert table, wiping his sweaty palms on his jeans before greeting Kevin's dad.

CHAPTER FIVE

"You okay, son?" Mr. Hinkley asked. "You don't look so good."

"Yes, sir. I'm great!" Eli returned. He began to load two plates, one with his favorites and one with Ivy's. His hands were shaking, and his face felt hot. He knew exactly why Mr. Hinkley expressed concern for his well-being. He was definitely living an old movie moment. He'd never in his life wanted to tap dance or sing Frank Sinatra songs, or dance in the rain or any of that other cliché mushy stuff from the movies, but, in that moment, his spirit was soaring and he'd gladly make a fool of himself for love.

"Alright then, good. Go get your seat, we're about to get started."

"Thank you, sir. Will do." Eli balanced the two plates on his giant hands, and when Ivy spotted him, she stood quickly to help him.

"I'm so sorry, I should have helped you, but my head was spinning." She smiled at him, and he gave her a knowing look before he smiled back. The two sat down, and Mr. Hinkley stood to say grace over the food. When the silence fell, Eli's stomach made itself known to the entire room. His classmates snickered with whisper-like voices. Mr. Hinkley cleared his throat in a signal to the group to get it together. Little did anyone know, the gurgling in Eli's stomach had nothing to do with the food and everything to do with the company. In fact, at this point, food was the last thing on his mind.

"Thank you, God, for this day, for these students and for the promise of bright futures that lie ahead. Thank you for Your presence and Your guidance as they navigate the harshness of the world without the cover of their parents' homes and supervision. Thank You for Your Son, and thank You for this food. We pray it nourishes our bodies, so that we may serve You in strength and in health. In Jesus' name, amen."

When grace was over, Ivy leaned in to Eli and said quietly, "You cannot be hungry."

Eli leaned over, as close to Ivy as he could get without being inappropriate and replied, "I'm not, but I am in… love." He almost laughed at himself. "This is a good day." Ivy squeezed his hand and began picking at her plate, though she wasn't sure she'd be able to eat a single bite.

After the prayer, as the students began digging in, Mr. Hinkley addressed the group, "Welcome graduates!" Eli looked around the room and counted about twenty of his fellow graduates, from a peppering of different schools, present and accounted for. For a moment, his thoughts wandered to his brother and the hundreds of other seniors who were likely already partying on the pasture at the lake. He'd never really been interested in the party lifestyle, and the only time he'd ever been part of the party crowd was to make sure Beau didn't wind up behind bars.

Eli's stark contrast to his brother had become even more evident after he committed his life to Christ when he was fourteen, the summer before his freshman year, around the same time Beau said goodbye to Julia. If not for that commitment, Eli may have been tempted too. Two months later, Beau was sneaking out at night to do things that would have made his mother faint, if Eli hadn't been covering for him. Though Eli knew he was doing his brother a disservice in the grand scheme, he still covered for him every time he asked. Despite all his flaws, Beau was his best friend. Such a friend, in fact, that Eli would ignore his knowledge of right and wrong to protect him. Eli knew that everybody loved Beau. He was the perfect marriage of sweet and funny, tough and valiant, and he was so free-spirited that it made him magnetic. His fun-loving nature and sense of humor caused even his most embarrassing behavior to seem almost endearing, which made it even harder for Eli to condemn him.

"Before we get back to socializing, we're going to do a quick Bible study." Mr. Hinkley put on his reading glasses. "If you have your Bibles, turn with me to Psalm 37, verses three and four." Eli could hear thin pages turning all over the room. It was a sound that could not be mistaken for any other. He hadn't brought his Bible, but then, he hadn't gone home either. He did have his phone, and he did have a Bible app, but he wanted to be close to Ivy, so he left his iPhone in his pocket.

Ivy's long hair was hiding her face like a soft brown curtain as she looked down toward her tablet. She always had a Bible, because she always had her tablet in her purse. Eli scooted closer to her and she held out the device so he could look too. When he got close to her, he could smell her shampoo, or perfume, or something. Whatever it was, it smelled good, really, really good — and once again his thoughts shifted away from the present, to a place he knew he shouldn't go. He shook his head as if to snap out of his love-trance and tried desperately to redirect his thoughts and forcibly pull his attention back to Mr. Hinkley's lesson.

"It's no secret that most of you will embark on your freshman year of college this fall. It's not uncommon for college life to pull students away from their faith. Temptations run high, and other students with various backgrounds and beliefs can inadvertently — and sometimes advertently — plant seeds of doubt in the mind of a believer. It's important that young people enter the world with the mindset of a soldier going into battle. You will encounter spiritual warfare. You will be challenged. How you respond to those challenges will be a personal choice and a measure of your faith. Scripture tells us we must set our hearts, which means make a decision about who we are *before* circumstances try to tell us differently."

"You are a free agent when it comes to your thought life. Nobody can dictate where your mind goes without your permission. Your mind, which is directly related to the thing we call "the heart," is a gateway between God and your spirit. If your mind is cluttered with doubt, sin and disbelief or an affection for the study of gods other than the one Most High, there is no way your spirit can maintain an intimacy with The Creator. The choice is yours. It always has been, and it always will be. Will you accept His gifts and answer His knocking, or will you shut it out and ignore it? What do you believe? How will you let that belief influence you in the next phase of life? Tonight's passage reads:

Trust in the LORD, and do good;
Dwell in the land, and feed on His faithfulness.
Delight yourself also in the LORD,
And He shall give you the desires of your heart.

I don't want any of you to head into your adult years with the attitude of doom and gloom. So, while we understand that we will face hardship, we must also remember God's promises. We are seeds of Abraham, which means we are heirs to those promises. I chose this passage because it speaks so poignantly to young adults heading out into the world — and it closes with a wonderful promise! Don't stray from the path —

there's a reason it's called the "narrow way." It's easy to get off course, so surround yourself with believers who will hold you accountable. Hold yourselves accountable to be the person GOD says you are and not the person society says you are. And for goodness sakes, call your mothers, often."

Spots of laughter bubbled up from various people in the room. "Alright, that's all I have. You're free to celebrate at will. Just make sure you do it in a way that doesn't end with me calling the fire department or the police." Mr. Hinkley turned and began to head toward the stairs. Kevin immediately ran to the stereo to find something "to move the masses," and the group began to move about the room, buzzing with excitement and anticipation. Most everyone seemed to be having a great time. Though, a few of the girls were crying. Eli assumed it was because, well, that's what girls do when things get emotional.

As soon as they were free to return to the pressing subject at hand, Eli was laser focused on Ivy. She nibbled at a cheesecake bite, but her hands were shaking too. Was she cold? Nervous? Eli wondered if she regretted telling him. His heart was totally exposed and he wasn't sure how to process the feeling. Ivy felt his eyes on her, and she looked up. When she caught him staring, her cheeks flushed, and she smiled to herself as she glanced back down at her plate.

Kevin made his way toward Eli, but he could clearly see who held the man's attention. He stepped into Eli's path and cleared his throat, "If I were a female, would you talk to me then?"

"Just to say 'excuse me' while I make my way to *that* girl." He nodded toward Ivy.

"Ugh. Gag me."

"You're just jealous."

Kevin paused for just a moment and began shaking his head, "You're right! God help me, you're right. Excuse me while I go drown my sorrows in some Cheetos and Mountain Dew." Eli laughed. As soon as Kevin was out of earshot, Eli took the short walk to be near his love. He leaned toward her and used his big fingers to pull her long hair behind her ear.

"I love you," he whispered. "Oh man, I said it. I said it out loud. I said it." He laughed a weird, nervous-mixed-with-excitement laugh. "I'm a total dork, but I did it, I said it."

"I love you too." Ivy responded with the same giddy enthusiasm Eli had. She made an "eek" sound.

"Do you feel weird?" Eli needed to know he wasn't alone.

"A little, but good weird." She smiled up at him.

"Oh, good. Me too. But definitely good weird. Def-definitely good." Eli had no idea what made him channel Rain Man. Ivy's face expressed her confusion, but she laughed enthusiastically anyway.

"Dork," she said, "I'm in love with a dork."

"Say it again," Eli begged.

"Dork." Ivy smiled. She knew exactly what he wanted, but she couldn't miss her chance to razz her Rain Man.

"No, not 'dork,' Dork. The other thing."

“You mean the ‘I’m in love part’?”

“Yes! That’s the thing. Who are you in love with?”

“With you.”

“Ah,” Eli sighed. “That hit the spot.” He sat the paper plate he was still holding on one of the folding chairs nearby. He held his big arms open and gave Ivy the signal to step inside them. She didn’t hesitate and quickly placed her plate on a chair. Eli’s big arms wrapped around her like a fortress of protection and warmth. This hug felt different. The whole world felt different. In this embrace was the confirmation that, together, there was nothing the two of them couldn’t accomplish. This hug was the doorway between high-school romance and life-long love.

CHAPTER SIX

"That's four! Your turn!" Beau exclaimed enthusiastically as he smashed yet another beer can between his mammoth hands. He tossed the can onto an already impressive pile and looked toward Heavy, visibly signaling the impending challenge.

Heavy had been called "Heavy" since he was little, and, as one might guess, he was aptly named for his size. He was most definitely heavy and always had been, but he wasn't heavy in a muscular McKnight way. He was heavy in a fast-food-every-day way. Heavy loved to eat… and drink. He was known for his ability to put away whole pizzas, and he carried around a box of oatmeal cream pies everywhere he went.

"Give me that, wench!" Heavy snatched another beer from the well-manicured hand of the cheerleader-turned-drinking-game-servant standing to his left.

"Wench?" She shouted back at him. She swung a shapely leg in his direction as the circle of onlookers laughed.

Heavy quickly stabbed the lower edge of the can with a pocket knife and pressed the forthcoming beer-geyser to his lips before popping the top. The crowd of surrounding teens went nuts. Heavy had just upped the ante. Beau looked on, never wavering from his arrogant stance. He smiled. Within what seemed like seconds, Heavy slammed the now-empty can down onto the white, plastic folding table in front of him. "Back to you, Princess," he spouted, looking at Beau through glassy eyes that signified pride, and perhaps a touch of nausea.

Without being prompted, the cheerleading bar maid from the current junior class walked over to Beau with a beer in hand. She held it out to him, but instead of taking the can, Beau reached down and grabbed the petite girl around her waist. "For my next trick, I'm going to need an assistant." He swept the girl off the ground with ease and efficiency. She squealed from the suddenness of the experience as Beau sat her onto the table in front of him. He stepped close to her and leaned in, placing his left hand on the table beside her. She leaned away from him instinctively.

"Whoo-whee!" She said, "I declay-uh," pantomiming a fan with her hand. The adoring circle of spectators made every kind of caterwauling noise imaginable as they looked on.

Beau pulled out his pocket knife and placed it between his teeth. His plan became immediately obvious and his assistant made it known to the onlookers that she certainly had no problems with the arrangement.

Heavy called out, “Oh, c’mon — that ain’t fair! You’re a dirty cheat McKnight!” Heavy stumbled back and the boisterous crowd of teens howled with laughter.

Beau’s assistant leaned in to fulfill her next duty, with a smile on her face that Beau had seen up close before. As she threw an arm over his shoulder, Dan Shepherd’s voice rang out loud and proud over the hired band’s sound system, “Ladies and gents, the pig is done! Let’s eat!”

“Ah, saved by the pig!” Heavy hollered out. Clearly, the dinner bell meant the challenge was over. “We’ll continue this after I fill my poor famished self,” he eyeballed Beau and smacked his ample belly, and then set out in a not-so-straight bee-line, stumbling and stammering his way to the food.

Beau laughed and called behind him, ‘If we have to wait till you’re full, we might be waiting all night.” Heavy didn’t turn around and instead gestured his retort with a single, predictable finger.

As darkness fell over the lake, there were three large fires burning at various intervals and the music was loud. Beau was secretly surprised at the number of his classmates who had generators that were confiscated for the event, “Why do so many people keep generators in this town?” he thought.

Spirits were high — there was beer, food and more beer, and to Beau’s delight, there were also girls, lots of girls. There existed a vast divide between the young men who became tongue-tied idiots around the opposite sex and boys like Beau McKnight, who somehow managed to become even cooler around women than he was every other day of the week. Beau seemed to have a natural, easy way with women of all ages. Little girls adored him and elderly ladies loved him, and so did every lady in between. Beau lived happily on the high side of that vast crevasse between the sexes.

His appeal was credited to not only his stunning looks and high-school notoriety, but also to his confidence and his free-and-easy sense of humor. He'd never wanted for a date, and truth be told, he'd never really worried about the consequences that might come from his romantic conquests. As he shoved another bite of his pulled-pork sandwich into his mouth, he got the feeling he was being watched. He wiped a spot of barbecue from the corner of his mouth and looked up.

He looked around slowly and his eyes met Maggie's. She looked away quickly, and visibly reacted to being "caught." Beau found it endearing and her stunning good looks didn't hurt — target acquired. He set down his plate, plunged his massive hands into the nearby cooler and pulled out two beers.

Maggie was sitting on the tailgate of a random pickup parked near the location of the forthcoming bonfire, swinging a pair of legs that any red-blooded man would appreciate. Her flip-flops hung precariously from her perfectly painted toes and she twirled a strand of long brown hair around her equally well-maintained finger. She refused to look up. Embarrassment flooded her entire body as Beau walked toward her, but she was determined to play it cool.

Beau liked Maggie, in general. She'd always been nice to him, and what's more, she'd never expressed a romantic interest in him, which made her all the more appealing. In fewer strides than seemed possible, he'd reached her perch. He turned and sat down next to her. The bed of the truck dropped rather dramatically. Maggie grabbed onto the tailgate with both hands.

"Good Lord!" She laughed.

"I got nothing," Beau admitted. "Can I buy you a drink though, mi' lady?" Beau set one of the beers he'd snagged on the tailgate next to her.

"Um, thanks."

Beau opened the bottle for her, and then asked, "Having fun?"

Maggie shrugged, "Eh."

"What? How can you possibly not be having fun? Everyone is here and there are drinks and a ginormous pig roasting on a stick over an open flame. And then there's me. I mean, I'm here. That's got to be as awesome as it gets, right?"

Maggie rolled her eyes, but smiled, "Is that right?"

"Seriously, what's eatin' at you?" Despite the fact that he never seemed to take anything seriously, Beau's muscled chest hid a very good heart — a heart he did his best to conceal.

"I guess I was just thinking about the fact that this is the last time I'll be here, with my friends, doing this kind of thing. It's kind of sad." She pouted a little. "I don't think I want to grow up."

"Are you kidding?" Beau sounded dismayed. "We're about to enter that time in life our parents call 'the good ole days.' We're old enough to make our own decisions, but young enough to get away with making some really stupid choices." He raised his beer and held it out toward her, "Here's to stupid choices and our good ole days. Cheers."

Maggie laughed and clinked her bottle against his, "I like the way you think Beau McKnight."

Beau cursed under his breath, "I'm just getting warmed up. You stick with me tonight. I think tonight is the perfect night to start making those stupid choices." He took a swig of his beer and threw an arm around Maggie. "Let's go eat."

"Didn't you just finish eating?" She hopped down off the tailgate.

"One is never actually *finished* eating." Beau stood and stuck his arm out for her. The pair began walking toward the large crowd gathered at the picnic tables. "Do you smell that? It's about to go down."

Mags smiled. "Okay, McKnight, I hear you." She paused, "Wait!" She let go of Beau's arm and rushed back to the truck, "I almost forgot my drink."

CHAPTER SEVEN

Eli and Ivy road in silence for the first few minutes of their journey back to Ivy's house. It wasn't an awkward silence, instead it was a silence of understanding. The implications of the night's events would change the course of the future. They both knew it. Finally Ivy said, "I knew it would be exciting, finding your match in planning your future, but I didn't know I should expect it to feel so comfortable. It's almost like that feeling you get when you've been traveling for a while and you finally get back home."

"Really?" Eli questioned. "At this point, I'm more like ninety percent excited and ten percent nervous." He stopped himself and added, "Good nervous, not bad nervous. Good nervous like you feel when you really want to do well at something. Like, game-day nervous."

Ivy made a sort of sarcastic face before shaking her head and saying, "Boys!" She laid her head on Eli's shoulder, and though she was incredibly tired, she couldn't have slept even if she'd tried. The couple rode in silence a while longer before Eli turned on the radio. As he turned into the driveway and passed the long rows of beautifully lit trees, he could see the house was dark except for one light in an upstairs window.

"I bet mom is kicking herself for lifting my curfew tonight. This is probably the latest she's been up in the last decade." Ivy chuckled at her own joke. Knowing that her mother always waited up was both comforting and annoying at the same time. She started to get out of the truck but Eli interrupted her.

"Wait!" He jumped out of the truck on his side and sauntered around to open her door. "I'm pretty sure opening the door for you when you get out of a vehicle is one of those love rules I'm supposed to follow." He held out his arm.

"While that is adorable, I'm pretty sure it's unrealistic. One day, when we have a car load of kids, groceries, and it's raining, the last thing you're going to want to do is get out and run around to open my door so I can run into the pharmacy to pick up…" Eli was smiling broadly and she interrupted herself, "What?"

"You said a car load of kids. And we both know where babies come from. And that means that somewhere inside yourself is the anticipation of sex, with me, sex with me." He was raising both eyebrows simultaneously over and over again in Groucho Marx fashion. The smile on his face had not abated, and Ivy, though she tried to be coy, could not stop herself from laughing.

"Well, we can always adopt. I mean, you know how I feel about overseas missions." She smiled at him and he crossed his arms, cocking his head to the side and putting on a deflated expression. She laughed again and threw both arms around him. She stood on her toes, signaling her desire for his kiss. Eli moved his face closer to hers.

"I'm going to marry you. You know that right?"

She looked into his eyes, "I'm banking on it." He kissed her, and she kissed him back, for what felt like an eternity. He ran his hand over her hair and held her close to him. He felt protective and powerful and, somehow, vulnerable at the same time. As he processed these new feelings, his bliss was interrupted when Ivy's mother began tapping on an upstairs window with her reading glasses. Ivy chuckled and pulled away, she bowed her head and placed her forehead against his chest for just a moment.

"I guess that's my cue. Will you text me when you get home?" She asked for his text in the form of a question but with the endearing tone of an expectation.

"Of course." Eli kissed her forehead, "Good night."

"Good night." Ivy turned to walk inside, she climbed the stairs to the porch and just before reaching for the front door, she turned and said, "Hey Eli, I love you."

Eli's smile was bigger than his face, "I love you too." He watched her walk inside and turned to take the twenty paces to his truck. His mind raced and he knew things would never be the same after that. It was late, but he wasn't the slightest bit tired. His mind bounced from thought to thought, from college to marriage and what it would be like to propose, and even how he would propose.

When he got back to his truck, his phone alerted him to two text messages. The most recent one, from Ivy, read <BE CAREFUL GOING HOME, IT'S LATE.> The second text was from his mom. It was just one word, <SAFE?> He quickly responded in the affirmative before deciding that he was in the mood for a milkshake. Knowing his mother would want one too, because she'd be up until Beau came in, which was bound to be past his curfew, he texted, <TAKING ORDERS FOR THE SUGAR SHACK.> She responded quickly with two smiley faces and the words <CARAMEL, NO WHIP.>

He made the three-point turn it took to maneuver out of the Zellway's driveway and headed back up the long driveway toward the main road. When he reached the end of the driveway, instead of turning left toward home, he turned right toward town and his intended destination, the Sugar Shack. A local favorite, the Sugar Shack stayed open late and made the best milkshakes money could buy. He reached to turn on the radio, but before he did, he dropped his hand and prayed, "This has been an excellent day, Father. Thank you. Thank you." His big finger probed the radio buttons and the sounds of classic rock poured out of the speakers. He cracked his window slightly and drove toward town feeling like the world was at his feet.

CHAPTER EIGHT

Beau pulled his truck a little farther back into the woods because Maggie had voiced her concerns about being seen. He turned off all the lights, but left the battery engaged and the keys in the ignition. His A/C was on and his radio was tuned to country music, which he turned down low before cracking the windows slightly.

"Let's just talk, okay?" Maggie said the words with an air of obligation that gave her away. She tucked her hair behind her ear and looked up at Beau with big doe eyes.

"Of course," Beau instinctively put his arm across the back of the seat and turned his body toward Maggie. "What's on your mind?"

Maggie took a sip of her beer, wiped the back of her mouth with her delicate hand and inhaled deeply through her nose. Beau smelled exactly the way a boy should smell and he was, without a doubt, beautiful. In her moderately inebriated state, Maggie reasoned her choices within her own mind, deciding that this was the last night of her high school career and quite possibly the last night she would ever see Beau McKnight. "I've always liked you, Beau."

"I've always liked you too Mags." He smiled and parted his lips to conjure some flattery, but before he could open his mouth to pay her a compliment, her lips were firmly pressed against his. He placed one hand on the back of her head, intertwining his fingers and her hair. Without missing a beat, or coming up for air, he took the beer from her hand, placed it into a cup holder and then put his hand on her waist. He pulled her close to him and began kissing her neck. Maggie let her head fall back and then she reached across his body to find the lever needed to recline his seat. When she pulled it, Beau's seat fell back — hard. He jumped and they both began to laugh. Beau pulled Maggie onto his lap, "You sure you want to do this?"

"More than sure. But do you have…"

Beau interrupted her, "In the glove box."

As the evening wound down, Beau and Maggie were both drunk, hot and exhausted. Maggie looked out the back window of the truck toward the glow of waning bonfires and said, "I'm pretty sure my ride's gone."

"No it's not!" Beau exclaimed as he slapped her on the backside.

Maggie yelped, giggled and grabbed her rear end, "Are you going to drive me home?"

"Well, you're certainly not going to drive, you lush." Beau rolled his eyes at her.

"Look who's talking," Maggie retorted. As she spoke, she fell off of the seat and onto the floor board, while simultaneously attempting to redress herself. She began to laugh at herself hysterically in an intoxicated way as Beau pulled her back up onto the seat.

"Well, I'm clearly not as drunk as you are," he joked. "It's fine, I'll take you home." He pulled his t-shirt over his head, buckled his seatbelt, started the truck, put it into reverse, and backed out of his cozy spot in the tree line. "Don't forget to buckle up." He patted the seat right next to his right thigh and Maggie slid over. She pulled the seatbelt across her lap and clicked it in place, laid her head over onto Beau's shoulder, and before they even turned onto the dirt road out of the field, she was out cold.

Ten minutes later, Beau was beginning to feel the effects of the night. He rolled down his windows to let the air hit his face. He fumbled with the items in the driver's door compartment until he found the bag of menthol cough drops he kept there and popped two of them into his mouth. He slowly reached his arm out toward the dash, so as not to wake Maggie, and used his fingertips to turn the radio up. Maggie didn't move a muscle. As Beau turned into Maggie's neighborhood, he realized that, while he knew the neighborhood was right, he had no idea which house, or even which street she lived on. He put his big hand on her left knee, "Wake up Mags." She stirred a little, but didn't wake. "Maggie," his quiet, whispered tone grew slightly louder. Nothing. He shook his right shoulder to jostle her head. “MAGGIE,” he spoke loudly, though not angrily. She finally raised her head.

Almost immediately upon opening her eyes, Maggie said, “I don’t feel so good.” She looked up at him pleadingly.

“Don’t you dare yak in my truck, woman!” Beau quickly pulled over. She threw her body toward the door of the truck and peered out through the glass.

“Ha!” She slurred, poking at the glass with a well-manicured fingertip, tapping her nail against the surface clumsily, “That’s my house! How did you know that?” Beau marveled slightly at his own luck, but focused the bulk of his energy on hitting the unlock button. Maggie pulled up on the door handle while leaning on the door. When the door flung open, Maggie fell out of the truck onto the asphalt like a marionette.

Beau yelled an expletive and then loudly inquired, “Are you okay?” He got no response, so he opened his door and trotted around the front of the truck, passing through the two beams of light like a human eclipse, casting a shadow on the trees in the curve ahead. Maggie was pushing herself up onto her hands and knees. She turned her head to look up at him and her expression revealed that she definitely wasn’t “okay.” She looked back at the ground beneath her and proceeded to vomit. “Oh, geez.” Beau had to turn away. His own stomach churned at the sight, and sound, of Maggie’s misery.

“I’m okay,” Maggie said, as she looked up at him a moment later, “I just need to lay down.” Without another word,

Maggie took her own advice and let her body fall onto the ground. Half of her body was in the grass and half of her was on the asphalt. Beau's own head was swimming a bit and he stumbled toward her.

"No you don't. Get up. Come on. It's just a little farther." Maggie moaned and rolled over onto her back. Beau stood over her, she looked helpless in a pitiful, but somehow still attractive, way.

"Alright. That's it then." Beau bent down toward Maggie, his truck still running and his driver's side door wide open into the street, and hauled her up off the ground. He lifted her into his arms and carried her all the way to her parent's front porch. "Should I ring the bell?"

"No!" Maggie yelled as she slapped at his hand. Beau turned toward the porch swing and started to make his way to it when Maggie began to gag again.

"Wait!" He let her feet down to the porch and she sank immediately to her knees. "Off the porch! Don't puke on the porch!" He urged her toward the edge of the decking and then stepped back to rub his face. He was losing his patience.

Maggie looked up at him again with her big doe eyes and he instantly felt guilty for being upset with her.

"Ugh, c'mon," he sighed. He hoisted her up again, put her right arm around his shoulder and basically dragged her over to the swing, then he helped her settle in. Maggie reached toward the afghan on the back of the porch swing, but before she could get her hand on it, she was unconscious again.

Beau grabbed the soft, compact fibers of the blanket in the palm of his left hand and spread it over Maggie's legs and torso. It then dawned on him that she'd passed out extremely abruptly and he thought to himself, "Is she dead?" He knelt down beside her, placed his right hand on the porch, and laid his head on her chest and listened carefully for a few minutes. When he concluded that she was, in fact, still alive, he hooked his big index finger under the collar of her shirt and peeked inside, aided by the light of the moon, and giggled to himself, "Yep, I've always liked you Mags." He had taken three steps toward the stairs when he stopped dead in his tracks and turned back. He walked over to Maggie and rolled her whole body onto its side. He whispered, "Can't have you going all, Hedrix, Helix, Hendrix — whoever."

Beau trotted back toward his truck, which was still running in the street. As he climbed inside, he noticed Maggie's bag on the floorboard. He leaned across the seat and reached for the bag. He snatched it out of the truck, and, as he pulled it toward himself, the strap got hooked on one of Maggie's half-finished beers in the cup holder. The bottle flew out of its plastic cubby and slung beer in all directions. "Seriously?" Beau exclaimed before coloring the night air with a string of profanities. He shoved the bag under his arm, snagged the spilled bottle and two others from various locations in the truck and then started to stomp back up the sidewalk toward the house when he paused and decided to stuff the bag into the mailbox instead.

“Screw it,” he said, as he slammed the mailbox door shut and turned on his heels toward the storm drain across the street. He threw the beer bottles into the drain and made a beeline back toward his truck. As he climbed into the driver’s seat, the weight of the night fell on him like a heavy blanket, and he wanted nothing more than to sleep it off.

Beau glanced at his phone as he put the truck into drive. He had four missed texts and it was already past curfew. He didn’t bother to read the texts and, instead, threw his phone onto the passenger seat and set out for home.

CHAPTER NINE

Eli pulled out from the Sugar Shack drive thru and made his way to the exit. Given the hour, it was no surprise that the roads were basically deserted. After pressing the back end of a straw against his thigh and forcing it through its paper encasement, he reached toward his cup holder and popped a straw through the top of the plastic lid protecting his milkshake from the outside world. He rolled the straw paper into a ball between his big fingers and dropped it into the console. He lifted the cup to his lips, took a long, slow gulp and let the sweetness of the drink permeate his taste buds for a few moments before swallowing.

He delighted in the sensation of milkshake hitting his stomach as he made the right hand turn onto the two-lane highway that ran the length of town. He turned on the radio and, for a change, tuned away from rock, and away from the contemporary Christian channel to which he'd been a loyalist for the last two years, and instead settled on a random, upbeat pop song. He didn't know the words. In fact, he didn't think he'd ever heard it before, but it had a decent beat and reminded him of Ivy somehow, so he let it play out.

Eli replayed the night's events over and over again in his mind. He felt oddly light — a rarity for someone of his stature. He also felt a little nervous, almost like he was daydreaming and if he made one wrong move, he'd be snapped back into the mundane reality associated with any other day. He tried to imagine what college would be like, living on his own, without Beau. Because his brother had accepted a football scholarship, he'd be in a different set of dorms and the two would have to make an actual effort to spend time together.

Eli had loved sports from a very young age. His mother kept framed pictures on the wall depicting a diapered Eli, before he could he even walk, with a little football tucked under one chubby arm and a baseball held firmly in the chubby fist of his other hand. And though he could have played his way through the next four years, in his spirit, he knew the academic route was the right choice for him. He envisioned playing intramurals, without the pressure of wins and losses looming over his senses, and pictured what it would be like to be in the stands, rooting for Beau with Ivy by his side and his parents yelling their brains out in the two seats behind him.

He envisioned breakfast with Ivy every morning at the student café and imagined discussing the future with her at dinner every night. He also wondered if maybe, just maybe, he'd have a roommate who didn't leave sweaty socks on his pillow for laughs the way Beau had done every night since they were nine. A wave of weirdness welled up inside Eli's veins as he thought about how strange it would feel to live apart from his twin, after all, they'd been fighting over the same living space since the womb.

Eli reached out with the middle finger of his left hand to engage his left turn signal. He placed his milkshake back into its cup holder and slowed down to make the left-hand turn toward home. As he eased into the turn, he was momentarily blinded by the reflection of oncoming high-beams in his rear view mirrors. Squinting into the reflection, Eli rolled on, but as he moved across what was supposed to be an empty oncoming lane of traffic, the blinding headlights that had just been behind him were suddenly on top of him. They were, quite literally, coming through the driver's side door.

In less time than it takes to formulate a single thought, Eli could hear the sound of metal careening against metal, moaning and screaming like a wounded animal. His hands were forcibly ripped from the steering wheel, the bones in his fingers pulled from their sockets as smoothly and easily as a foot pulls from a sock. He recoiled at the thunderclap his head made as it ricocheted off the air bag. The angle of the impact and the momentum of his body moving across the cab of the truck caused the rough material of the bag to scrape across his right cheek, searing his skin like raw meat on a hot grill.

Eli's back slammed against the inside of the passenger door like a sack of flour being dropped onto the floor, broken glass rained down over his forehead as the back of his skull smashed against the partially open passenger window. At the same time he blinked the glass fragments out of his eyelashes, he could feel the driver's side door compressing against his chest and abdomen. The sound inside his head was a high-pitched bell, almost like a distant fire alarm. He looked down to see a part of his body lodged between his stomach and the driver's door, but he couldn't tell what part of his body it was, and though it was dark, he could see what looked like a sticky, crimson oil slick slowly making its way down his neck and onto his shirt.

Eli felt an intense pressure rising in his chest and, as he lifted his head, he vomited forcefully, without warning. The sound inside his head remained a constant warning bell, but he felt no pain. His left arm was pinned at the elbow, between his stomach and what might have been his left leg, but his right arm remained free, though there was very little space to move it. He tried in vain to push against the door in front of him. He could almost taste the odor of something burnt as he tried to inhale through his nose. Dizziness crept into his being slowly as he lifted his right hand toward his face. As he moved, he finally felt the onslaught of pain pulsating through every nerve in his body.

His useless fingers dangled from his palm like bananas in a bunch, but as his hand neared his skull, he felt the back of it brush against the rough texture of a tree trunk. Suddenly, his arm went limp, falling heavily back to his side. As he leaned his head forward again, into the nineteen inches of space between the truck doors, he felt the warmth of a thick liquid running into his eyes. The inky darkness of the night closed in around him from all sides, and the world went black.

CHAPTER TEN

Beau blinked against the morning light of another day, tasting his own foul breath as the pounding in his head drummed him into consciousness. As the wheels in his mind began to turn, he realized the pounding in his head was not the same as those familiar morning-after drumline headaches he'd experienced before. As he opened his eyes, he became aware of his surroundings — unfamiliar surroundings. Gaining his wits, he noticed the transparent, snake-like tail of an IV emerging from the bend of his left arm. Then the faint beeping of a nearby medical monitor became clear inside his pounding head. The room came into focus, and there, seated next to him in a tan vinyl recliner, he saw his mother. She was curled into a ball, feet in the seat, knees to her chest, head down, with her forehead resting against her knees. She was wearing jeans and one of her favorite sweatshirts. Her hair was tucked behind her ears.

"Mom?" Beau's voice hung in the air. Valerie's head shot up.

"Oh, thank God you're awake!" She uncurled her body and moved to his bedside.

"What's happening? Where am I?" Beau's voice was pleading.

"You were in an accident, Beau. How much do you remember?" Valerie's response was almost awkward, as if she was fighting the silence to grasp at words that wouldn't come. Her face was the picture of exhaustion. She spoke hesitantly, with an uncharacteristic reservation that made Beau subconsciously uneasy.

"Remember? Nothing! What's going on?"

Valerie's expression was serious, but Beau could see loving concern in her eyes, "You crashed your truck last night."

"I did? How?"

Valerie grabbed his hand, tears beginning to fill her eyes, "They think you may have fallen asleep at the wheel. You were in and out when they brought you in."

"I did? How long have I been here? How's my truck?" Beau pushed himself up in his hospital bed with his hands, "Dad's going to kill me, isn't he?"

Valerie broke into a sob, "Son, I…" She stopped and covered her clearly-weary eyes with her left hand, letting her head fall to her chest. Valerie took a deep, staggered breath and continued, "Son, you had alcohol in your system and you…" She had to stop. "You hit another truck, Beau. You hit your brother's truck." Beau was silent. He stared at her. His expression personified the confusion he felt on the inside. He could tell there was more to say, but his mother was having difficulty breathing, let alone speaking.

"Wait, what? Just tell me, Mom."

A sob caught in his mother's throat, "You hit Eli's truck. He's hurt. He's really hurt, Beau. He was airlifted to Houston Methodist. Your dad went." She broke down and didn't even try to hold back her tears. "That's all I know." She glanced at her phone. "Dad will call when there's more."

All the air was sucked out of the room and Beau suddenly couldn't breathe. "Eli was…" He began to feel nauseated, "I... I." He covered his mouth with his hand, leaning over the bed. Valerie pressed the nurse call button.

"Could I get some help in here, please? He's nauseated." She fell silent again, wiping her eyes.

As the door to the room came open, the nurse entered carrying a pink, plastic container. She walked over to Beau and put her hand gently on the back of his head, guiding him back toward his pillow with the container under his chin. He instinctively reached up to hold it, as he dry heaved and gagged, producing nothing.

"Keep this handy, but there's likely very little in your stomach." She turned toward Valerie, "We had to pump his stomach last night." Valerie nodded a thank you in the nurse's direction and, as the nurse opened the door to leave, Beau could see a police officer standing in the hallway outside his room.

The officer spoke to the nurse and Beau watched as the door slowly closed behind her, as if to conceal a secret everyone knew except him. He wretched again.

Valerie walked to the window, her arms hugging her own body. The morning sun came through the blinds in a wash of color that, under any other circumstances, would have brought her joy. She closed her eyes to pray, but her mind reeled and she couldn't form the thoughts necessary to pray, so instead she cried deep, silent sobs.

Beau was silent, his mind reeling. His heart began to beat inside his chest with such force it quaked his entire body as shock flooded his being. He watched his mother through dizzy eyes, crying at the window, but neither of them made a sound.

Not a word was spoken, because there was nothing left to say.

CHAPTER ELEVEN

The silence in the room was shattered by the sound of Valerie's cellphone ringing on the windowsill. She snatched it up with an urgency unlike any she'd ever experienced. Beau could almost feel his mother's heart sinking as she said, "It's your Nan." She pushed the green slider to the right and answered, "Mom? Yes, he's awake, he's going to be fine… I'm not sure. No, Joe said he'd call as soon as he knew something. I haven't… Wait!" Valerie pulled her phone away from her ear to look at the screen before continuing her call. "Mom, it's Joe. I'll call you back. I love you, too." She looked at her phone again and switched lines, "Hello? I'm so happy to hear your voice. What's happening?" There was a long pause before Valerie lifted her arm and lightly covered her mouth with her left hand. She closed her eyes and the tears began to flow. "Thank God. Thank God. But…" She fell silent again.

Beau, who was leaning forward, listening in earnest, propping himself up with his only untethered arm, couldn't hold his peace any longer, "He's okay? He's good, right? Mom, he's okay, right?" Valerie lifted her hand abruptly, her palm facing toward Beau in a gesture that was unmistakable. Beau immediately fell silent, resigning himself to the wait.

"How long? What did they say? Do they have any ideas? What are they going to do?" Valerie asked. "I don't know. He hasn't called yet. I haven't mentioned that. Joe, I… I don't know what to do. I feel so helpless." She looked down toward the cold, sterile floor tiles and took a ragged breath, trying to hold back her tears. "I understand. I'll figure it out. I love you, too. Please, call soon. I love you."

"Well? How is he? Haven't mentioned what?" Beau demanded answers from the confines of his telemetric prison.

"We need to go. We need to get there, but…"

"Mom! What is happening?" Beau's agitation was palpable.

"He's alive, but it's not good. He's been unconscious since they found him and he's still in surgery, okay? We need to get there!" Valerie spoke loudly, brusquely, shrilly, in a tone Beau had never heard come out of her mouth before. The audible sound of her obvious pain was like a dagger in his chest. "I have to speak to the police, and since the lawyer hasn't called me yet, I need to call him. We have got to go."

"Police? Lawyer? What?" Beau fell back onto his bed, his mind racing, still unable to comprehend his current reality. Valerie paced around the room, thinking, but not speaking.

Beau interrupted her internal process with a loud plea for clarification, "Mom?"

"Beau, listen, you're technically under arrest. You had alcohol in your system last night. You are under age, which means that, no matter what, you're going to be in trouble. As far as the police are concerned, you broke the law and hit another vehicle. Someone called 9-1-1, and, well, here we are. The fact that it was your brother's truck means nothing legally. Since you're both eighteen, it's out of our hands. Your dad got you a lawyer and he's supposed to call me, or come by, or something. I hope they let you go with me. I don't know when they'll discharge you. I don't know if you'll have to go straight to jail. I… I don't even know what to do next." Valerie was in hyper-drive. She was on autopilot. Her emotions had given way to stoic, yet, manic, shock. She spewed hard-hitting, rapid-fire information all over Beau and then she suddenly, without warning, opened the door to Beau's room and stepped out into the hallway.

Beau struggled to organize the onslaught of information he'd just received. He could hear muffled voices in the hallway. "This isn't happening. This cannot be happening," he spoke the words aloud in a feeble attempt to convince himself they were true. He covered his face with his hands, pressing them into his flesh like he always did when he had a nightmare, but instead of waking up to the safety of his room, he woke to the same nightmare. He laid back against his hospital bed and closed his eyes. He heard the door to his room open and he expected to see his mother's frame, but he didn't. The nurse walked over to his bedside and began checking his vitals in awkward silence. Beau didn't speak either.

After what felt like an eternity, the nurse broke the vacuum of quiet in the room and asked, "Do you think you could eat something?" She reached out and touched his head with the back of her hand, gently and with compassion. Beau knew her compassion spawned from pity and that knowledge alone burned like a hot coal in his belly.

"No."

"Buzz if you need anything." The nurse turned to leave and, as she approached the door, she turned back toward Beau, as if she had something else to say, something on the tip of her tongue, but she didn't say it, and, instead, she took a deep breath and turned away again.

The door hadn't closed all the way when Valerie stuck her hand out and stopped it, pushing it open again. She crossed the threshold and let the oak-toned barrier click shut behind her. She didn't move. She didn't speak. She stood, looking at her son, breathing deeply. In this moment, he was more a boy than a man. He looked like a frightened toddler — *her* frightened toddler. Her heart was torn between fear, anger and compassion for her child, her children. She walked toward his bed and lowered the side rail. She sat down next to him and slid her slender arm behind Beau's head. He instinctively scooted over to give her more room. She slid off her shoes and raised her feet from the floor, stretching her legs out on the bed beside his. As they reclined there, in silence, she bent her arm at the elbow, behind his head, and rested her hand gently in his hair, patting him lightly. They sat together quietly for an hour, not moving, not speaking.

"Is Eli going to die?" Beau's question shattered the silence like a hammer through plate glass.

The words pierced Valerie's very soul. Through her pain, her doubt, her fear and her knowledge that, yes, Eli may very well be dead before she could hold him again, feel the warmth of him in her arms, kiss his face and tell him she was there, she mustered the strength to say "no." Surprisingly, when she heard her own voice say the word, she felt her heart quicken within her. Something about speaking that word, speaking life aloud, gave her an unexpected and unlikely strength. She didn't fully even believe the word herself, but saying it renewed her spirit. It revived her fighting instinct. Just when she had resigned herself to the possibility of losing a child, she was accosted with a newness of purpose because of one simple word, a word she herself had considered to be a lie before she spoke it. "No! He's not! He will live and not die!" She spoke emphatically this time.

Beau heard her words and his mind recoiled. He knew that scripture. He knew she was speaking from a place a hope, which meant hope was all she had to go on. The reality of what was happening began to settle in his gut. A feeling of self-loathing flowed over him like a liquid, chilling him and scalding him at the same time. As the feeling strangled him within its deadly grasp, he struggled to breath. He quickly slipped into a strange limbo between denial and self-blame. He didn't believe his own reality, but at the same time, he hated himself for creating it. As his mind mutated within the confines of his skull, the door to his room opened.

CHAPTER TWELVE

A slim man in a dark pin-striped suit, maroon tie and exceptionally shiny shoes stepped into Beau's downcast view. When Beau lifted his eyes, he was met with a solemn gaze and slick hair. Valerie rose to her feet immediately.

"Mrs. McKnight, Beau, I'm John Paul Sapuro. Most people call me JP. I believe you've been expecting me."

"Yes, we've been waiting." She reached out to shake the hand he offered. "I assume my husband filled you in on what happened. We just don't know where to turn next or what to expect. The bottom line is that I, we, need to get to Houston to be with Eli. We should really be there already."

"As you probably already know, the officer outside the door is here to arrest Beau when he's released. He'll then be booked and, with your permission, I will petition the judge to release him with a PR bond. Given the circumstances, I don't think it will be an issue. I will make sure that in-state travel is permitted and he can join you in Houston. There may be some restrictions on his ability to drive at that point, especially since he's looking at a vehicular assault charge on top of the underage consumption. The fact that his BAC wasn't over the top will help us, because falling asleep at the wheel, which is what I will argue and what the doctors actually believe, is not the same as negligence due to intoxication." JP led Valerie away a few feet and spoke to her softly. Beau could still hear him, but he pretended not to. "Mrs. McKnight, this is a hard thing to discuss, but if your other son passes away, the DA will likely argue for a vehicular manslaughter charge. I know this DA and I'm hoping the circumstances will work in our favor, but we would be in for a fight."

"That is *not* going to happen." Valerie *sounded* confident, but she rubbed her face to mask her anxiety nonetheless.

JP nodded. "Unfortunately, he will probably have to stay overnight at the jail at least one night, unless we can expedite the hospital release and get this all done today. I can speak to the doctors, but that part is really out of my hands."

"I will handle that." Valerie sighed, "I'm guessing all of that takes hours though, right?"

"Yes. Most likely, but assuming I can assure his travel privileges, which shouldn't be a problem since your son has only been charged but not convicted, he will be free to go to Houston." He paused, "If you need to leave now, you can arrange for transportation and Beau can meet you there."

Beau finally spoke up. His words emerged from his body coated in a thick layer of ice, "Stop talking about me like I'm not here. Mom, just go." In his heart, he didn't want to go to Houston. Going would make the situation real. "I need to be in jail, right? So let's go." He fell silent as abruptly as he began. Even as the words emerged from his lips, Valerie noted a palpable strangeness about her son. She could audibly *hear* him loathing his own existence.

"Beau, don't. Just, stop." She shook her head toward JP, who easily keyed in on the fact that the young man in the nearby hospital bed was a very different person from the one she knew.

"I will speak to the officer outside. Mrs. McKnight, you may want to talk to Beau's nurse to speed up his release. It might also be prudent to arrange for transportation for your son's trip to Houston, hopefully, this evening."

"Will he be able to drive?" Valerie asked.

"He should be. I'll know more soon." JP turned to exit the room and neither Valerie nor Beau acknowledged his departure.

"Are you sure you want me to go ahead? I don't think I can do that. How can I leave you?" Valerie walked over to Beau and put her hand on his arm. He pulled away and nodded.

"Go!" Beau practically shouted, pure anger in his voice. The tone pierced Valerie's spirit, but she chose to ignore it.

"They towed your truck, but I think they got your wallet and phone first. I will try to find out. We'll have to get a rental car, or something. Dad was going to call your grandparents. They're probably already on the road. Ivy is going today, too." She trailed off. Beau lost focus on her words and instead let his heart soak in the inky dark shame like a sponge.

CHAPTER THIRTEEN

Beau, in a daze, walked silently through the arrest process, the pat down, the booking and the waiting. He was torn between the pressing, eager desire to return to his own freedom and the desire to hide from the world, coupled with the repressive reality that he deserved to be right where he was. Before Valerie left the hospital, she had placed a plastic bag containing Beau's cellphone and wallet on the bedside table. With the exception of a tiny crack in the upper right-hand corner of his phone screen, his personal effects were unscathed. If it weren't for the agony of the reality unfolding before him, it would have felt like any other day.

By the time his arresting officer had processed his belongings at booking, Beau's phone screen registered more than thirty unopened text messages. He knew that the entire school had likely already heard, but he was long since past caring. He didn't care enough about the curious masses to return messages or phone calls. Nothing mattered.

It was almost like he was sleepwalking, yet he remained wide-awake. He had not spoken. He had been silent during the fingerprinting process. He had been silent when a female officer had asked him if he wanted some water. The male officer, who had waited outside his hospital room, for probably the entire night, had been sympathetic and had let Beau ride in a wheelchair all the way to the hospital doors, while he trailed behind at an unassuming distance. When Beau slid into the backseat of a squad car, he had expected handcuffs, but the officer had closed the door behind him, never touching the cuffs that dangled at his waist. Still, Beau hadn't uttered a word.

"Do you want to call someone now?" Another attending officer gestured toward the phone, offering Beau his customary "one phone call" before, ultimately, being locked up. Beau simply shook his head. "You sure? Last chance." Again, Beau shook his head. He then turned away, silently ending the would-be conversation. "Oh-kay," the officer drew out the word in a tone that obviously minimized the situation in such a way that seemed almost offensive to Beau, whose very life would soon be defined by the experience, "suit yourself."

A few minutes later, another jailer came out into the booking area from behind a steel door, gestured casually toward Beau and said, "It's going to be a few minutes before I can take him back to holding."

"No problem," a female officer responded. She pushed herself up from a squeaky, gray office chair, opened a file drawer to retrieve some handcuffs, and sauntered around to where Beau stood, "Hands behind your back, please." Beau silently, immediately, but somehow slowly, complied. The female officer escorted him over to a short row of plastic chairs, each of which was bolted to a cream-colored cinder block wall and also to each other. "Sit tight," she said. She nodded as if to imply "sit tight" was more of a question than a command and smiled slightly before returning to her spot behind the counter.

Beau leaned back against his new jewelry, scooting low in his seat, and rested his head against the cold block wall behind him. He could see through a glass partition into what looked like a waiting area for family or friends. In the corner, he spotted a small television set. He couldn't hear the sounds, but he could read the words on the screen. The channel was set to local news. At the bottom of the screen he read, *Tragedy Befalls High School Hometown Heroes*. The screen then flashed an image of Beau and Eli McKnight, arms over each other's shoulders, standing in front of their school. Beau recognized the photo from their yearbook. A reporter stood at the crash site and Beau could see the remnants of glass in the road behind her. She gestured and a picture of Eli flashed above her right shoulder. Beau's stomach turned. He stood quickly, "I'm sick. I'm gonna be sick," he blurted the words even as the cold sweat beaded on his forehead.

A clerk in civilian clothes kicked a metal trashcan toward the edge of her desk and an officer, who had been casually chatting her up, snatched it up and moved swiftly in Beau's direction. "Sit down," he said, as he pushed the trashcan between Beau's knees with his foot. Beau leaned over the can, but when his head went between his knees, his nausea subsided some. He rested there, breathing. It almost looked like he was bobbing for apples. He didn't move from that position for a solid ten minutes. He half hoped he'd die right then and there.

The steel door swung open again. "I was sent to walk one back to holding, but I don't have a name," a familiar voice called out into the room. Beau looked up, he knew the call was for him, but he remained in his bowed position. The jailer waiting to walk Beau back recognized him instantly and almost jovially sang out, "No way. McKnight? Is that you? I haven't seen you in at least two years! What are you doing here?" Nausea overtook Beau's body again, and he turned his face back toward the floor. When he looked up again, Jessee, a former teammate from years ago, had a file folder in his hands, reading. He looked up from the file into Beau's eyes, dismay whittled into his expression. His voice was almost a whisper when he said, "Let's go."

CHAPTER FOURTEEN

Valerie screamed into the parking lot at Sapuro, Stephens and Popp on rails. She snatched the rental car keys from the seat beside her and tucked them into an envelope containing a note for her son before launching her body out of the car and across the lot like an Olympic sprinter.

"I'm Valerie McKnight. I'm here to see JP Sapuro, please." Val didn't wait for the receptionist to acknowledge her presence before she made her urgent announcement. The young, sweet looking, slightly heavy girl behind the counter glanced up.

"Mrs. McKnight. JP told me you were coming. Give me one moment."

"Please hurry. It's urgent. I don't have time to waste." Valerie managed to blend politeness and matter-of-fact like some kind of southern-speak smoothie.

"Yes ma'am." Valerie waited for two minutes, but it might as well have been two hours and it felt like two days.

"Mrs. McKnight, follow me." Val followed the receptionist down a short hallway and through open double doors to a conference room where JP was waiting with a large stack of papers and file folders.

"Mrs. McKnight," JP greeted her.

"Call me Val, Mr. Sapuro."

"Only if you call me JP."

"Okay. JP, tell me what's going to happen to my son." She pulled out a chair and sat down. "I've got to get to Houston and I'm literally falling apart inside. I haven't slept and I can't seem to get my head around all of this."

"For starters, I'll say that you really should sleep before you drive to Houston." Valerie's incredulous look spoke volumes, and JP knew she didn't want to hear this.

JP cleared his throat, "Well, Beau has been booked. He's in holding and I'm about to head over there. We will meet with the judge in about an hour and the judge will determine whether or not your son is cleared for a PR bond."

"You mentioned that earlier and I didn't ask. What is a PR bond?"

"It's a personal recognizance bond. It will save you money, and it will allow Beau to be at home with you for the duration of his case. I have to tell you, it's only the unusual condition of this case, and the urgency alone, that has allowed me to move this through so quickly. PR bonds are something of a rarity, but so is this situation. I am confident the judge will be sympathetic. Right now, he's charged with reckless driving causing serious bodily harm and he's got a minor in consumption charge, what we call an MIC ticket. It is a very good thing that he wasn't legally intoxicated and, of course, that your other son is alive, or we'd be having a completely different discussion. I sent your son's history, along with my statements, over to the court for the judge to review about an hour ago. We're putting a rush on everything, working as fast as we can."

"When will you see him? I spoke to my husband again and I really, really need to be on the road. But, I feel terrible about leaving at the same time."

"Don't worry. I'll see him very soon. He and I both will meet the judge. If all goes as planned, he'll be on his way to you by evening."

"That long?"

"Unfortunately, yes. Well, probably. We'll try to move it along quickly, but these things do tend to crawl on for a while."

Valerie slid the key to the rental across the table. The mere tone of the bright yellow tag labeled *Nissan* made her squint. The exhaustion and the strain of both the tears and the situation had settled into her temples and showed no signs of easing up. "It's parked in our driveway. They actually delivered it. I had no idea that was a thing. But, I have no idea how Beau will get to the house. I suppose I could leave some cash for a taxi..."

JP interrupted her, "Don't worry about that. I'll get him home. He and I will get to know each other really well over the next few months. We might as well start tonight."

"Thank you." Val was almost in tears again. "I just can't believe this is all happening."

"You'll get through it. We will get through it."

"That's very kind." She paused, "My husband said something about a retainer that needed to be paid."

"That's right. My retainer for felonious criminal defense is normally $10,000. Your husband called on a recommendation from Bill Roberts. Bill and I go way back. After speaking with Mr. McKnight and hearing the nature of the case, I have settled on a retainer of $7,000. It translates to about twenty-five hours of billable time and will be put toward the total bill. After that amount is exhausted, I bill at $280 per hour."

"Felonious?" Valerie repeated the word in the form of a question, with an obvious tone of worry. She knew what a felony was and what it would mean to Beau's future.

"Yes ma'am. I am working this as a felonious case because he is charged with, essentially, vehicular assault, which can be a felony in Texas when serious injury is involved. I am hoping to secure a misdemeanor charge, but we just don't know yet. It's too soon. I promise you though, I will do everything in my power to minimize this situation as much as possible." JP was sympathetic, but also remained professional. He had kids of his own, and though they were much younger than the

McKnight brothers, his heart ached at the thought of something so tragic happening in their futures.

"I understand. Bill is a deacon at our church. He's such a nice man. Joe has always said, 'it pays to know people who know people,' but I don't think this is what he had in mind." She pulled the check book from her purse and began scrawling, but she paused and glanced up, "Make this out to?"

"We have a stamp."

"Okay, thank you. Can I ask a favor? We will need to move some money over from another account. Can you wait a bit to deposit this? Maybe forty-eight hours?"

"Sure. Just date it for two days out."

Five minutes and $7,000 later, Valerie McKnight was behind the wheel of her car. She typed the address for the hospital in Houston into her GPS and drove two blocks down to the notorious double arches. She hadn't consumed anything except a cup of coffee from the nurse's station in the ER since this nightmare began and hadn't eaten fast food in at least a year. She ordered a #2 with a large sweet tea and hoped the sugar and caffeine, coupled with her adrenaline, would be enough to get her to Houston unscathed. She didn't really feel like eating, but she knew she should.

As she pulled out of the parking lot, she instinctively began a prayer of thanks, the words of her prayer caught in her mind like a fish caught in a net. She forced them out and then immediately, from somewhere deep in her gut, she gave thanks for her blessed life. She had always heard people quote the verse about giving thanks in all things, and she was determined to do just that. She thanked God for His promises. She thanked Him for JP. She thanked Him that they had the financial means to hire a good lawyer. She thanked God for faith. It was, after all, the only reason she hadn't completely fallen apart — and she had a long way to drive. She couldn't think of a better person to talk to than the Almighty.

CHAPTER FIFTEEN

Joe McKnight hadn't left his knees in a solid two hours. He knelt alone, head down, on a cold vinyl chair in the waiting room outside the surgery ward. He knew Val was on her way. He knew Beau was in good hands, at least as good as he could manage at the moment, and he knew Eli was alive, for now. At this point, he didn't know what to pray. He couldn't form the thoughts necessary for coherent prayers, but somehow, in his agony, he felt a certain peace. A peace that assured him the cries of his heart were heard, acknowledged, despite his own inability to be rational.

Joe knew that any minute, someone in Eli's medical camp would walk in and give him a report. He couldn't imagine dealing with any more *news* without Valerie by his side. It dawned on him how much he needed her and how times of tragedy seem to magnify how much people take one another for granted during everyday life. How many times had his partner in life carried the family through difficulty without a thank you? How many dinners went unappreciated? How many loads of laundry?

And now, now that he needed her so desperately, all those missed opportunities to appreciate her came flying into acute focus. Though he knew it was supposed to be his role, Val had always been the driving force behind the spiritual pursuits of their household. She'd always been the studier, the prayer, the doer, the volunteer. She'd always been involved and she'd been the one to pour faith into their boys over the years. It wasn't that he didn't lead the family, and it wasn't that he didn't participate in the spiritual aspects of family life, he did — but somehow, she seemed to live it out in a way he never could, or never tried to.

As his mind reeled, growing more emotional and nostalgic with every passing second, he heard footsteps approaching. He straightened himself. "Where is Val?" he wondered. He could actually feel the doctor's imminent arrival and his stomach grew tight. He braced himself for what was to come, but he didn't want to be alone when the news came — whatever the news happened to be. His hands became clammy and his heart beat faster with every approaching footstep down the long, tiled hallway. Any second now, he took a breath and held it, and watched the corner in brutal anticipation.

When Val saw him, she dropped her bag and ran to him. He let out audible cries of surprise and relief. His heart began beating again. He kissed her over and over. "I'm so glad you're here. Thank God you're here. I am no good for anything." They held each other for a long time.

Finally, after they'd walked over to the row of chairs and taken seats as close to one another as possible, Valerie mustered the courage to ask, "What has happened? Is there news?"

"He's been in surgery for hours. They said it would be about four hours, but that was almost five hours ago now. I thought you were a doctor coming and had braced myself for the worst."

She leaned over and squeezed him, "Joe, I'm so sorry I haven't been here. I came as fast as I could. But, you must not say that. Never say that. Don't you dare speak anything but life over him now, over both of them! Not to me or anyone else. Okay?"

And there it was, exactly what he'd needed. He was now standing at a place of choice. Choose faith or choose to be a *realist*, as he'd often heard it called. Staring into his wife's eyes, he knew she needed him to choose hope. She needed him to choose faith. So, that's what he decided to do — even if he didn't feel entirely hopeful. "Okay."

Almost as soon as he'd uttered the words, a man in scrubs, with a medium build and slightly graying hair, came briskly around the same corner Val had turned fifteen minutes before. His head and eyes were downcast and he had a file in his hands. Joe and Val couldn't see his face. There was no visible clue as to how they should prepare. They stood immediately, hand in hand. As the doctor approached the corridor, he looked up. They tried to read his face, but it was impossible. He didn't look distraught, but he didn't look pleased either. He looked tired, but serious.

"Mr. and Mrs. McKnight?"

"Yes," Joe answered.

"I'm Dr. Davies. I am your son's neurosurgeon." Val and Joe stared at him. The typical niceties escaped them both, and Dr. Davies seemed to expect no less.

"The surgery went well." Valerie started crying immediately. "Your son is stable. But, I'm afraid his injuries are quite severe. He suffered a direct impact traumatic brain injury. Essentially, part of the back of his skull was fractured badly and the impact caused his brain to bleed. We removed a small portion of his skull and we've managed to stop the bleeding. We've inserted a drain for now and, depending on his progress, at some point in the coming months after recovery, we'll have to place a small plate to replace the removed portion of his skull. Most of the damage occurred to the occipital lobe and part of the cerebellum. These areas are responsible for motor functions and visual functions. We think there's a chance that his brainstem has also been damaged. The brainstem controls things like breathing and heart rate. Unfortunately, that means your son could suffer permanent damage to his ability to move and balance, and he could lose his vision, or both, or neither. He may have trouble breathing on his own and, worst case, he may never wake up. There's still too much swelling for us to make definitive diagnoses. Unfortunately, though we have learned a lot, the human brain is still a mystery in many ways — only time will tell how your son's brain will respond to treatment."

"His condition is still very critical. Right now, he's on a ventilator and, though we are still waiting on the effects of the anesthesia to wear off, based on his brain activity, we believe he'll remain in an injury-induced coma. Unfortunately, I can't tell you how long or provide more information than I have. I am optimistic though. I've been doing this a long time. Your son is a fighter, I can tell." Joe squeezed Val's hand. She was weeping silent tears but listening intently. Joe didn't know if she was grateful or fearful, or both. He raised his hand to his face and rubbed his brow.

"How long until we can see him?" Joe asked.

"Fifteen or twenty minutes. I'll send a nurse for you."

"Doctor?" Valerie spoke softly, but no other words would come.

Dr. Davies looked at her. No matter how many years passed, the look on a mother's face was always more than his heart could bear. He reached out his hand and she took it. Out of nowhere, not even he was sure what prompted him to say the words, he just couldn't stop himself, he said, "Don't lose faith, Mrs. McKnight."

"Thank you," she replied.

CHAPTER SIXTEEN

Beau sat in the corner of the cinderblock holding cell and made himself register his surroundings. There was a drain in the middle of the floor, a single stainless steel toilet and sink combo unit behind a barely existent cinderblock knee wall, and not much else. The bench in holding was a perimeter bench, which left the center of the room open. There were two other men in the cell, an older man, maybe in his early sixties, clearly intoxicated, and Beau thought the man looked like he might have been homeless, and a young man, mid-twenties with tattoos on his head, arms and hands. No one said a word. Beau did his best to avoid eye contact. All he wanted to do was stew in his own self-loathing and bitterness. He knew he'd soon be headed to Houston, and though he was anxious for news, he didn't want to see his father — he wasn't ready, and he definitely didn't want to see Eli.

None of the three incarcerated men spoke and barely made eye contact with one another. Eventually, an officer appeared on the outside of the cell, "McKnight, your attorney is here. Come with me."

Beau stood and walked toward the door of the cell. He expected the door to open, but it didn't. "Place both arms through this opening. I have to cuff you," the officer spoke matter-of-factly. Beau did as commanded and stepped back, with his wrists bound in front of him this time. The officer opened the cell door and Beau stepped through it. The officer took him gently by the elbow and walked him down a hallway and into a small office-like room. It struck Beau that his jail experience had been nothing like what he'd seen on TV his whole life. Everything was much less dramatic. The absence of drama gave Beau ample time to stew in his own self-loathing. When they walked into the room, JP was already seated at a small rectangular table.

"Beau, I assume you remember me?"

"Yes, sir," Beau murmured.

"Can you take the cuffs off him, please?" JP looked at the officer expectantly.

"Turn, please." Beau turned toward the officer and instinctively held his wrists out. The officer unhooked his cuffs and placed them back on his belt. "I'll be right outside," he said, and walked casually through the door, closing it behind him. Through the narrow, vertical window in the center of the door, Beau could see the officer's profile briefly, and then he appeared to sit.

"Have a seat." JP motioned toward the table and Beau complied. "Look, we're moving fast today to get you out of here. I managed to get a meeting with the judge in the jail court they have here. Normally, this wouldn't happen, but your case is unique. The goal is to get you released on a personal recognizance bond today, with clearance to drive to Houston. You'll be arraigned in three days, so you'll have to be back for that. Do you understand all that?"

Beau nodded, "What's 'arraigned' exactly?"

"That's when you'll hear the formal charges against you, enter your plea, and they'll revisit your PR bond. It's the first rea…"

"Guilty," Beau interrupted. "I'm pleading guilty."

"We haven't heard the formal charges yet, Beau."

"It doesn't matter what they say, I'm guilty."

JP took a deep breath. "Okay, let's just take a breath and burn that bridge when we come to it, okay?" Beau nodded.

"Our meeting in the jail court is minutes away. Do you have any questions for me? Anything you need to go over first?"

"Have you heard anything about my brother?" Beau's expression was stern, but JP sensed his pain.

"No, I'm sorry," JP said softly. Beau nodded his understanding again.

The PR bond process was a relatively painless process. JP did most of the talking. It only took about forty-five minutes for the judge to meet the pair, look over everything JP presented, and, ultimately, agree to release Beau on his own recognizance as long as he remained in state. Beau signed a formal agreement stating he promised to be back for his arraignment in three days and that was that. When they were dismissed, the judge expressed sympathy for Eli that seemed genuine, but he also reiterated the importance of using good judgement while traveling to Houston, which, to Beau, seemed obligatory.

Beau followed JP out of the jail court and they headed back toward the office. JP had a stack of papers in a file folder under his arm and looked generally pleased. "It will probably take them a couple hours to get you processed out. I think you can be on the road to Houston by five or six."

"How am I supposed to get there?"

"Oh, I forgot to tell you. I have the keys to a rental car that your mother brought by. It's at your house. I will drive you there once you're out. Right now, I'm going to go grab a burger. I'll get you one and have it waiting when the time comes."

"I'm not hungry."

"I'll get you one anyway." JP declared his intent in his best attorney voice.

"What's going to happen now?"

"You'll go back to holding for a little while and wait for them to do what they do. Then, they'll let you out, return your phone and keys and all that, and we can leave." JP tried to make the whole process seem less terrible by keeping his tone light. Beau's depth of emotion was palpable, he nodded again.

The jailer seemed to appear from out of nowhere. He didn't speak to JP or Beau audibly, but he was a master at non-verbal cues. Beau stepped toward him and turned around, without having to be asked. It struck JP that, though he could still see a frightened child behind Beau's eyes, he somehow also looked resigned, natural almost, as the jailer put the cuffs on his wrists to walk him back to holding — almost as if he wanted to be there. Then JP remembered Eli, and the thought made chills run down his spine.

"When they release you, I'll be here. I promise, Beau. Okay?"

Again, a nod.

CHAPTER SEVENTEEN

Ivy made her way down the long corridor toward the ICU using the vague directions Mrs. Valerie had given her over the phone. As she walked, she regretted telling her mother that she wanted to go alone. This walk would have been easier with her mom by her side. Her mind wandered. She didn't know what to expect. Should she be heartbroken? Should she be hopeful? She had no idea. All she knew was that Eli's life hung in the balance and it had taken one of the finest neurosurgeons Houston Methodist had to tip the scales in his favor. She paused when she saw a sign hanging across the corridor that read *Intensive Care Unit*, with an arrow confirming she was on the right path.

When she turned the corner, at the end of the hall, she saw Joe, leaning against the wall with his eyes closed. "Mr. Joe!" she called out in hushed tones as she picked up her pace. She threw her arms around his neck when he stepped toward her. Fear gripped her, “What’s happening? Why are you in the hall?”

“Oh, they’re doing something with his catheter. I can’t bear even the thought of that.”

“I’ll wait with you then. What’s happening? Please, tell me everything you know. I don’t know how to feel and it’s making me crazy!”

“Well, it’s not good honey.” He put his hand on her shoulder gently but decided to give it to her straight, because he knew that’s what she wanted. “He’s hurt. He’s got a traumatic brain injury. They had to remove part of his skull in surgery to relieve the pressure on his brain, because he was bleeding. Now, he’s in a coma, on a ventilator, and they think the part of his brain that controls his heart and lungs might have been damaged in the accident. He’s also got a broken wrist, sprained fingers, lots of cuts and bruises, and a sprained knee.”

The tears welled up in Ivy’s eyes immediately. “A coma?”

Joe nodded, “They keep telling us they’ll know more when they do more scans. But because he just had surgery and he’s a trauma patient, they want to give it a little time before they do more.”

“But he’ll be okay, right? They fixed everything in surgery, right?” Ivy began to weep, which caused Joe to tear up as well.

“We don’t know. They said he might not be able to breathe on his own. That’s why he’s still on a ventilator. He’s been on it since surgery and they didn't take him off it because, after seeing his brain, they thought we might lose him if they did. Apparently, he was barely breathing when they found him." Joe hugged Ivy again. She leaned into his shoulder, crying, trying in vain to process what she'd just heard. It didn't seem real.

"This isn't right. This can't be right! This isn't God!" She was screaming inside her own mind, but her mouth remained silent. She thought about the night they'd had less than twenty-four hours earlier. She had lain awake, excited, for an hour, imagining herself in a long white gown as Mrs. Eli McKnight. She thought about their plans. She thought about Eli's mind and how she loved his wit and humor and his potential to do anything he wanted. Just as her mind began down a dark path, the door to Eli's room opened and a nurse walked through it. She smiled at them as she rubbed hand sanitizer onto her palms and silently turned back toward the ICU nurse's station.

Ivy didn't wait on Joe. She turned into the room without hesitation, but she wasn't at all prepared for what she saw. Eli's head was wrapped, his wrist in a cast, his eyes had tape on them, he had stitches over his eyebrow, he had tubes and wires of every kind coming out of him and there were machines beeping and buzzing on the wall behind him. His chest rose and fell softly and his arms rested on pillows at his sides.

Ivy's breath caught in her throat as she panned around the room. Valerie was in the vinyl chair opposite the bed. The

TV was on, but the sound was too low to be heard. Valerie's head was back and her eyes were closed, but she opened them almost instantly when Ivy moved closer. She stood and hugged the girl, an embrace that squeezed sobs out of them both. Joe slowly walked in behind Ivy and moved toward the window, staring out into the sky.

Joe felt his phone vibrating in his pocket. He pulled it out and put it to his ear, "Hello?" Valerie and Ivy broke their embrace and watched him in silence. "Oh, thank God. Good. Yes. No, I understand. Thank you." There was another pause before Joe said, "Not too good, I'm afraid. I will. Thank you."

He hung up and turned toward the ladies, "That was JP. The PR thing was approved. He's waiting on Beau to be released and then he'll be on his way here."

By the time Ivy had pulled out of her parent's driveway, the entire county had heard that Beau McKnight was responsible for a terrible accident and even though the local news hadn't mentioned names, the entire student body, recent grads and freshmen alike, had been spreading the gossip about how Eli was air lifted to Houston and it was Beau's fault. She knew the word had probably spread through the youth ranks first, because Joe had called Mr. Hinkley, who happened to be watching a late-night infomercial with Kevin, who happened to have invited Chris Barker, one of his many *adopted* brothers, to stay the night, and Chris Barker happened to have the biggest mouth in three states

Though he was an active member of the church youth and vehemently loyal to the Hinkley family, Chris had always carried a grudge against Beau, calling him a "smug s.o.b." to everyone except Eli. Getting the chance to sully Beau's name would be too tempting for Chris to pass up. Nobody knew why Chris had such disdain for Beau. As far as anyone knew, they'd never fought or feuded. Eli had always speculated that Chris held a grudge against Beau over one of two things, a sport, or a girl, but he never dared ask.

As she thought about the relative smallness of their town, and people like Chris Barker, who ran his mouth like it was a paying gig, Ivy knew it wouldn't be long before the news stations had all the detail they needed to run a full story.

She did her best to feel compassion for Beau, but as she stood there, looking at Eli, as he laid motionless in the bed before her, knowing that Beau's selfish carelessness had put him there, she felt nothing but contempt. She was so angry. She was riddled with pain and compassion for Eli, but her anger toward Beau threatened to rip her apart at the same time. How could someone who looks exactly like her sweet Eli be so, so different from him?

Valerie looked up from her phone, "My mom and dad are here, Joe. They only want three back here at a time. Maybe you could take Ivy to get some coffee downstairs and then we'll rotate? Your parents will be in late tonight, but said they'd get a hotel room and come first thing in the morning."

"Sure. Do you want some coffee?" Joe walked over to Val and put his arms around her. Ivy watched them and it dawned on her how young they seemed, almost like kids themselves. As she watched the McKnights, her heart ached in her chest as her mind instinctively longed for Eli's embrace and the promise of a future with him — a future that only hours before had seemed so certain.

CHAPTER EIGHTEEN

After her parents had gone, having insisted upon getting Val and Joe some non-hospital dinner, Valerie sat alone in a vinyl chair, staring at her son. She'd tried to read, but couldn't stay focused. She'd tried TV, but it was useless. Finally, as she searched the web for ways to "have faith," she found a podcast that managed to keep her attention. She sat, staring at Eli with her earbuds in place. The podcast was nothing more than a recording someone had made of a preacher as he spoke at some seminar in Colorado. But there was something so captivating and simple about his way of teaching that Valerie could easily follow along, despite her current mental state.

"I got a hotel room a few blocks from here. It's a two bedroom, with a living room. I figured we could use it as a hub and take shifts here. Between you, Joe, Ivy and me, we can keep someone here all the time probably." Pete's announcement was made matter-of-factly as he walked through the door. He didn't even look to his left. He couldn't bring himself to see Eli yet. When Val saw him, she yanked out her earbuds and jumped to her feet.

"Pete!" She hugged him tightly, holding back her tears.

"There's a little kitchen at the hotel too. I'm going to stock it with a few essentials, cereal and milk, waters, snacks, maybe some bread and lunchmeat, and probably some donuts and stuff. You know, sugary food you eat late at night when you can't sleep."

"I didn't know you were coming! You didn't call."

"Of course I was coming. That's why I didn't call. Like anything else was an option. I've got a week off for now, but I'll be here as long as you need me, even if it means a leave of absence, no matter what."

Valerie hugged him again. The two had always been close, and though most people knew him for his crazy, cut-up personality, Val knew that he didn't get the nickname "Sweet Pete" for nothing. As she let go of him, she turned toward Eli. Pete took a deep breath and turned toward the hospital bed for the first time since he walked through the door. To fight back his emotions, he turned away again and looked at Val, "What are they saying now? The last info I got was from Mom, and that was before they even got here."

"He's in a coma. They took part of his skull off in the back, to relieve pressure. There's a drain there now. His vitals are okay, but his heart rate is a little low. They have him on the ventilator because they think there was so much swelling and damage to the back of his head that the injury may have impacted the part of his brain that controls breathing. They didn't take him off the vent after surgery because they didn't think he'd breathe on his own. They still don't. But they've also admitted that they just don't know. His neurosurgeon told us that despite all they've learned about the brain, it's still a big mystery sometimes." Valerie didn't well up with emotion this time around. The "how is he doing" monologue was becoming too familiar. She took a staggered breath and stared at her son as she crossed her arms across her body and put a hand over her mouth.

"Listen, why don't you go downstairs? I saw Joe and Ivy in that little lobby café. That little girl is a mess. She could probably use you, and you could use a cookie, one of those big ones that they only sell in hospitals because they're so good they're liable to kill a person. I'll stay here, give you a break, and when you three come back, I'll head out to find a grocery store to stock our home base." Pete put his hand on his sister's shoulder and said, "Take a break, Val."

Valerie started to protest, but then resigned herself to the fact that a few minutes outside that room to clear her head might be good for her. "Okay. I won't be long though." She kissed Pete's cheek, grabbed her purse, and headed into the hall. As she walked, she felt strangely hopeful. She also felt tired, and when she reached up to rub her eyes, she thought about how terrible she must look. She pulled an elastic hair tie from her bag and slung the bag over her shoulder as she did her best to pull her hair into a high pony-tail.

Joe and Ivy sat in two chairs that made up a foursome at a low table outside the lobby café, Val picked up her pace when she saw them. Ivy had clearly been crying. When Joe looked up and saw Val coming, he jumped up, "Oh God! Is everything okay?" Ivy abruptly stood up next to him.

"What? Oh my goodness. Yes. It's fine. No change. I'm sorry, I didn't even think." She walked over to Joe and hugged him. She hugged Ivy, too, and held her for a minute. "Pete said I needed a break. Did you know he got a hotel room, a suite, to have as a home base for us?"

"He did? I hadn't even thought that far ahead." There was genuine gratitude in Joe's voice.

"You must be exhausted," Valerie said. "You've been awake longer than I have. Ivy, have you spoken to your parents? You should probably call them. How long will you get to stay in town?"

"I haven't called them since I got here." She sniffed. "I'll go out to that courtyard and call in a minute. I need some time to pull myself together anyway. I brought enough clothes for a couple days, but I could technically stay longer. Mom will probably want me to come home every few days anyway. She and Daddy said they'd drive up tomorrow if I wanted or if you needed them, but I said no because, because I don't know why. Is that mean?"

"No, Honey. It's not mean. I'm sure they don't think that. They just want to be here for you." Valerie motioned for Ivy to sit again. Joe followed suit and Val put her purse in one of the free chairs and her body in the other. She took a deep breath. "I think I will have a cookie. I'm not really hungry, but Pete mentioned them and they do look good."

"You seem different than you did before I came down, Hon. Lighter or something." Joe's statement wasn't accusing, but he was aware that something had changed about his wife's outlook. Ivy nodded approval of Joe's statement, agreeing with his observation.

"I feel a little different, hopeful somehow. Nothing has changed at all. Literally nothing. But I was listening to this podcast where the pastor talked about the realities of this world being different from reality in the spiritual, and how faith means knowing that God has already moved and that just because we don't see something in the natural yet, doesn't mean the prayer hasn't already been answered. He made a reference to Daniel's prayers that one time took three days and another time took three weeks, though scripture says each prayer was answered immediately and that there was a spiritual hindrance…" She realized she was rambling on and stopped herself, "Anyway, I was listening to this guy and then Pete walked in and he was so kind and, as I walked down here, something felt different. Like no matter what, it's all going to be alright."

Ivy sat up straight. She realized she'd allowed herself to feel hopeless and anxious, even though it helped nothing. She made an internal vow to get a handle on her emotions, instead of letting them control her, but she could tell it would be easier said than done. "I'll go call home now." She stood up, walked over to Val and bent down to hug her. She then hugged Joe and made her way down a ramp and through the sliding glass doors to the courtyard outside the gift shop.

Joe ordered a coffee and a cookie for his wife at the café and returned to their spot. As he sat the coffee onto the table in front of Val, the sliding lobby doors behind her opened and Beau appeared between them. "It's Beau!" He immediately raised his right hand into the air and trotted over toward his boy. He threw his arms around Beau, but Beau barely responded. He simply couldn't muster the enthusiasm to return his father's embrace. He saw his mom walking toward them with coffee in her hand. She handed her coffee to Joe and squeezed Beau around his middle.

"I need to see Eli." Beau's voice was somber. Joe nodded. Beau couldn't make eye contact with his dad. He didn't want to see shame staring back at him.

"Alright." Valerie sent a quick text to Ivy <GOING BACK UP> and led the way toward the elevator.

The McKnight trio walked silently, Valerie taking the lead, Joe walking beside her, and Beau a few paces behind. Beau didn't know what to say. What could he say? His mind was twisted with guilt, blame and anger. He was bitter. He blamed himself, he blamed God, he even blamed Maggie. He knew it wasn't rational, but that didn't stop him.

As the group walked past the nurse's station, nobody said a word about the number of visitors. In fact, no one looked up from their work. Val pushed opened the already-ajar door to Eli's room in ICU. What she saw caused her heart to rend in her chest. Her eyes filled with tears. As the three filed into the room, they witnessed Pete bent over Eli's bed, touching him ever so gently, whispering into his nephew's ear, his eyes closed, holding the very tips of Eli's fingers in his chubby fist. When he felt them in the room, he opened his eyes. He whispered again, "We'll finish this later." He let go of Eli's fingers and lightly patted his shoulder.

Valerie started to ask what Pete had been saying to Eli, but she stopped herself when she saw him looking at Beau. It was the first time he'd ever seen Beau broken. Pete walked over to his nephew and looked up at him. He put a hand on each of Beau's shoulders and looked him in the eye, "I love you Beau. We all do — no matter what." He turned to Val, "I'll make that grocery run now. I left a key card and the address over on that table. I expect you to come shower and sleep, all of you. I'll be ready to come back and do another shift tonight." Valerie hugged him again, expressed her thanks, kissed his cheek, and with that, he was out the door.

Beau took in the sight of his brother. He gritted his teeth, his stomach in knots. He wanted to weep, but couldn't. His eyes grew wet, but his face felt hot with guilt and rage. He walked over to Eli's bedside. Valerie and Joe watched in silence. When Beau reached out his hand and laid it on his brother's chest, neither Val nor Joe could hold back their tears. Finally, the tears that had escaped Beau since he woke in the hospital came in a fury, the hand he'd laid on Eli's chest formed a tight fist, greedily gripping Eli's hospital gown. Through uncontrollable sobs, Joe and Val heard Beau form the words, "I'm sorry. I'm sorry."

The moment stretched on for what felt like an hour, though only minutes had passed. When Beau finally turned toward his parents, his face was red, his jaw was set, his eyes were hard, but his tears had stopped. His expression was impossible to read, it was like an emotion neither Val nor Joe had ever witnessed was welling inside their son.

"I have to call JP. He said if Eli was bad, he'd try to get a continuance for my court appearance. Right now I have to be back in a few days." He pulled his phone from his pocket. Valerie and Joe listened and made a few pertinent interjections as Beau explained Eli's condition. There was a long pause as Beau listened. It was hard for Joe not to take the phone and intercede. "Yes sir. I understand. Thank you." He ended the call, but didn't speak immediately.

"Well?" Joe asked.

"He said he'd take care of it and he'd get a continuance. He's going to try for four weeks and thought it might be possible under the circumstances. But he also said to be ready to come sooner, if it doesn't work the way he wants it to. He sounded pretty sure he'd be able to get the time."

As they stood together in a torrent of emotion, unsure of how to process the sudden onslaught of strain they were experiencing in every facet of their lives, Ivy stepped through the door of Eli's room. Her eyes were downcast as she tucked her soft brown hair behind one ear. She lifted her head and saw Beau. Beau looked over at her. Their eyes met, and Ivy could feel her heart rate increasing instantly. She felt heat rise up from deep inside her body and she became physically ill from an overdose of hate. This would be a very long night.

CHAPTER NINETEEN

By the fourth day in ICU, the McKnight family had been officially granted the option of up to five visitors in Eli's private room at a time. So many people had come to see Eli that the nurses had no choice but to raise the limit. So far, there'd been no issues. Even when a dozen of his teammates from both the basketball and football teams had filed in together, they'd waited patiently in the waiting room and moved in and out as if under mechanical power. The McKnights had, so far, been ideal patients.

As evening approached, Ivy announced that she would have to return home to spend some time with her parents and repack for a longer stay. The entire group had put Pete's hotel room to good use. They had filed in and out, showering in shifts, resting and eating and using the room exactly as Pete had intended. At around eight o'clock, the short-term guests had all gone home and only Valerie, Joe, Pete, Ivy and Beau remained.

Eli's neurosurgeon came into the room while doing rounds, followed closely behind by the ICU fellow, Dr. Weston.

"Dr. Davies!" Joe and Valerie both stood. Joe extended his hand and the rest of the McKnight clan stood back, just waiting for news on Eli's condition. Dr. Davies had been by a few times during the past four days, but this was Beau's first encounter with the man. As Dr. Davies looked around the room, he finally made eye contact with Eli's identical twin.

"I didn't know brother meant *twin* brother!" He made a few strides and held out his hand to Beau. Beau reached forward and shook his hand, nodded, but said nothing. Dr. Davies continued as he walked over to Eli's bedside, "We need to discuss moving forward and what happens from here."

"Alright, please, go ahead." Joe affirmed, nodding his consent for the doctor to speak freely, as he moved closer to Valerie. He grabbed her hand instinctively. Pete and Ivy stepped closer. Beau remained perfectly still, breathing in and out through his nose, with a blank expression on his face. If anyone had been watching him, they'd have been hard pressed to tell what he was thinking or how he was feeling.

"After around seven days on a ventilator, the chances of having difficulty in weaning him off it accelerate, though, technically, we could potentially keep him on the vent for up to fourteen days. Research seems to indicate that mechanical ventilation longer than that can lead to brain damage and possibly delirium. Unfortunately, given his recent scans, his occipital lobe," he paused, glancing around, "that's this area," he said as he placed his hand on the back of his own head, making eye contact with Pete who clearly wanted additional details, "is still showing limited function. It seems to be healing slowly, in terms of inflammation, and the swelling and acute pressure there has largely subsided, likely resulting from the craniectomy." He paused and braced his own mind for his next statement, "But, we didn't get to him fast enough to prevent the brain from swelling downward and we're just not seeing improvement in the area of the cerebellum and the underlying regions. There's still a lot of swelling there, though no signs of active bleeding."

He moved his hand a little lower and rested his slim fingers in the middle of his skull. "This is the area of the brain that controls motor function. But my greater concern is the fact that the swelling around this area is still putting pressure on his brain stem, and looking at his recent scans, we can now say for sure his medulla was impacted by the injury as well. As you know, we were concerned about his brain stem from the beginning. The brain stem is responsible for his heart and lung function. He's not on a heart bypass, and his heart is functioning on its own thus far, even though his heart rate *is* repressed, slowing more so in the last couple days. Still, my greater concern is respiratory." He paused and took a deep breath. It became obvious to Joe and Val that his words up to now had been nothing more than an attempt to delay the inevitable.

"Mr. and Mrs. McKnight, I'm afraid it's highly unlikely your son will breathe on his own when removed from the ventilator. Unfortunately, it's also likely that his coma will persist, as with the continued swelling, there is seemingly irreparable damage to his reticular activating system. Basically, the part of his brain that controls awareness is injured."

Ivy burst into tears. Pete seemed to have trouble accepting the doctor's words at face value, giving off a vibe that one might expect during an encounter with a con man. Joe and Val stood shoulder to shoulder, hand in hand. Stoic — but seemingly in shock.

"So, you're saying he might not wake up?" Valerie questioned. "Or he might not breathe?"

"Unfortunately, the chances of both scenarios are likely. It's clear now that both his heart rate and respirations have been affected by his injury. He could remain in the coma. He may never breathe on his own. If he doesn't wake, he'll be in a vegetative state. He's not currently responding to stimuli, which is a bad sign. If it persists longer than four weeks, the chances of permanence to his vegetative state increase dramatically." Dr. Davies hated this part of his job. He knew he was one of the best surgeons in his field, he had an office full of awards and diplomas to prove it, but some wrongs were beyond even his ability to right, and it was days like this that made him feel useless as a physician.

"I recommend that we give his body as long as we safely can, to heal as much as it will, before we think about taking him off the ventilator. We can push this another week here in ICU. At the two-week mark, if we've seen no progress in his condition, it will be time to decide where we go from here. If, medically, we determine there's no improvement and little chance of recovery, the hospital will formally recommend we forego all life support. But, overall, it will be your decision. If we remove him from the vent, you will need to sign a DNR. If you do, and he does pass, you will need to decide if you want to donate his organs. If you push to keep him on the ventilator, you may have to deal with administration, but we can burn that bridge if we come to it. Between now and then, I promise you, I will do everything in my power to help him. At the end of the day, though, I'm afraid it's in God's hands, as they say. I'm sorry."

Dr. Weston added, "Of course, myself and your son's nurses will sit down with you to discuss the actual process and what to expect before the time comes, and you can rest assured that we will continue to provide the best care possible, no matter what."

Dr. Davies had learned not to wait around after these conversations. Recalling that four days prior, after surgery, he had been so openly optimistic about Eli's case made his stomach ache. He felt as if there were some kind of outside force at work, something dark holding the boy in his current state. Based on his initial surgery, *this* day should never have come. They should be planning therapy, not a funeral. Something didn't feel right about any of this. And though Dr.

Davies was agnostic, something about this case made him hunger for a higher power. He walked briskly and silently as he left ICU. He simply raised a hand toward Weston and kept moving.

The room was silent, except for the sounds of Ivy's weeping. Pete took a deep breath, trying not to become emotional, "I need a minute. I'm going to call James and Mom." He turned to walk into the hallway, but left the door open behind him.

Joe felt like a deer caught in the headlights. What had just happened? Though he'd half been expecting some bad news, it had still surprised him. He felt ill, dizzy, a cold sweat beaded on his forehead. "I need to sit." He walked over and sat in the vinyl chair by Eli's bed and reached his hand through the slats in the rail to rest it on top of Eli's hand. The nurses had turned him recently to prevent bedsores, and he was leaned, on an angle, against a wedge. If Joe didn't know better, he'd think Eli would speak at any moment.

Beau stood motionless. He thought to himself that if Eli died, he'd want to die too. He wondered if he could go through with ending it all. Then he looked at his father, and his mother, and he knew he couldn't. He wouldn't. He needed to live with his guilt. At this point, guilt had become a drug to him. He *needed* to feel the full force of his shame.

Finally, having remained frozen in the same spot she'd been in since receiving the news, Valerie spoke, "You heard him. It's in God's hands. That means we have hope. God promised healing. He said it was already ours, right?"

"Val… I want to believe that, but we have to be practical, too." Joe looked at her with compassion.

"Why? Why do we need to be practical? What good will that do Eli?"

"I don't know if I can muster that kind of faith," Joe said. "What if we get our hopes up for nothing?"

Valerie looked at Joe, at Ivy, and even at Beau. She had impassioned tears rolling down her cheeks. I've spent about eighteen of every twenty-four hours for the last four days right there in that chair," she pointed to Joe's chair, "with my Bible in my hands, listening to every statement of faith I could find online and praying for my son. That one pastor I've been listening to has totally changed my perspective. For so long we've been fed a weakened version of our faith, and now I say 'NO!' Satan will not win this battle. Eli will live and not die. With or without you, I am standing on this promise." She was sobbing now, but her words were somehow flat. She hoped beyond hope that her family would stand with her. "If it's in God's hands, then it's right where it needs to be. Right?"

Ivy stood and walked over to Valerie. Valerie reached out her hand and Ivy grasped it intently. Joe sighed, but he stood and walked over to where the two stood. He took Valerie's other hand and reached out to Beau.

"I can't." Beau didn't move. He looked down and spoke in a hiss, "How can you trust a God who would allow this to happen?"

Ivy had been holding in her rage against Beau for the entire week. She'd tried in vain to forgive him. She wasn't ready to forgive him, though she knew she should. She dropped Valerie's hand and nearly ran to face Beau. She shoved him. She was small, but she was powerful. The momentum of her shove pushed him back. "You arrogant, selfish…" she slapped his face, hard. "How dare you? How dare you blame this on God? This was not God! This was you! You! You did this! Look at him! Look at what you did! You did this! This happened despite God, not because of Him. It happened because of *You*!" Ivy screamed with all the force her lungs would muster. Bloodcurdling sounds emitted from her lungs, and not even she had believed she was capable of such rage. She shoved Beau again. She was sobbing angry tears.

Pete had stepped in from the hallway when the commotion became loud enough to draw the attention of the nurses down the hall. He stood in the doorway, motionless. Beau didn't move. Ivy began to beat his chest with her fists, and as she flew out of control, Joe ran over to her, wrapping her in his arms as she collapsed to her knees in a pool of her own tears. Joe looked over his shoulder at Valerie. Val's cheeks were tear stained, but her eyes were closed. Her lips moved slightly and Joe knew she was already in prayer.

Beau stepped around Ivy and his father on the floor and made his way toward the door. Gently, Pete tried to stop him, but Beau put his big hand on his uncle's chest and pushed him backward. Pete watched as he shoved his hands into his pockets and stalked down the hall, head down, toward the elevators.

CHAPTER TWENTY

The days rolled by faster than Valerie could fathom. *D-Day* was bearing down on them like a locomotive. Valerie had called it "D-Day" since hearing Pete say "Decision Day" during a conversation with her other brother, James. Valerie was struggling to keep her faith afloat. She spoke the right words, but a thousand doubts swam in her head, like a school of piranha taking nibbles out of her brain every time she heard an alarm sound in the hospital or witnessed a family mourning in the hallway. Except for the healing of his cuts and bruises, Eli showed no signs of improvement.

JP had managed to get a continuance for Beau, but had not yet been successful in getting four full weeks. The family knew he had another meeting with the judge, but they didn't know when. They held out hope that he'd be able to secure the month, but, truth be told, they'd all been too preoccupied by Eli's prognosis to put real thought into Beau's court date.

Two days before their hospital-imposed deadline, Joe mandated a family discussion. He refused to conduct the meeting inside Eli's room, and despite Valerie's desire for round-the-clock bedside support, she joined the group for dinner at a nearby twenty-four hour breakfast place. Joe requested a table in the back where they might have some quiet. There was no wait, and the hostess led them to a large, round table in a back corner of the restaurant.

The entire McKnight clan knew where this discussion was headed, and as a result, coffee and muffins were all they could muster the appetite to order.

"In forty-eight hours, they're going to ask us what we want to do. He's been in that bed for two weeks and, despite their best efforts, parts of his brain are still swollen. They still think his brain stem is damaged and he's still very much asleep. Those are the medical facts..." Joe spoke softly, visibly controlling his emotions.

Valerie interrupted him with a stern whisper, "Medical facts are not spiritual facts, and we all know it." She was determined to speak life over her son, even though all her human reasoning and logic told her it was futile.

"Right," Ivy affirmed Val's statement, as her eyes welled with tears.

"What do you think Eli would want?" Pete leaned in and spoke softly. "I think we owe it to him to think about what he would want if he had the power to say." Joe listened intently to Pete's words. Somehow, over the course of the last two weeks,

Val's insane, wacky, totally juvenile brother had become the rock upon whom they'd all leaned, morning, noon and night, for the last twelve days. He'd taken care of meals, kept the hotel room stocked with essentials and creature comforts, taken late night shifts at Eli's bedside, made runs for coffee, bagels, and cafeteria food, and he even drove all the way back home to get more time off work, check on everyone's houses and make sure the mail hold was taken care of at the post office. Ivy's parents had visited the hospital, officially getting to know Pete and several other members of the McKnight family as they came and went, so during his trip back home, he'd even gone by the Zellway's to give an in-person report, having assumed they too felt a bit lost and helpless. Now, Joe found himself regarding Pete's opinions as words of wisdom, something he would have considered an impossibility three weeks ago.

"He wouldn't want that, to be stuck in that bed, no way." Beau pointed in the general direction of the hospital, shook his head and spoke curtly, rapidly — it was the most words he'd spoken since his confrontation with Ivy. "You know it, and I know it." He looked Ivy in the eyes, unwavering. He was almost angry. She knew he was right. She and Eli had discussed it once after going on a visitation with the youth from the church. On the way back, mortality had become a topic, and Eli had confirmed that he knew where he was going and questioned anyone's desire to stay on earth as a shell of a man when the hereafter held so much promise. Ivy's eyes filled with tears as she was confronted with this memory and reminded of a truth about Eli that she'd chosen to repress since arriving at the hospital.

"He's going to be alright. We can't give up on him or on God. We can't." Valerie laid her right hand on Joe's firm forearm and squeezed it, "We can't!"

"We aren't. We won't, I promise." He put his hand on Val's. "But we can't just keep him on the vent forever. You heard the doctor say that it's almost a guarantee of further brain damage to leave him on it too long. I mean, if his brain is already injured, are we doing more harm than good by prolonging his dependence on the ventilator? Does it hurt his chances of recovery even more? I don't know. All I know is we have to decide whether to fight the recommendation or not, whether we want to or not."

"So, we're hoping he'll breathe on his own, but the doctors say he won't. And since that means we're potentially choosing to end his life, I can't. I don't want a vote. I can't do this." Ivy broke into sobs. She couldn't bring herself to choose. She knew Eli wouldn't want to be kept alive by machines, but she couldn't agree to remove the ventilator and just *see what happens* either, especially if it meant losing him, and according to his doctors, it would.

"He will breathe on his own! He will!" Valerie spoke loudly. She made eye contact with everyone at the table, one at a time. She'd been the cornerstone of faith-filled words since they made the decision to fight for Eli's life spiritually, as hard as they would fight naturally. She regularly had trouble believing her own words, but that didn't stop her from speaking them. She had poured over scripture for hours every day. She had studied effective prayer and had been doing her best to be bold and confident in her conversations with God. After all, if she's a co-heir with Christ, she had direct access to all the blessings of Heaven. She had developed a deep desire to be a miracle working disciple like those she read about in her Bible.

"So, you think we should remove the vent and trust God to heal him?" Pete asked. He looked at Valerie with pleading eyes. He didn't know the right answer either. Valerie was silent. She couldn't form the word "yes." It was beyond her ability as a mother.

"Here's what I think. I think we all commit to praying about this tonight. I know we have been praying all along, but I think we need to pray about this specific thing. What's the right choice? What does God want here?" Joe rightly ascertained that nobody, himself least of all, was ready to make a choice, and a night of fervent prayer might be just what they needed.

Beau shook his head in agreement, but in his spirit, he seethed. If there was a God, Beau wanted nothing to do with Him.

Joe reached his hand out straight in front of him and Valerie put hers on top of his, squeezing it lightly. Pete placed a hand on top of Valerie's delicate fingers and Ivy followed suit. Beau watched the scene and finally slid his hand across the table and, keeping the heel of his hand on the wood, rested his fingers across his mother's hand, near her wrist. But he did it for her benefit, certainly not for his own.

CHAPTER TWENTY-ONE

Valerie hadn't slept all night. She walked down the long, sterile hallway toward ICU with a coffee tray in one hand and a paper bag with cheese Danishes in the other. She had her earbuds in place, listening to the pastor she'd come to adore over the last couple weeks, in part to hear the message but also to drown out the sounds of hospital care all around her. She couldn't take the beeping and the clanking and the sounds of rolling carts anymore. When she rounded the corner to Eli's room, she found Pete standing in the hallway outside the door.

"What's going on?" Valerie asked with a minor sense of urgency, pulling the earbud from one ear with her shoulder.

"Oh, nothin'. They're doing their thing with the catheter and all that. I just stepped out to make it easier on them."

"Oh. Okay." She handed him the coffee tray. "Mine has the marked lid. How was the night shift?"

"Long." Pete rubbed his chin with his free hand. "I didn't sleep at all. Normally, I can doze in the recliner, but my mind just kept going. I couldn't stop thinking about tomorrow. I prayed, but I still don't know how to feel."

"I know what you mean. I can't bear it. I keep feeling like we're missing something. Have we done everything, I mean, everything we can do?"

"What else can we do, Val? I mean, he has the finest doctors in the country who have all gone out of their way. They're still giving him that IV Vitamin C hoping it will help with the inflammation, and you heard Dr. Davies say it was experimental and he had to push the hospital to even go for it. What else *can* we do?"

Valerie started to respond with the phrase, "I don't know," when she heard the pastor's voice in her left ear, the voice she'd been tuning out since seeing Pete in the hall.

"You either believe the Word fully and do what it says – or you don't. It's that simple."

"Oh my goodness!" Valerie looked dismayed and excited at the same time. "I know what we haven't done!" She pushed past Pete and through the door of Eli's room. The nurses quickly turned to look but didn't seem surprised to see her.

"Good morning, Mrs. McKnight," one of Eli's nurses, Amy, always greeted each individual member of the group. Valerie had greatly appreciated this small act of kindness during her time at the hospital, but today she was too distracted to be personable.

"Morning," Val responded without making eye contact while she dug in her bag.

Pete came barreling through the door, completely ignoring the exiting hospital staff. "What? What haven't we done?"

"We haven't done what the Bible says!" Valerie pulled her fist from her bag and, in her grasp, was her leather-bound Bible.

"What?" Pete sighed. He was a believer, but he sorta felt like Val was going off the deep end with Bible stuff lately.

"Pete, do you really believe what you say you believe? Do any of us? I mean, really? Do we believe it's really real? Every word? Do we take it seriously?"

"Well, yeah. I think so." Pete reached into the bag of Danishes.

"Then why do we seem to minimize its significance so much? If we really believe what it says, then why don't we do what it says, too?" She opened her Bible and began flipping. "We either believe it and do it, or we don't."

"Okay. And?" Pete spoke with his mouth full as Val flipped frantically.

"Alright, listen." Valerie began reading aloud. "*And these signs will follow those who believe: In My name they will cast out demons; they will speak with new tongues; they will take up serpents; and if they drink anything deadly, it will by no means hurt them; they will lay hands on the sick, and they will recover.*" She looked up at Pete, "Did you catch that? They will lay hands on the sick, and they will recover! If we believe what we say we do, then this entirely applies to us! It's a question of our trust in God's word. If we believe His promises, then why wasn't this the first thing we did?"

"You mean lay hands on him?" Pete wiped his fingers with a cheap paper napkin.

"Precisely."

"I don't have an answer for that question, Val."

"Do you believe what this says?" She poked the pages of her Bible with her index finger.

"Well, yeah. But, I've never seen it. I mean, I've always kind of thought that was meant for, you know, his disciples and followers back in the day."

"Exactly! That's what everybody seems to think, but that view is not scriptural, there's absolutely no Biblical evidence of that doctrine being truth. This podcast I'm listening to talks about it so much. We're copping out. We're selling Jesus short here. I really believe there's a God reason I found this guy at this exact time. I mean, truly, scripture has completely come alive for me since we got here."

"Okay. I hear you. I'm with you even, but what if…"

Valerie cut him off, "Shhh! Don't speak doubt. Even if you feel it, don't speak it. It won't help. It won't help me or him." She pointed at Eli.

"Fine, right, okay." Pete conceded. "Now what?"

"When Joe and the kids get here, we'll just do it. We'll all lay hands on him and pray. I'll be reading about it in the meantime. Maybe there's a technique or something? I'm learning as I go here. And I don't care if it seems crazy to everybody else in the world, this is my baby and I'm not giving up." Val's eyes were wet when she looked up from her phone. "I'm just not."

Pete put his hand on her shoulder, "Neither am I."

Valerie walked to the familiar vinyl chair and sat, placed her Bible on her lap and began reading. Pete reached into the Danish bag, Val glanced up when she heard the paper. He gestured as if to ask permission for seconds. Val nodded and returned to her reading.

CHAPTER TWENTY-TWO

Joe used his foot to prop the door open for Ivy as they entered Eli's room. Beau reached out from behind him and grabbed the door so his father could enter. Joe was holding a cellphone and was in, what appeared to be, an intense conversation. His other hand gripped his briefcase. Valerie opened her mouth to greet them when they walked through the door, but Joe dropped his briefcase onto the rolling tray at the foot of Eli's bed and held up a hand requesting that she wait.

"I understand, we will work it out." Joe hung up the phone without saying goodbye. When he looked up, he was shaking his head and he was visibly frustrated. Beau didn't say a word, nor did Ivy. Finally though, Joe said, "That was JP."

Suddenly, Valerie had a new concern on her hands. She spoke with resolve, "And what did he say?"

"Beau's continuance can't be extended any further. When he arrived here and relayed Eli's condition to JP, JP did his best to push his arraignment out four weeks. Unfortunately, the judge and the DA aren't going for that and said two weeks is long enough for something that's normally done within two days. He has to be at the arraignment at nine o'clock in the morning, the day after tomorrow."

"The day after tomorrow?" Pete rubbed his face hard. "So much for compassion," he spewed with disdain.

Ivy didn't say a word, but she was staring a hole in Beau. In her heart, she was just as angry at him as she had been the day they arrived at the hospital. He was the reason they were here. And in her mind, he deserved everything that was coming to him. But, she also felt guilty about her opinion, for the sake of Valerie and Joe, whom she knew would be heartbroken if things didn't go well for Beau. Dealing with his legal situation on top of Eli's medical situation had to be overwhelming.

Beau stared at the ground, hands in his pockets, with a look on his face that mirrored exactly how he felt on the inside. Even his appearance had changed over the course of the last two weeks. He was no longer the fun-loving young man he had been at graduation. Now, he seemed to carry the weight of the world on his shoulders, and he looked as though he'd aged ten years in a matter of mere days. His face was scruffy, his hair was unkempt, his eyes appeared dark and sunken, and he didn't care.

"Well, I guess that makes tomorrow a 'D-Day' all around for us, doesn't it?" Valerie's words fell flat. She didn't know what to say and every word seemed ill-fitting for the situation. Attempting to make eye contact with Beau, she looked around and smiled slightly in his direction. "It's going to be all right, son." She received no response.

"Okay, we're all here now. What is so urgent?" Joe's demeanor softened, he walked over to Valerie and kissed her, then grabbed her hand, realizing he'd been less than personable when he arrived and feeling a pang of guilt for being so short with his words, despite their current level of stress.

"Pete and I have been talking, and I've been doing a lot of studying, and I think the Holy Spirit has revealed something to me." Valerie looked at Pete, who nodded in agreement.

"Please tell me there's a miracle coming, tell me this is all some tragic mistake and we'll all just wake up at any minute," Ivy spoke with a weak, pleading voice. It was abundantly clear that Ivy Zellway was not emotionally equipped for what the next few days would hold.

Beau took a deep breath. He didn't roll his eyes, he didn't scoff, but Valerie could feel the hardness of his heart from across the room.

"We say we believe that the Bible is true. We say that we trust every word that came from God and every word that Jesus spoke. We say we believe it, but do we live like we believe it? Do we really truly believe it? And if we do really believe it, why don't we live like we believe it? My point is, there's a very clear message in Scripture that says we, through Christ, should have the ability to accomplish all the same miracles and good works that the disciples accomplished, but, somehow, we've let that die. We've swept it under the rug and it's not even a discussion anymore. Not in most places anyway."

Joe looked at his wife. He was taken aback. They had attended church together for most of their lives, they'd shared so many spiritual discussions over the years it was impossible to count them, and yet, he'd never heard her say anything like this before. "I hear you, Honey, and I suppose I don't disagree. But, where is this coming from and where are you going with it?"

Ivy perked up a bit, she felt a strange surge of hope in hearing Val's words. She and Eli had been studying the minimization of Christ's power in group Bible study. They had discussed how Christ, and what he actually did for his followers, had, over time, become a footnote of life — instead of the pinnacle.

"What I'm getting at is that we don't do the things the Bible says to do. And we don't do them because deep down we don't actually believe them. If we did, we'd still be seeing miracles, healings and other amazing things, but somehow, we've watered down that message and our collective level of faith to such a point that it doesn't really even work for us anymore. I'm not talking about just us in this room, I'm talking about Christianity at large. I know not everybody is on this same sad path, but most of the people we know are. I also know that this pastor I've been listening to for hours a day over the last two weeks serves an entire congregation of people who have taken their faith in a different direction, and there are testimonies by the hundreds of amazing things that have happened. I know what you're thinking, and I know you can't believe everything you hear, but I believe this guy and literally everything he says is backed up by scripture. And where I'm going, well, I think we owe it to Eli, and to ourselves, to approach this coming day with a different perspective."

"Earlier, I read a scripture to Pete: *'they will lay hands on the sick, and they shall recover.'* — These are the words of Christ himself. And for some reason, we didn't even consider this when we arrived. Yes, we've been praying, but we didn't actually do this. So, that's what I want us to do right now." She paused, "All of us." She looked hard at Beau. She knew he didn't feel the way she felt, and at this point, she wasn't sure if he even believed in God at all. But she also knew his upbringing, his good heart, and his desire to please her and Joe. If for no other reason, he'd do it for her.

"You want to lay hands on Eli, is that what you're saying?" Joe was still processing his wife's words.

"Yes. That's exactly what I'm saying," she answered.

"Okay then, where do we start?" Joe didn't know if it would work, he doubted he could muster enough faith to turn on a light switch, let alone produce a miracle. But, Val was intense, and something in his heart told him to trust her petition.

"I've been reading about it. It's pretty straightforward. We just put our hands on him, speak the Word over him, and assert God's will to heal him." Val stood to her feet.

Joe paused, looking at his wife with a burning question on his tongue. He dared not ask, but he didn't need to, Valerie seemed to read his thoughts.

"You want to know how I'm sure it's God's will to heal him, don't you?" She asked. Joe nodded in silence. "Because of the Bible, that's how I know. If we really believe this book, then we know God's will for us is good. Jesus paid the debt of death for us and He said He wants us all to be in good health. He healed people, He never hurt them. Not once. There is no scriptural evidence of the post-Jesus doom and gloom so many people subscribe to. If God sees only Jesus when He looks at us, because Jesus paid for all our sins, then there's no way anyone but Satan, and his influence in this world, is behind our pain."

Joe wasn't sure what to think, but Pete kept nodding. He'd been with Val all day, and she'd clearly been reading him scripture since sun up. He had to admit, all her points made sense, even though it was vastly different from what he'd heard for decades. As he looked at Eli, he decided they had nothing to lose.

"Before we do this, let's talk about tomorrow. We've heard from Dr. Davies, the hospital is pressing us to take him off the ventilator. Every medical person we've talked to has said it's time. According to his scans, he's not going to make it and we'll be saying goodbye anyway. While some of his brain is healing, his brainstem is still damaged. On the other hand, doctors don't know everything, and we," he paused, looking at

Val, "have the Great Physician on our side. If we admit to ourselves that Eli wouldn't want to live this way, and add the hospital pressure, he will be better off if we give him back to God." Joe took a deep breath after speaking, his exhale was shaky. He was fighting tears. It was time to let Eli go. They all knew it, but nobody wanted to admit it.

Ivy was crying again. She'd cried so much in the last two weeks she'd almost forgotten what it was like to have a tearless day, "So, we're going through with it?"

Pete put a hand on her shoulder. They all knew it was time, but saying it out loud was another thing entirely. Joe nodded.

Valerie inhaled and wiped her eyes to blot the forming tears. "He will recover," she spoke bluntly, flatly and adamantly as she moved to Eli's bedside. Her family followed her. They all laid both hands on Eli, even Beau, despite his resistance. As they did, Valerie prayed like she'd never prayed before, but she asked for nothing. Instead, she thanked God for healing her son, thanked Him for His promises, and she thanked Him that His word promised the sick would recover at the laying on of their hands.

By the time she was finished, everyone was crying. Emotions ran high, feelings were mixed. There was hope and grief at the same time. Everyone stepped back from the bed, staring at Eli as if testing their progress, half expecting him to open his eyes, sit up and talk to them… he didn't.

CHAPTER TWENTY-THREE

The morning of *D-Day* was bleak, overcast and befitting of the day's unfolding events. No one had slept and, having been informed of what may come, family had been pouring into town throughout the night. Valerie and Joe expected Dr. Davies to arrive midmorning. They would speak with Dr. Davies and Dr. Weston in private and then sign a thousand papers before setting the time of day that the machines keeping breath in Eli's lungs would be turned off.

In the meantime, they spent minute after minute visiting with aunts, uncles, cousins, nieces and nephews, all of whom expressed tearful regrets about time not spent and things not said and then shared emotional goodbyes. Valerie spent the majority of her time avoiding people, and nobody complained. Everyone assumed her distance was the result of intense, debilitating pain. They were right, to an extent.

As the morning unfolded, Pete found Valerie hiding by the vending machines down the hall.

"What are you doing out here?"

"I can't stay in there. I can't listen to everyone saying goodbye, like his death is a foregone conclusion. I swore I wasn't giving up and I'm not, but, listening to all that heartbreak makes it really hard to think faith thoughts. I just can't deal with it."

"I came down here to tell you that you can't hide all day, but instead, I'm going to hide with you." Pete put an arm around his sister's shoulder. She chuckled and hugged him back.

"Let's sit. We can split a honey bun." She nodded toward the row of chairs along the wall in the little vending room.

"Um, have we met? I don't share honey buns." Pete lifted a serious eyebrow in her direction. She smiled and sat down, leaning forward with her face in her hands, rubbing her skin while taking deep breaths through her nose. Pete sat next to her and for a long while, they simply sat together in silence, breathing in and out, because they lacked the strength to do anything else.

As Valerie leaned her head back against the wall to rest her eyes, Ivy came hurriedly around the corner.

"Ms. Valerie, Dr. Davies and Dr. Weston are here." Ivy didn't know whether she should speak with urgency or dread. She somehow managed both.

Valerie looked at Pete, and he looked back at her. "Okay." She sighed and stood to her feet. She grabbed Ivy's hand. When they walked into the hallway, Valerie saw that Ivy's parents had arrived. Mrs. Zellway stepped toward them and grabbed Ivy's other hand. Mr. Zellway waited for them to pass and followed them somberly down the hall. Pete joined him. When they arrived at the ICU, nurses were filtering family through Eli's room in groups. Joe was standing in the hallway with Dr. Davies. When he saw Val, he walked toward her. She dropped Ivy's hand and moved into Joe's arms.

"Dr. Weston went ahead of us to the conference room." Joe looked at Dr. Davies, who nodded and turned toward an opposite hall. In all the time they'd been in Houston, Valerie had never walked this particular hall, though it was right across from the ICU. When the trio arrived at the conference room, Dr. Weston was waiting inside. He wasn't sitting, but instead, he stood with a file folder under his arm. There was a pitcher of water and a box of tissues on the conference table, and a buffet table with disposable insulated cups, a coffee pot and all the trappings was under the window.

Dr. Weston pulled out a chair and gestured for Valerie to sit. She did, and Joe chose the chair next to her. Dr. Davies sat at the head of the long, oak conference table and Dr. Weston took the seat across from Joe.

The conversation unfolded just as expected. The doctors reported that Eli's condition had not improved, a fact that Joe and Val already knew, and in what seemed like minutes, and felt like far too brief a time to make it legal to cut a young life short, the decision had been made to remove Eli from the ventilator at six o'clock that same evening. Valerie and Joe signed a DNR and filled out all the paperwork necessary to donate their son's healthy organs. When the decisions were made, and all the documents signed, Dr. Davies offered sincere apologies that he couldn't do more to help Eli. His honesty was palpable. He stood to leave, leaving Dr. Weston behind to discuss the finer details of the evening.

Joe and Valerie weren't as emotional as they had expected to be. Somehow, they both felt a weird peace throughout the discussion. Dr. Weston assumed they'd grown somewhat numb, but he'd seen "numb" hundreds of times, and the McKnights seemed different from the rest. He went through the entire process, and told them they'd get very little time with Eli after the machines were turned off because the surgical team would be standing by to harvest his organs. It was abundantly clear that Eli's doctors gave him no hope of survival. Doubt began to creep into Valerie's heart. Hearing the details of the medical science made it difficult for her to hold out hope. Maybe this really would be her last day with her son.

After the meeting, Joe and Valerie walked back to ICU, hand in hand. Joe looked at his wife, "I'm not ready for this. I'm not ready to let him go. It's not supposed to be this way." His eyes filled with tears.

"Me either… Wait, what am I saying? We can't give up Joe!" Valerie spoke emphatically.

"Val, you have to prepare yourself."

"Stop it! Don't do that!" She almost shouted.

“Valerie, I’m worried about you. What if you’re lying to yourself?”

“If I’m wrong, then I’ll lose my child, who everybody says I’m going to lose anyway. What will it hurt to let me believe in his healing until the very end? I would rather live with hope now and mourn later than to mourn twice.

Joe thought about his wife’s words. What would it hurt? Nothing, it would hurt nothing. Why should she give up hope? What good would it do? The only thing it would do is make everyone more comfortable with Eli’s death, and he didn’t want *anyone* to be comfortable with it. “You’re right. You’re absolutely right.” He put his arm over her shoulder and pulled her close.

~

Once the family heard Eli’s time on earth would end at six o’clock, they rallied around him again, sharing the same tearful goodbyes and expressions of regret as before. To Beau, it all seemed so pointless. Eli didn’t even know they were there. They shed tears and spoke wistful words for their own benefit, not for Eli. Not really, anyway. He tried to appreciate their points of view, but his insides had turned to stone. He sat in the corner of his brother’s room, thinking about what he might say if he could see all this from the outside. He wondered if Eli would hate him. He wondered if Eli would maintain that chronically happy persona if he knew his own brother had killed him. Beau had already forgotten how to feel happiness, his emotions were in tatters. He thought about watching his twin take his last breaths at six o'clock, mere hours away. As he looked at his brother, his mind traveled back in time to when they were six years old, and Eli had saved him from falling off the footbridge in the park. They were never supposed to be there in the first place, but Beau had insisted and, when he lost his footing trying to climb over the rope railing, Eli had been there to pull him back. Eli had always been there to pull him back from the ledge.

The last two hours with Eli were reserved for immediate family, but Joe and Valerie wanted Ivy and Pete to stay until the last hour. The five of them sat in Eli's room, looking at him and at each other. Ivy wept, watching the clock with a sense of dread that made it difficult for her to focus on Eli, which filled her with guilt. Her parents were waiting for her down the hall, and for the first time since the ordeal began, she wanted nothing more than to be in her mother's arms. Pete was a rock. He poured waters, procured chairs, and fielded calls from friends and distant family. He made the occasional trip down the hall to brief the waiting grandparents, James, and the Zellways. If he were breaking, he didn't show it.

When the clock struck five, Ivy stood and walked over to Eli's bed. She brushed her fingers over his cheek and leaned down to kiss him, one last time. She then turned to where Valerie sat by Eli's bed, holding his hand through the slats in his bed rail. She bent down and hugged Valerie's neck, breathing in her sweet smell and mourning the loss of a lifetime as mother and daughter-in-law that they would no longer share. Somehow, through the course of this day, Ivy had abandoned her hope. Her faith now wavered like a reed in the wind. She moved from Val to Joe, who returned her embrace with a warm hug and a quick peck to her forehead.

The gesture caused her eyes to fill with tears once again.

Pete stood and followed suit. He knelt in front of his sister, unable to muster words of comfort. He patted her knee and rose slowly, as he stood, he reached out and lightly pinched her chin between his thumb and index finger. “I’m not giving up,” he whispered. He held his hand out to Joe as he headed for the door. Instead of returning his grasp, Joe threw both arms around Pete’s neck.

“Thank you, Pete, really.” Joe had been seeing Pete with new eyes for the last two weeks and wanted him to know his efforts hadn’t gone unnoticed.

During the last hour, Joe, Valerie and Beau were by themselves. They decided each one of them would take ten minutes alone with Eli, and then they’d come together for the last twenty minutes as a family.

Joe went first. He kissed his son’s head, ruffled his hair like he used to when Eli was small, and told him how proud he was to be the father of such an amazing son. He told Eli that God had blessed him with the chance to see Eli grow and that, no matter what happened today, Eli’s life mattered and had made a difference in the world. He didn’t want to waste what little time he had shedding tears, but he couldn't help the teardrops that fell onto Eli's hospital gown as he looked into his son's face. And though he struggled to muster just a little bit of faith, he needed to breathe some words of strength. He leaned down into Eli's ear and whispered, "You are a wonderful son, Eli. And, if you can hear me, I want you to fight. Do you hear me? Fight, son. Fight. It's now or never."

Beau entered his brother's room without the slightest clue of what to do or say. He sat next to him in silence for a few minutes before he finally spoke, "You're a real jerk, you know that? How can you just lay there? How can you be the one in the bed, clueless to any of this, while I'm here, wishing to God I could trade places with you. You've always, always bailed me out. I deserve that bed, but here you are, bailing me out again. You're just a jerk. Just once, I wish you'd let me get what I deserve…" Beau began to feel nauseated. He ran to the trashcan and suffered dry heaves for about a minute. "I can't do this Eli. I can't. I can't stand here and watch you die knowing it's my fault. That's what they say, you know, that you're gonna die." Beau paced by the window, he punched the wall with everything in him, leaving a healthy hole in the sheet rock. "Just once, this once, could you break the rules? Disobey doctor's orders? Just this once, jerk?" He reached into his pocket and pulled out his wallet. In it, he had a photo of Eli and him at about eight years old, shoulder to shoulder, watching the sunset.

He walked to Eli's bedside and placed the picture under his hand. Then, he sat in that familiar vinyl chair and took off his shoes. He removed his socks, and as he'd done every night for as long as he could remember, he laid his socks on his brother's pillow. He sniffed hard, fighting back the grief that swelled inside him, "Don't think that just because you're in a coma, I'm going to miss this chance." He bent down and tried unsuccessfully to hug his brother, it was more like leaning over him, with one arm under his back and the other supporting his weight against the bedrail. He noted Eli's warmth and took it in, for what he expected to be the last time.

When Valerie's turn came, she first took note of Beau's socks, a scene that made her both chuckle and ache at the same time. She walked over to his bedside and smoothed her son's hair. She told him she'd loved him fiercely from the moment they'd heard two heartbeats on the Doppler. She told him that she'd learned so much from him and that she was so grateful for the young man he'd grown to become. But then, she changed her tone, "That's why I refuse to let you go. God has big plans for your life Eli McKnight, and I will not let that promise die today. I refuse to let the Enemy have his way. In the name of Jesus, I claim the healing that Jesus died to pay for. I command your brain and your body to work perfectly." She laid her hands on him, smoothing his blankets and gown, speaking lovingly, but firmly, "I am not ready to see you go, and I don't believe the doctors know everything. And Eli, don't forget Ivy. She's been here the entire time. She misses you. I miss you. Dad misses you. Beau misses you. Fight back, son. Please. I am begging you to fight." Val's faith flopped back and forth like a fish out of water, violently slapping from hopeful to hopeless in a way that made her angry with her own mind. "You know I love you son, you're one of my favorite people in the world." She leaned over the bedrail and laid her head on his chest, listening to his heartbeat and hoping beyond hope that his heart wouldn't soon be beating in another man's body.

The minutes of the last hour ticked by quickly, too quickly. Joe, Val and Beau were standing around Eli's bed, looking at him, when Joe said, "He's always loved the story of the day he and Beau were born, let's tell him that story." Valerie smiled and Joe began recounting the comedy of errors that was their debut into the world. His words were like fiery daggers to Beau's chest, a bittersweet reminder of better days and, at the same time, a foreshadowing of a life that would never be the same.

At five past six, Dr. Weston and his nurses quietly came into the room. Valerie and Joe had already been briefed on what to expect, but the staff was kind and compassionate and talked them through everything that would happen again. "We'll do this over the course of an hour, so as to minimize distress within your son's body. We want his experience to be as peaceful as possible, regardless of his level of awareness. This is called 'extubation.'" They spoke in turn, softly, as they moved around the room. "The surgical team is standing by. You can choose to stay here in the room, or leave."

Dr. Weston spoke up, "Mr. and Mrs. McKnight, based on the most recent scans of your son's brain stem, you'll likely have only a few minutes with Eli after ventilation is withdrawn, before he passes. We will leave you for just a few minutes after pronouncement, before we move him to surgery. Is there anything you need? Do you have any questions?"

Valerie shook her head. Joe and Beau were stoic.

The staff moved about the room, and over the course of the next sixty minutes, life-giving ventilation was slowly withdrawn. Finally, one of the nurses made a hushed announcement that extubation was complete. The nurses monitored Eli for signs of distress, but the beeping had been turned off and there were no sounds in the room besides those belonging to the living. Dr. Weston sent a page to the surgeon on standby as Joe, Beau, and even Valerie watched and waited for their beloved Eli to step out of this world and into the next. Valerie lowered the bedrail and sat next to her son on the bed, holding his hand. Beau and Joe stood closely behind her.

Valerie didn't realize she'd been holding her own breath until Eli had taken his third. One minute passed, then two, then three, then four. At the five minute mark, Eli was very clearly breathing on his own. "He's breathing! He's breathing, isn't he?" Valerie needed the nurses to confirm what she was seeing, because she thought she might be dreaming. Eli's chest rose and fell, his cheeks were still pink, his lips were not turning blue.

The nurses were visibly shaken by such a remarkable turn of events. The doctors had been so certain that they'd not prepared themselves for the need of a different protocol. Finally, Dr. Weston, who'd been quietly observing and expecting Eli's oxygen levels to begin falling, walked over and checked Eli's vital signs himself. There was a long pause before he finally spoke, "I'm speechless. His heartrate is better than it was just ten minutes ago, and his respirations are strong. His O2 levels are stable. I… I don't know what to say." He waited for a moment and tried to get his head around the situation. "I want another look at those scans." He turned to one of the nurses and requested she retrieve Eli's file. She darted from the room as her coworkers began attaching heart monitors and blood pressure cuffs to Eli's body. Dr. Weston turned to Joe and Val, "Well, he'll have to breathe on his own for at least an hour before we consider him fully weaned and stable, but, I have to say, this goes against everything his brain scans have indicated. We are witnessing an actual miracle. That's the only explanation I have." He pulled out a phone and began punching numbers with speed and authority, "Davies, you're not going to believe this. Eli McKnight is breathing on his own. Yes, I'm serious. No, no — just over six minutes now. Okay. Will do." He looked up from his phone, and in a tone that held a blend of disbelief and borderline excitement, he said, "He wants a full report of the night's events. If Eli is still with us in the morning, he'll come by as soon as he gets here."

Valerie felt her heart leap in her chest. She jumped up from Eli's bed and turned to Joe and Beau, "Do you see? Do you know what this means?" The relief and hope in Joe's eyes lit him up from the inside and Valerie could see it.

Beau, however, was hesitant and fearful. He wouldn't allow himself to feel hope. Instead he stood in silence, waiting for the "but," waiting for the other shoe to drop. Ten minutes passed, then twelve, fifteen, twenty, and finally Eli had been breathing on his own for a full hour. Valerie was elated, a new person with a renewed spirit. Nothing could shake her faith, not anymore.

At the hour mark, Dr. Weston cleared her to tell the waiting family. She burst through the door and sprinted down the hallway at a dead run. When she turned into the waiting area, the look on her face said it all — Ivy jumped to her feet. She could tell by Val's expression that the news on her lips would be good. "He's breathing! He's breathing on his own!" The room erupted with cheers, applause, tears and laughter. Ivy squealed and hugged her mother as tears erupted from her eyes like a volcano of emotion, but this time, they were tears of joy. Even the nurses at the nurse's station cheered. Pete ran up and hugged his sister. She made her way around the room, sharing her love and her renewed faith with everyone.

Meanwhile, back in Eli's room, Beau was sitting by Eli's bedside, staring at his own socks on the pillow, wondering why none of the nurses had mentioned them, all the while remaining silently fearful that Eli would stop breathing at any moment and silently bitter that his coma lingered on.

Joe stood staring at his son, watching his chest rise and fall at a steady clip. Eventually, he turned to Dr. Weston, who still appeared to be in disbelief, "I'm going to need that DNR back."

HANGDOG
Shoulder to Shoulder

PART TWO

CHAPTER TWENTY-FOUR

In the months since she and Joe brought Eli home, Valerie had amassed an abundance of skills she never thought she'd have, let alone need. She became a full-time nurse, seemingly overnight. Home health visited once a week, but predominantly, she was Eli's primary caregiver.

In some ways, she felt like a prisoner to her son's coma, but the entire family had agreed that Eli would receive the most love and devotion in the comfort of his own home. So, three weeks to the day after the ventilator was removed, medical transport had escorted Eli McKnight back home. They helped Joe get him up the stairs and into the waiting hospital bed, in the room he'd known since childhood.

Private nurses came for a few hours a day until Valerie got acclimated to her new routine. Val had to learn how the feeding tube worked, how to manage Eli's catheters, how to move him and roll him to avoid bedsores, how to bathe him and handle the full weight of his ever-shrinking frame all by herself.

Gradually, home health visits were dropped to just once per week.

Joe helped out in the evenings, but he had returned to work shortly after Eli came home and late nights weren't an option. Ivy, though, had become a permanent fixture. She practically lived in the house, helping Valerie manage the household, while also caring for Eli. She and Val would work in tandem, like a well-oiled machine, and their relationship had grown into something reminiscent of Ruth and Naomi.

Ivy's parents hadn't pushed when she chose not to start school in August, but they had recently begun encouraging her to get out more, visit friends, get a part time job, and begin preparing herself for classes in the spring. Her mother tried not to resent the McKnights, but it had become difficult. Joe and Valerie couldn't blame them. After all, Ivy and Eli weren't married, and she shouldn't be expected to put her own life on hold simply because he had been forced to. In fact, in many ways, they could empathize with the Zellways.

Beau had been on a downward spiral since he'd pleaded no contest to aggravated assault, a class B misdemeanor, and received a MIC ticket. JP had done a beautiful job with Beau's defense, getting his jail time down to twenty-eight days, to be followed by thirty hours of community service and a driver's class. The judge had been sympathetic and had considered the mitigating circumstances of the case to be punishment in and of itself. The judge had even suggested that Beau should spend some time in counseling, "for his own health and wellbeing."

Valerie and Joe had encouraged it, but Beau wanted nothing to do with it, explaining that no amount of "chit-chat with a stranger" would right his wrongs.

JP had requested that Beau's report date for the county jail be expedited, so as to improve his chances for a normal transition in the fall. Both the DA and the judge had agreed without issue, and Beau was behind bars within two weeks. He had been allowed one half-hour visitation per day, and either Joe, or Val, or both of them had gone every single day, without fail. Jail made Beau's vocabulary even more withdrawn, as he rarely spoke to anyone unless he had to. He'd also grown a bit leaner behind bars.

He told his parents the food was inedible, but in truth, he'd not had much of an appetite since the day he woke up in the hospital. Val and Joe put money on a commissary account for him, in the hopes he'd find commissary fare more palatable. Beau spent the money on junk food to share with his cell mate, a young man of twenty-five who had been convicted of armed robbery, but swore his innocence, alleging he'd been in the wrong place at the wrong time. He never had visitors and said he'd lied to his mother in Florida, telling her he'd taken a temporary job as a deckhand on a fishing boat and would be out at sea for two months without phone access or internet. Beau had never bothered to ask why he concocted the story, or if his mother even knew he was in Texas. Joe secretly worried that Beau's seemingly high comfort level with the jail environment was a bad sign.

Joe had taken money, a lot of money, from their savings to pay for Beau's legal fees, but JP's work had made it worth it. Beau's life would not be ruined. His future could still be bright, and he would be able to bounce back, except for one devastating caveat. His football scholarship had been revoked. Not long after sentencing, he'd received a call from his would-be head coach informing him that, as a result of his legal situation, the athletic department, in conjunction with the Dean of Students, had chosen to revoke his scholarship, as well as his offer to become part of the football program. Because he'd violated the Code of Conduct and the Honor Code prior to officially becoming a student athlete, he was told his admission to the school still stood, but his financial aid and football opportunities were behind him.

Considering that football was the only real reason Beau wanted to go to college in the first place, losing that chance in the eleventh hour had snuffed out his will to do anything. He'd been sleeping most of the day, and even though Val and Joe had taken his truck away, he was out all night, presumably partying until dawn. Occasionally, he'd go to the gym with a buddy and lift weights, but then he'd be gone for hours doing God knows what. Without Eli there to bail him out, he was making one poor choice after another. Thankfully, none of them had resulted in legal consequences, at least not yet.

Val and Joe were at a loss. Beau was angry and distant, bitter about his own losses, but also still punishing himself for what he'd done to Eli. They'd always been so close as a family, but Beau had become a stranger. Val spent most of her spare time trying to build up her faith. But, every day that passed without visible progress, for either of her sons, made it more difficult to remain positive.

Somehow though, she pressed on, speaking words of faith and hope over both her children, her husband, Ivy and her household every single day. Joe admired her. He'd been on the verge of screaming for a full month and had lost his temper with Beau more than once. Their relationship had become so fractured, Joe didn't know if he'd ever be able to look at Beau the same way as he had merely months before. But, somehow, Valerie was still tender and loving toward Beau, as sweet and giving as she'd ever been. She once told him that she chose to serve Beau, and it didn't matter if he was deserving or not.

Still, despite it all, the family had managed to establish a routine. The local news had finally stopped running stories about them and things were slowly falling into a new normal. Friends, the true kind, had started to come around again, and Val had even hosted dinner once or twice for their small group. It wasn't a particularly good normal, but it was consistent, and that alone provided some comfort.

CHAPTER TWENTY-FIVE

The Saturday morning sun was pouring in through the windows as Valerie cooked up some eggs and bacon. The house smelled of fresh bread, as biscuits baked in the oven. She only prepped enough food for Joe, Beau and herself, because Ivy had agreed to take Saturday and spend it with her parents. She and her mom were getting pedicures and then they'd meet her father for lunch and a matinee. Val welcomed Ivy's presence, always, but she was also grateful for some alone time.

When breakfast was ready, Joe decided Beau should join them. He rose from his chair at the table, where he'd been sipping coffee and filling Valerie in on his current projects at work. He walked through the family room and turned to climb the stairs, stopping to grab a basket of towels Valerie had folded the night before while watching late-night TV. When he reached the top of the stairs, he placed the basket in front of the linen closet and made the sharp right toward Beau's room. He cracked the door open and stuck his head in. The shades were drawn, but even in the darkness, he could see that the room was in complete shambles. It even smelled a little. He spoke softly into the darkness, "Beau? Are you awake?" He was met with silence. "Beau?" He shuffled over the mess in the floor to be closer to the bed. "Beau, your mom made breakfast. Come eat."

Beau let out a groan, "Later."

"No, now. It's after ten already, come eat with us." He laid a hand on Beau's back.

"I don't want to! I don't feel good." Beau moaned and groaned and Joe knew immediately he was hung over. The realization made him see red.

"I don't care if you throw your guts up for the rest of the day, you will get up, out of that bed, right now, and come downstairs to eat!" He stalked over to the window and threw open the shades, allowing sunlight to bathe the room. "Now, Beau!"

Though technically an adult, Beau had enough respect for, and fear of, his father that he didn't dare ignore the command. Despite his current state, his reflex to honor and obey his parents was ingrained at a young age and he simply wasn't wired to overthrow their authority — especially Joe's. He began moving and pushed himself into a seated position.

"You have five minutes. Wash your face, put on a fresh shirt, and for everyone's sake, brush your teeth." Joe left the room calmly, having gotten himself under control, and made his way back downstairs. When Beau made his appearance a few minutes later, Joe was once again seated at the table, sipping coffee, and this time, flipping through the pages of a *Golf Digest.* "Val, I know it's not practical, but I'd really love to play a round or two before the weather turns cold. Will it be too much if I try to play tomorrow after church?"

"I think that will be okay. I'm sure Ivy will come over, and we've still got a week before we have people over, plenty of time for cleaning." She sounded happy, hopeful and normal. To Beau's ears, the tone of the conversation was like nails on a chalkboard. Not because of his headache, but because of the normalcy of it all. He refused to accept his current circumstances as normal, and yet, everyone else seemed to be moving forward with life and adjusting to a new pace. They smiled, they laughed, and he wanted to scream every time they did.

Valerie walked over and placed a full plate of bacon and eggs in front of Beau, along with a small glass of orange juice. She patted his shoulders and turned to Joe, "Hon, do you want some juice to go with that coffee?"

"Sure! That actually sounds really good."

Beau couldn't take it anymore. He lifted both his arms and slammed his fists onto the table, causing utensils to jump and clatter, orange juice to splash, and causing Valerie to shriek in fear. "Stop it," he yelled, as loudly as he could muster, "Would you just stop? Stop acting like everything is normal! Stop acting like we're all okay! Just stop!" He put his elbows on the table and his hands over his face. His outburst was peppered with expletives and Joe had to restrain himself from jumping across the table and onto his son.

Valerie took a deep breath to calm her nerves, but instead of speaking, she went back to the eggs. Joe put his glass onto the table and used a napkin to wipe the coffee splatter from around his mug. He breathed deeply, wanting desperately to handle this situation the right way. He didn't want to push Beau further into the dark hole he was in, but he couldn't let him continue on the destructive path he was walking, nor could he allow his son to speak to them, especially his mother, the way he had. Not just this morning, but for weeks. He lifted his eyes to look at Beau, who was still covering his face.

"Son, I'm only going to say this once, and you're going to listen." His tone was gentle and reassuring, "I know you're hurting. I know you're angry. I know things are tough right now, but son, if you ever speak to us like that again, you'll wish you hadn't." He paused for a quick second, still calm, "I'm telling you right now, the only person who can turn things around for you is you. It's time to take some responsibility for your life. Your behavior has been deplorable. We know you're drinking, often and a lot, which, by the way, is a really, really stupid choice under your circumstances." He put heavy emphasis on the *stupid*. "You're not pulling your weight around here. You're not taking care of your own stuff. You're disrespecting me, your mother, your brother, and yourself. We love you, but enough is enough. It's time for a change."

Valerie walked over and sat down next to Beau, who had a blank, but somewhat thoughtful, look on his face. “Son, what would Eli say about all this?”

“Don’t! Don’t do that Mom.” Beau’s response was flat. “He can’t say anything and that’s my fault too, and you know it. Why don’t you two just come out with it already? It’s my fault and I’m getting exactly what I deserve!” He raised his voice slightly, but not enough to warrant backlash from Joe.

“No. It was an accident,” Val said. “Sure, you caused it, but it was not intentional and that is all we need to know. Now, it’s time to dust yourself off. Your brother will be fine. He will be!”

“You don’t know that,” Beau said.

“I choose to believe it.” She looked at Joe.

“Listen, son. Here’s the bottom line. We wouldn’t be doing our jobs as parents if we let you just carry on in this, whatever this is, without stepping up. So…” He took a deep breath, “You have two weeks to make a decision about where you’re going from here and take action on it. Either you’re going to get a job, or enroll in school, or something — just make a decision and move on it… Two weeks!”

Beau was silent. He seriously considered asking his father what would happen if he didn’t comply with the deadline, but he could tell by the look on Joe’s face that it would be a mistake. Truth be told, he didn’t really want to know what the consequences would be.

“Am I clear?” Joe intended the question to be rhetorical, but Beau nodded a response.

Valerie decided she wouldn’t let tension ruin her little family Saturday, so she spoke up, “Now, let’s eat, okay?” She grabbed both Beau’s and Joe’s plates and walked over to the microwave, having correctly assumed the eggs would be cold by now. As the plates heated, she topped off Joe’s coffee and popped an ice cube into Beau’s glass. When she pulled the plates from the microwave, she carried Joe’s to his place first. Before she took Beau his plate, she stopped at the skinny cabinet by the refrigerator and opened it. She popped the top on an aspirin bottle and put two of them on Beau’s plate. As she put the plate in front of him, she gave him a little wink. Though Beau didn’t respond, she could see that his demeanor softened a bit. She put her own plate into the microwave and glanced at the clock, “After we eat, I think I’m going to change Eli’s sheets and read to him for a while, and then maybe we’ll rent a movie. How would that be?”

“Sounds like a good day to me,” Joe responded. “And just to keep it extra low key, let’s order pizza for dinner tonight.” Beau sat and took in his parents’ casual conversation at the breakfast-turned-brunch table, marveling at how peaceful they seemed. How could anyone going through what they’re going through be peaceful? Why were they not angry? What was wrong with them? Their peace was part of his torment. Where would he go from here?

CHAPTER TWENTY-SIX

"Joe! Will you turn that crock-pot down to low, please?" Valerie called across the kitchen as she buzzed over a drink station, setting up ice and cups and two-liter bottles buffet-style.

"Done. What else ya' got?" Joe called back in a jovial voice.

"Maybe see if Beau finished vacuuming the living room? We only have an hour before everyone arrives."

"Will do," Joe responded, as he spun on his heels to head out to the living room.

It was the first big event Joe and Valerie had hosted since the accident. Except for a few smaller gatherings, they'd not been up to entertaining. But, since getting into a rhythm within the confines of their new normal, they'd decided it was time to start opening their home again.

Every quarter prior to the crash, Valerie and Joe had hosted an open-house fellowship for anyone and everyone from their church who wanted to attend. The event usually lasted three or four hours and spanned an entire afternoon. People would come and eat a buffet of hors d' oeuvres and sweets, watch whatever pertinent sporting event might be on at the time and hang out with friends. The events had been a huge success, in part because the McKnights had a great house with lots to keep folks entertained, but also because of who they were. Everyone loved being around them.

Valerie was apprehensive this time around, though. People seemed to look at them differently now. They'd been forced to attend church in shifts, because they couldn't leave Eli alone, and now people seemed drawn to them for a different reason — pity. Instead of laughter and banter, they got questions like, "How are you holding up? It must be so hard, right?" Valerie expected the get-together to have a different vibe than it did before the accident, but she was determined to make it a good time anyway.

"Did you get that vacuuming done, Beau?" Joe asked, having found his son laid back on the sofa with a remote in his hand.

"Uh-huh," Beau's response was despondent.

"I expect some of your friends will be coming tonight, right?" Joe longed desperately to get a glimpse of the Beau he used to know. He prayed a silent prayer that God would intervene on Beau's behalf and shake him loose from the prison he'd built for himself.

"I don't know," Beau shrugged, never making eye contact with his dad.

"Mom wants to get Eli into some fresh clothes before people arrive. Why don't you go help her?"

Beau didn't say anything, but he put the remote down and stood. He stretched for a second and slowly moved out of the room. Joe sat and rubbed his temples for a moment, lost in thought over Beau and his future. Everything had changed so quickly and now, well, nothing seemed certain.

~

When the doorbell rang to signal the first guest's arrival, Valerie had everything done. She felt prepared for the party, but not so much for the company. She knew she'd be answering a thousand questions about Eli's care and prognosis, and though she was standing on faith that he would wake up, she could feel the pity of others, others who thought she was in denial, or expected Eli to pass away, or, even worse, thought he'd be better off dead already. None of the McKnights were blind to the talk, but they wanted to move past it, because stepping out in faith for healing meant living as though it was a done deal.

After about twenty-five minutes, the McKnight home was filled with the sounds of entertainment. There was talk, laughter and lots of eating. Valerie had fielded a few questions, but far fewer than she'd expected, and she was actually enjoying herself. Ivy had arrived with her parents and had made a bee-line for Eli's room. She did the honors of hosting guests who made the climb to visit him. She talked to him as though he'd answer, held his hand and managed to make every visitor feel at ease and somehow more hopeful about Eli's condition.

When Kevin Hinkley arrived, he didn't bother ringing the bell. He opened the door and held out his arm, Maggie put her arm through his and reluctantly stepped to the threshold. As the pair made their way through the crowd of guests, Valerie noted a twinkling in Kevin's eyes she hadn't noticed before. Kevin came by at least once a week, sometimes with his dad, and sometimes alone, but he never mentioned a girl. She walked up, hugged his neck and asked, "Kevin, aren't you going to introduce me?"

"Ms. Valerie, this is my girlfriend, Maggie Cox. And, she's the bees' knees." He winked and put heavy emphasis on the word girlfriend, as if the official coupledom was a new development.

Valerie chuckled, "I have no doubt that she is." She held out her hands to Maggie, taking one of Maggie's hands in both of her own. "Welcome Maggie, there's tons of food in the kitchen."

When Kevin and Maggie turned the corner into the kitchen, Maggie stopped dead in her tracks as her heart took an expedient leap into her throat. Beau was seated at the table. He looked up from his plate and made eye contact with Kevin first. But then, his glance shifted to Maggie. She stood next to Kevin, staring at Beau with a pleading look that was unmistakable. She swallowed hard and it was evident to Beau that Kevin had no idea about what had happened between him and Maggie after graduation, and Maggie definitely preferred it to stay that way.

Kevin handed Maggie a plate and began loading his own, while asking questions about her preferences and simultaneously making small talk in Beau's general direction. Kevin had never been at a loss for words, even when the second party in one of his conversations had nothing to say in return. Mr. Hinkley had always joked that Kevin could bond with a fencepost thanks to his conversation skills.

Beau sat silently, chewing, and looking at Maggie. He had no intention of telling anyone about what had happened between them, and for the first time in his life, the power of being the keeper of such a secret didn't appeal to him. He didn't feel proud of his conquest. He could tell Maggie was terrified. After a while, he gave her a silent, but reassuring, nod. He watched as her stress level visibly lessened. She turned her attention back to Kevin and seemed to trust his nod enough to spend the rest of the evening at peace.

Beau pushed away from the table and walked into the living room. The party guests had given him a wide berth for most of the evening. But, his mother patted the sofa next to where she was sitting. In the small circle were Mr. and Mrs. Hinkley, Mr. and Mrs. Zellway, and his parents. He sat down next to his mom, keeping his greeting to a quick nod. Soon, the conversation turned to the future. Kevin and Maggie came into the living room and joined the group.

“There’s a mission trip coming up next year that I think Ivy would be perfect for. It’s an agricultural mission in Zimbabwe. She’d literally be helping feed people, which is right up her alley.” Mr. Hinkley directed his statement toward Ivy’s parents. “It’s still quite a few months away, but I know she’s postponed school so it wouldn’t interfere. But, she’d have to commit pretty soon, as there’s some extensive training to complete first. I spoke to her about it a few days ago and she expressed an interest, but she was adamant that Valerie needed her and she couldn’t leave Eli.” He turned his gaze to the McKnights.

Mr. Zellway nodded. Mrs. Zellway didn’t know how to respond. She wanted Ivy to move forward, but she didn’t dare say so in front of the McKnights.

“She should absolutely go,” Joe said. “Poor kid, she’s putting too much burden on herself.”

“Yes, she should go,” Valerie wholeheartedly agreed with Joe. “I love her, she’s a great help, and, of course, we’ll miss her around here, but she should absolutely take this opportunity. There is no way we’d want to stop her from following her heart.”

Mrs. Zellway exhaled in an almost-laugh and put a hand on Val’s forearm, “Oh my goodness, I’m so relieved to hear you say that. I’ve been encouraging her to get out, but didn’t want to seem insensitive. I think this trip will be so healing for her, and I’m just relieved that you agree.”

"Absolutely," Mr. Zellway chimed in. "We didn't want to come off as jerks, for lack of a better word."

Joe laughed, "Never! Ivy is such a huge help, but I'm sure we can manage the household chores while she, you know, feeds the hungry and spreads the gospel. Priorities!"

The group shared a laugh as Beau listened in. He wondered if Ivy would actually go.

"Excellent! Maybe we can all sit down with her next week to talk it over. In the meantime, we'll all be praying."

"Is Kevin going on this one?" Mrs. Zellway thought it might help if someone Ivy knew were going on the trip.

"No, actually, we've got some big news." Mr. Hinkley looked toward Kevin, knowing his son wouldn't be able to sit idly by and let someone else do the talking.

"I've decided to join the Air Force. I'll be leaving for basic training next month." Kevin smiled and sat up straight, he looked over at Maggie who smiled back at him. It was clear to everyone in the circle that Kevin and Maggie were smitten in a way that might lead to something permanent. Valerie smiled and Kevin continued before his dad could get a word in edgewise, "College is expensive, which is why I didn't apply this year. I want to live my life without a bunch of student loan debt, and I feel like this is a good way to get my college paid for while making a full-time living doing something that matters."

"Oh my goodness, Kevin! Congratulations! That's a big step!" Valerie stood and took the two steps to Kevin. She bent over and took his face in her hands. He stood and hugged her in return.

“It was a big decision, but he made it all on his own. We couldn’t be prouder. Or more worried,” Mrs. Hinkley chuckled at her own statement. The group followed suit. For the first time since sitting, Beau perked up. He leaned forward, placing his elbows on his knees.

“So, what will your job be?” Beau asked Kevin with seemingly genuine interest. Joe and Val looked at each other but tried not to act surprised that Beau showed any interest at all, let alone that he was speaking full sentences for a change.

“I did pretty well on the ASVAB, so I qualified for a lot of jobs, but since I think I want to study electrical engineering one day, I picked mostly electrical jobs and,” he pointed toward the sky, “got my first choice. I’m going to be an Electronic Computer and Switching Systems Specialist. I really don’t have any idea what that means specifically, except it has to do with electronic security and stuff, but it sounds like it’s important and it’s definitely in my wheelhouse.” Everyone listened intently, and Kevin was obviously thrilled with the attention. “I’m pretty excited.”

“What’s the ASVAB, exactly?” Beau asked another question. Joe and Val stayed quiet, watching the scene play out.

“It’s a test...” Kevin responded.

Beau interrupted, “I hate tests.”

“But it’s not like a regular test. It’s a test to see what you’ll be good at. It’s an aptitude test.”

"So they look at your scores and say, 'This is what you'd be best at'?" Beau asked. All the adults watched the exchange as if God himself had ordained it, because they all knew how Val and Joe had struggled with Beau since the crash, and they knew he only had a week left on Joe's deadline to take some kind of action toward living again.

"Yeah, kinda," Kevin answered.

Joe and Valerie didn't really think Beau would consider the military, not seriously anyway. Partially because he bucked authority, but also because, in the past, he had said he'd never want to live anywhere but Texas. But neither of them cared that it wasn't a serious consideration, at least he'd shown signs of life.

Beau sat back on the sofa, nodding to himself, arms folded across his chest. He leaned his head back and looked at Kevin. He offered a single nod of thanks, and that was it. The conversation was over as quickly as it had begun. There was a long pause before Mr. Hinkley opened the door for conversation again, but when he did, Beau's focus faded back into himself.

CHAPTER TWENTY-SEVEN

"Are you sure you don't want to include your parents in this process?" Throughout his entire time as a recruiter, Cpl. Cash had never had an applicant complete the entire enlistment process without including at least one other person in the process, be it as a support system or even just a ride to his office. Granted, he'd not been in recruiting long, but it was strange to sit across from someone who wanted zero input from anybody. Stranger still was the fact that an eighteen-year-old kid would travel forty miles outside his own home town to visit a recruiter.

"Yes. I'm sure," Beau responded. "What do you need from me?"

"Okay then, well, we'll need to get you to MEPS," Cash picked up on Beau's facial expressions and added, "that's short for Military Entrance Processing Station, to take the ASVAB. But, first, I need to ask you some questions." The recruiter went on to ask Beau about his life's history. Was he a high school graduate? Did he use drugs? Had he ever been in trouble? For some reason, Beau found it uniquely easy to come clean with Cash. The story poured out of him like water from a pitcher. He was an open book, a downtrodden, monotone open book. He told his newly appointed recruiter all about what had transpired after graduation, the accident and the charges he'd faced, his conviction and the judge's ruling. It didn't take long before Cpl. Cash began to piece together the likely reasons Beau had traveled so far outside his own town. If he were in Beau's shoes, he'd be flying under the radar as much as possible, too. At the same time, it dawned on him that Beau might be running from his mistakes or, at least, trying to hide from them.

Despite that fact, Cpl. Cash had a good feeling about Beau. He genuinely liked him, even if he did come across as depressed. As far as Cash was concerned, Beau had earned the right to be melancholy. Having dealt with such tragedy, a good mood would seem almost disrespectful. He was determined to help Beau. This time, it wouldn't be all about his quota — it would be about helping a kid get his life back on track.

As a bonus, Beau was exactly what one would expect from a Marine physically. Internally, Cash hoped he had the mental wherewithal to perform on the ASVAB. He seemed to be "with it," but the young corporal had seen "with it" people bomb the test in the past.

The interview progressed with Cash informing Beau that he would require waivers to get in, because of his legal issues. They discussed all the paperwork Beau would need to provide

— his birth certificate, proof of high school graduation, background check, Social Security card and medical records, especially those from his recent stay at the hospital after the accident. Provided his history didn't include additional medical issues, obtaining the records would likely be an easy task.

Finally, Cpl. Cash asked Beau, “What kind of work would you like to do as part of the USMC, provided you qualify?”

Beau wasn't exactly sure how to answer, he had no clue what he might want to do. All he knew was he wanted to do something that would take him far, far away from his home, away from his place under the same roof as Eli, and, hopefully, away from his guilt.

At the end of it all, Beau had another appointment with his recruiter, a list of things to bring, and a plan. He’d take the ASVAB after his next appointment and then he’d enlist officially. He was nearing his Dad’s deadline. He wanted to be fully committed to the Marines before he told his Mom and Dad about his choice. He knew they’d freak out or perhaps try to talk him down, and, though he knew he shouldn’t be happy about it, he felt somewhat justified in having made the choice without their input.

He’d always been impressed by the Marines. Their uniforms, their stoic expressions — the way they seemed to have it all together. They seemed to defy life’s chaos. Maybe that’s why he didn’t think twice about the branch he’d join. The very moment he asked Kevin about the ASVAB and the Air

Force, he'd made up his mind. Soon, he'd take his own exam and wait for a future he never expected to have.

~

Joe was hesitant to broach the subject of his ultimatum deadline with Beau. The two hadn't spoken much since that day, except for a few niceties one might expect living under the same roof. As his work day progressed, he found himself distracted, dwelling on his impending discussion with his son. Had he made any progress at all? Did he have a plan? How was it possible that he and his baby boy, once so close, now seemed like strangers living in the same house?

On the other hand, the accident, and Eli's state of being, had somehow reinforced his relationship with Valerie. They were now bonded in ways most married couples never experience. But whatever internal struggle Beau had been dealing with since the accident had driven a wedge between them all — truth be told, it had driven a wedge between Beau and everyone.

Joe felt moments of guilt. Perhaps he had not equipped Beau to handle stress — or his emotions. Perhaps he'd not prepared him to face his own mistakes with integrity or grace. Maybe he'd not been tough enough, or maybe he'd been too tough. Perhaps it was a mistake not to intervene more aggressively, even though he knew Beau was sowing wilder oats than Eli had ever dreamed of. His mind rolled over every questionable moment and every perceived mistake from his eighteen years as a father. Was it all his fault?

Joe and Valerie both knew Beau had pushed the boundaries of authority, and they'd chosen to give him some growing room. Knowing their son's personality type, they believed tighter reins would only drive Beau to greater rebellion. So, in some respects, they let him get away with things, reserving consequences for heavier issues. It was easy now for Joe to blame himself for what had happened. "If you'd only been a better father, maybe none of this would've happened. Maybe Beau would still be the joyful young man he had been a year ago," he told himself. In his spirit, he knew blaming himself was a waste. But he had trouble keeping the thoughts at bay.

Lately, he'd spent more time at work trying to come up with ways to hold his son accountable for improving his own situation than he had spent working. The only consequence he believed might have an impact would be to kick Beau out of the house. It was a heart-wrenching consequence, and Valerie would hate it, but, he didn't have any other options. How could he help Beau become a man, despite his circumstances, without destroying their crumbling relationship forever?

CHAPTER TWENTY-EIGHT

"I don't know. I want to go, and I don't want to go at the same time." Ivy looked across the table at Valerie, as she sat sipping her mostly-cream cup of coffee. "Twelve weeks is an awfully long time to be away. What if he wakes up and I'm not here? I can't bear the thought of him waking up and me not being here to witness it."

Valerie looked across the table through understanding eyes. She sipped her own cup of coffee and tried to put herself into Ivy's shoes. What if it were her? What if Joe was lying in that bed upstairs? How would she handle it? How would she have handled it at eighteen? "Eli would want you to go, and you know it. He would be going with you if he could. If God is calling you to it, there are no downsides to going. Besides that, Joe and I want you to go, you want to go, Eli would want you to go, your parents want you to go, Pastor Hinkley wants you to go. I literally see no downsides here." Val smiled her sweet smile and took another sip of coffee before she continued, "And

Eli wouldn't be able to bear it if he thought he was holding you back. He would definitely want you to go, especially knowing how much you really want to go."

"Is it that obvious?" Ivy felt a pang of guilt for having a desire to leave. She was torn between her desire and obligation to stay with the man she loved and had planned to marry, for better or worse, and her desire to take an opportunity she believed God had called her to take. She didn't want to be excited about it, but she was.

"It's okay to be excited. You should be excited. Besides, if God called you to it and Eli would want you to go, he would also want you to be excited," Valerie said. "I think, knowing Eli like we do, he would expect you to follow God's will and would hold you accountable to doing just that. Knowing all that, there's no way you're making the wrong choice."

Ivy made a face, "Then why, why do I, for some reason, have to fight back the feeling of guilt every time I think about it?"

"Every time you think about the trip?" Valerie asked.

"No. Every time I'm excited about something. Not just this, anything — for some reason it feels wrong to be excited about anything. So, when I do feel excited about something or happy about something, I also have immediate feelings of guilt, almost like I'm betraying Eli by being happy when I know he can't be."

"Ivy, honey, Eli would never forgive himself if he knew he was the reason that you weren't happy. You have to be happy. If for no other reason, be happy for Eli, not despite him. And how do we know he's not happy? Maybe he's having, I don't know, the greatest dream ever. We never did know what was happening in that head of his, why should this be different?" Valerie chuckled at her own statement. She liked the idea of Eli having a good experience, despite living in a perpetual state of medical crisis.

"I guess you're right," Ivy responded with a laugh. She smiled and thought about the fact that not going might be an injustice to Eli's expectations of her. He really would expect her to follow God's will for her life. Still, she had mixed feelings about leaving him for twelve long weeks. "But twelve weeks?"

"Yes, twelve weeks. That's just three months. I can handle it for three months. I promise." Valerie reached across the table and patted Ivy's hand. "I'm beginning to think you have no faith in me," she chuckled and Ivy smiled.

"Are you absolutely sure I'm not making a big mistake?"

"Of course I'm absolutely sure!" Valerie smiled and gave Ivy a reassuring nod. And with that, Ivy jumped to her feet and squealed as she ran over to the other side of the table and wrapped her arms around Valerie's slim frame.

"Thank you, Ms. Valerie! I love you!" Ivy said it, and she meant it. Mrs. McKnight had become one of the most important people in her life. "I'm going to go tell my parents right now! My mom is going to be so happy for me!"

"I know she will be! I'm excited for you, too. Don't forget to call Pastor Hinkley. You'll have to start the training right away. After all, with the holidays coming up, your travel days will be here before you know it."

Ivy squealed again and headed out through the kitchen door. On her way out, she reached over and grabbed her purse from the kitchen counter and called behind her, “Thanks again Ms. Valerie! I’ll see you tomorrow!”

Val watched her go and thought about how much life had changed in a few short months. It seemed like just yesterday she and Joe were planning a summer trip to Bora Bora, and now they were thrilled just to get dinner out when someone from the church offered to sit with Eli for the night. She sighed and grabbed her Bible from the table, along with what was left of her coffee, and walked through the glass door onto the back deck. She looked out over the back yard and took note of how little they’d used the pool and patio this year. She noted how neglected her flower beds appeared and how obvious it was that things just weren’t the same around McKnight Manor, as she liked to call it. She sat down in her favorite Adirondack chair, carefully placing her coffee cup on the arm of the chair, and opened her Bible on her lap. As she began to read, she thought it might be time to get into her flower beds. She’d heard her new favorite podcast pastor say that negative thoughts and faithless thoughts are like weeds in the mind. If you allow them to grow, they’ll take over. She’d been plucking faithless thoughts from her mind for months, or at least trying to, and now, it was time to pluck some actual weeds from her life right alongside them.

~

At the end of the day, Joe came through the door of his home and made a bee-line for the kitchen, where he expected to find Valerie preparing dinner. Instead, he found the kitchen empty. He called out, but received no response. He walked out onto the back deck and called again. To his relieved surprise, Valerie's head popped up between the slats in the deck railing, not ten feet from where he stood. She was wearing earbuds and her sun hat."

"Oh, hi!" she tugged at the earbuds and smiled at her husband. "I thought I would go ahead and take care of the weeds in this bed. It's a mess out here."

"You scared me for a minute!" Joe had grown accustomed to his wife's routine. It startled him that she'd chosen something different for the afternoon.

"I did a crockpot dinner for tonight, so I had some time. How was your day?" Valerie pulled off her gardening gloves and stood up. She made her way around the edge of the deck and climbed the stairs. Before Joe could say anything, she interjected, "Oh, while it's on my mind, I thought we might eat outside tonight. It's supposed to be nice and we haven't spent any real time around the pool all summer."

"That sounds nice. I wanted to talk to you about Beau anyway." Joe shook his head, he'd been dreading this discussion, but he knew it was time to share his opinion with Valerie about kicking Beau out of the house. "I wonder if Beau will be home in time for dinner, or if we might get the chance to talk, just us?"

"Why wouldn't we get the chance to talk, even if Beau is here?" Valerie cocked her head a little bit sideways, confused at her husband's statement. She sensed something was up. The family had always been so open in discussions that purposely leaving Beau out of a family dinner meeting seemed strange.

"Oh, we still could. I just have something I want to talk to you about privately first."

"I see," Valerie responded. She'd never been much on waiting. "Well, I'm not busy now." She sat down next to him in her Adirondack chair and put her hat in her lap, staring at him inquisitively. He looked at her and almost laughed at her expression and how logically she'd presented *now* as being as good a time as any for a conversation.

"Touché," he responded. "I'm going to grab us each a glass of tea. Then we'll talk, okay?" Joe untucked his shirt and began to take off his belt. He realized he was still dressed for work, which was not characteristic of him. Under normal circumstances, the first thing he did when he got home was take off his button-down and slacks, replacing them with a T-shirt and ball shorts or sweats.

"Oooh, that sounds lovely," Valerie practically sighed her response. Having her husband serve her an ice cold glass of tea while she sat and relaxed was like a song written in her love language.

Joe disappeared into the house and Valerie placed her sun hat back on her head. It was brighter outside than she had expected for late afternoon. While she waited, she walked over to the light switch panel and flipped the third switch from the left, which illuminated the lights in their pool area. She inspected them for burnt out bulbs, but found none. Instead of turning them off, she walked to the edge of the deck. The cobblestone patio and landscaping around the pool had been sorely neglected over the past few months, having received nothing more than an occasional visit from the weed eater. Nonetheless, it was still a beautiful back yard, private and very inviting. She walked down the steps of the deck and turned the corner, following the short, cobblestone path toward the patio and pool. She kicked off her slip-on shoes and stuck her toe into the water. Nice and warm. She reached down and rolled her cropped jeans a couple times before sitting on the edge of the pool, dropping her feet into the water.

Joe emerged through the glass door holding two glasses of tea. He immediately noticed his wife down by the water and, instead of calling for her to join him, he headed down the steps and onto the path himself. As he approached Valerie, she turned and reached out a hand for her glass. He handed it to her and sat his on the concrete. Now in his shorts and T-shirt, he kicked off his flip-flops and sat down beside her, letting his feet dangle in the water next to hers.

"Wow, the water feels great!" Joe looked at her with astonishment in his eyes. The summer had been a blur, their typical summer activities having been derailed by their abrupt change in circumstances, and he couldn't remember the last time he'd enjoyed their pool.

"Right?" Valerie responded. "We've been missing out!" She followed her statement with a sudden question. "Okay then," she said. "What's on your mind?"

"He's only got a couple days left, Val." Joe turned to Val and didn't have to clarify, she knew exactly what he was referring to. "He hasn't said anything to us about his plans, or whether he even has a plan."

"I know." Valerie took a deep breath and let it out.

"I've decided, if he doesn't deliver, I'm going to tell him to find another place to live," Joe just blurted it out. Flatly, quickly, like ripping off a Band-Aid.

"What? Kick him out?" Valerie's shock and displeasure was obvious. It was easy to hear in her voice. "Are you nuts, Joe? Why would you kick him out? Won't that only make things worse?"

"What else are we going to do, Val? What else do we have as leverage? Do you have a better idea? If we take his truck again, he'll just sit around here all day, with the excuse that he can't get a job because we took his truck. Or he'll just get rides and go to places we can't monitor. If we take his phone, he's not going to care. He hasn't turned that thing on since court. He doesn't want to see people unless they're partying, so we can't ground him from social stuff. He just won't care. But if we force him to stand on his own two feet, maybe he'll at least get a job. I'm thinking we give him another two weeks to find a place, secure it and pack his stuff. I don't want to do it, but I can't think of anything else. He can't keep living like this and expecting us to look the other way."

Valerie sat in silence for what, to Joe, felt like a long time. "I don't know. There isn't anything, really — nothing that would make an impact. I guess this might actually be the best, and maybe the only, option." Tears began to well in her eyes. She didn't want to feel fear, but she did. She now feared losing her other son as well, not to illness or injury, but to a hardened, and probably broken, heart. The idea that kicking Beau out could ruin their family's already fragile relationship caused her heart to pound and her stomach to turn.

"Maybe it won't come to this. Maybe, by some miracle, he's actually come up with a good, safe, healthy plan that we know nothing about." Joe tried to sound hopeful. They shared a glance.

"I certainly pray that's the case, because if he hasn't, I'm not sure I can bear that conversation," Valerie murmured.

Joe looked at her. He seemed wounded. "Val, I'm not going to yell or throw him out like a tyrant. What kind of a person do you think I am?"

"That's not what I meant, Joe. I know you'll do it right. I just don't know if I can take it, regardless of how it comes."

Joe understood her position and tried not to take her reluctance personally. He put his arm around her and, without saying a word, tried to tell her that everything would be okay.

CHAPTER TWENTY-NINE

When Cpl. Cash arrived at his office the next morning, he found Beau sitting outside on the curb. Beau had a small cup of what appeared to be orange juice in his hand and a file folder next to him on the concrete. "Lord Almighty!" Cash exclaimed. "How long have you been here?"

Beau shrugged, "Only about an hour."

"I thought I was doing good because I was able to get you in for the ASVAB tomorrow, but you've definitely got me beat. I tried to call your cell last night, but it went straight to voice mail and it was full. I didn't expect you to get all that stuff so fast." Cpl. Cash was astonished. Nobody had ever moved that fast for him before.

"I went straight home after we talked yesterday. My parents were out on the back porch so I snuck upstairs to the office. As Beau relayed the story, he thought about the things he'd found when he opened that metal file cabinet where his mom kept important papers. As he picked through the folders, he found everything labeled and easy to decipher. There were folders on him, his father and brother, and even his mom. He found shot records from when he was little, a cephalogram x-ray from his orthodontic days, and one entire file labeled "Beau - school to keep," which contained certificates and at least one piece of work from all twelve years of his school career. That file had also contained his diploma.

As Beau recalled all the things he'd seen while looking for his birth certificate and Social Security card, he felt a moment of remorse for not including his mom in his plan. He could tell by the effort she'd put into organizing all his paperwork and school stuff that she really did care about what happened in his life. Of course, he knew that already, but somehow seeing her effort with his own eyes made it real.

Cpl. Cash sat there with his mouth open as Beau went on to tell him that he'd only been able to find his release paperwork in his mom's file folder, so he took all the things he needed and snuck back out of the house while his parents were still outside. He then told Cash that he'd headed over to the hospital. It was pretty late in the day, but he knew somebody there would be able to get him his records.

He told Cpl. Cash that he'd arrived at the hospital at around six thirty and had been told by a nurse that the medical records office was closed and the staff was gone for the day, but he'd refused to leave without his records. Because he refused to leave, he became a thorn in the side of the nurses on duty and, after about three hours of his loitering at the nurses station, someone made a phone call. The next thing he knew, he had his records in hand and was on his way. He even stopped at Walmart on his way back home to purchase a folder to hold everything, which he kept in his truck overnight so he wouldn't forget anything. He'd gone in, had dinner, watched a bit of TV and headed up to bed early so he could be there first thing in the morning.

Cash laughed out loud at Beau's account of the prior day's events. "Well," he said, "I'll get all of your paperwork taken care of today, and tomorrow you'll take your ASVAB. But, be warned, it's highly unlikely your waivers will be reviewed this week, though miracles do happen. Once you have your scores in hand, give me a call and we'll go from there." Cash handed Beau a folder that contained some information about the test and Beau flipped it open.

"Is it okay if I just come by after?" Beau asked.

"I might be in an appointment, but I don't mind."

"Okay, good." Beau looked at the folder in his hands.

"Beau, can you just tell me what's really going on? Why are you in such a hurry?" Cpl. Cash could sense that something was up. Nobody is in that big of a hurry without a specific reason.

Beau told his recruiter about his father's deadline, and how he wanted to have his commitment fully made before coming clean with his parents about his plan. Cash wasn't sure what to make of the situation, but he definitely hadn't met a young man as eager and as driven as Beau had been the past two days, regardless of the reasons — whether it was spite, or anger, or guilt. He didn't really care what Beau's reasons were, he was impressed all the same. What kid camps out at the hospital and pesters nurses until they get what they need? No kid he knew, that much was certain.

"I'd really like to meet your parents. Once you tell them." Cash had learned early on as a recruiter that parents were the biggest influencers in his recruit's lives, and he didn't want to risk a last-minute change of heart. "Oh, and Beau, keep your phone on, for my sake, okay?" That open line of communication would lessen the chance that Beau would change his mind.

"I'm sure they'll come and meet you. That is, if they don't murder me first." Cpl. Cash laughed at Beau's joke, but the statement was also a red flag. Beau, on the other hand, was only half joking. He had no idea how his parents would react, but he definitely knew the Marine Corps was not on their current list of viable options.

~

As Beau exited the building with his ASVAB scores in hand, he couldn't help but feel proud of himself. A 77 was a very respectable score. In fact, Cpl. Cash had told him that anything above a 50 would qualify him for hundreds of different, desirable jobs as a United States Marine.

It was the first time since the accident that the feeling of complete self-loathing took a backseat to a positive accomplishment. In fact, it was the first actual triumph Beau had experienced in months. For the past few months, even showering and brushing his teeth felt like major accomplishments, so having earned a relatively high score on the ASVAB was quite literally the best thing that had happened to him since graduation.

As he pulled into the parking lot outside Cpl. Cash's office, he mentally anticipated the moment he would tell his parents he was joining the Marines. He wanted to be able to slide his scores across the table and prove that he had met his father's expectations, and that he had managed to do it without any input from either of them. Though he felt moments of regret for not including them in the plan, especially his mother, the vengeful side of him couldn't deny the warm and fuzzy feeling that came with defying them, and, in a way, proving them wrong. And though he knew it was likely the wrong way to be, he reckoned he'd gotten used to the wrong way of doing things, and, at this point, he was quite comfortable with that fact. Or at least, that's what he told himself.

Beau walked to the office doors, ASVAB scores in hand, and took a seat in one of the straight-backed chairs lined against the wall. Cpl. Cash was talking to someone else at his desk and Beau used the wait to look at all the accolades on the walls. He noticed awards Cpl. Cash had hanging above his desk and displayed in various places throughout the room. But it was a poster that drew his attention the most — a photograph of a young man who appeared to be half civilian, half Marine. Down the midline of his body, was a sword. On one side, he wore a crisp white hat, had a clean shave, and a polished demeanor. On the other side, the same man looked just like everybody else, a bit scruffy, and simply appeared to be nothing special.

As he sat there, Beau began to consider what he was getting himself into. He actually felt good about it. Not because it was what he truly wanted to do or even because he thought it would do him some good — instead, he felt good about it because it was going to take him away from his current reality. Far away, he hoped. He felt good about it because he thought he might die doing it. Morbid, and depressing though it may be, secretly, he relished the idea of going out a hero instead of a failure.

When Cash's appointment was over, Beau walked over to his desk and slid the score sheet into his line of sight. Cpl. Cash lit up inside. "Holy crap, man," he shouted. "You're just full of surprises, aren't you?"

"So that'll do, right?" Beau asked flatly, already knowing the answer.

"It's freaking outstanding. Your line scores look pretty darn good here. You were so quick on the draw with this paperwork." Cpl. Cash reached over and smacked Beau's shoulder. "Well done! I do have some news you're not going to like. I definitely can't get you back into the MEPS until sometime next week."

"Oh," Beau said, dejected.

"Once your waiver comes back, we'll move you right along, but that might take some time." Beau hung his head. This definitely derailed his plans to be *in* before telling his parents.

"Yes, sir." Beau stuck one of Cash's cards in his pocket and turned to go. "Can I keep this?" He pointed toward his score sheet.

"Sure. Let me make a quick copy though, I'll put it in your file." He wheeled his chair to the edge of his L-shaped desk and popped the score sheet into the feeder. "There you go." Cpl. Cash handed Beau his score sheet. "Congrats again. You're going to be an asset to the Corps."

"Thank you," Beau said, but he didn't seem as excited as Cash had expected when he turned to leave. Vindicated, maybe — but not excited.Beau tucked his score sheet into his folder and headed out through the office doors. He was dejected. He didn't realize how much red tape went into military service — it just wasn't something he'd thought about before. Now, all that red tape was forcing him to rewrite his plans.

Once inside his truck, he felt restless. He wasn't ready to go home, but didn't know where else to go. It was still early. His go-to drinking buddies weren't even awake yet. He decided to grab a burger and head to the park. He ate in his truck and then took a walk. He found a path that ran alongside the lake and followed it as far as he could.

When he came to a clearing with a picnic table and a hammock, he stopped. He looked around to see if anyone had staked claim to the items, but no one was within eyeshot. After looking left, then right, he climbed into the hammock, awkwardly. After almost falling out twice, he finally settled in. He thought to himself, “I’ve been alive for eighteen years and I’ve never been in a hammock.” He stretched out, arms behind his head, and looked out at the lake. As he swayed in the breeze, he dozed off. The last two nights had been long and exhaustion was starting to set in.

Beau was awakened by an unfamiliar sound. When he realized it was his phone, he clumsily fumbled in his pocket for it, tipping out of the hammock and onto the dirt. He’d totally forgotten his phone was on ring and he nearly jumped out of his skin. “Hello?” He said, breathlessly.

“Beau? It’s Cpl. Cash.”

“Oh, hi. How are you?”

“Dude, seriously, somebody up there must really love you, because I just got the notification that your waiver was approved. For real, in less than a day, don’t ask me how. I normally wait at least a week or two for those. You’re officially, by far, the luckiest recruit I have."

Beau chuckled to himself and rolled his eyes, "Trust me, sir, nobody up there wants anything to do with me." Cpl. Cash wondered about that remark, but didn't press Beau for an explanation.

"Now, we need to get you into MEPS. We'll try for Tuesday, okay? Will Tuesday work for you? I'll try to get you on the schedule right now." Cpl. Cash swiveled around toward his computer, and Beau could hear his keyboard clattering through the phone.

"I literally have nothing else going on in my life," Beau said. "You could schedule me for literally anytime and I'd be available." As he listened to the clattering keyboard, it dawned on Beau that Cash had called him "lucky." He was in the darkest place he'd faced in his life, and this guy was calling him lucky. He wondered how it was possible for one man's desperation to be seen as another man's good fortune. For a split second, his mind jumped to some of the things his mother had said about the benefits of God's favor and the power of prayer. He knew half the town had been praying for him, but he wouldn't let himself go there. The thought of it just made him angry.

"All right then, Tuesday it is. You'll have to come see me on Monday for a briefing, okay?"

Beau pulled out the card he had and flipped it over. He wanted to write this down, but, he panicked a little, no pen. "Okay," he said. "Can you text that appointment to me. I don't have a pen on me and I'm nowhere near a place to get one."

"Sure. I'll do it now," Cpl. Cash said. "I'll be calling you this weekend sometime to follow up. Please keep that phone on. The reason I mention it is because there's still a small chance this appointment will be canceled. If MEPS is super busy and not everything is in the schedule, it can happen." He paused for a moment, "But" he drew out the word, "somehow, with your crazy luck, I think you'll be just fine. Congrats you lucky son-of-a-gun. I'm pretty sure you've just broken some kind of record." Cpl. Cash laughed and finished with, "Have a good night," before hanging up altogether. Beau didn't even have time to return the sentiment before the phone clicked.

Beau dusted himself off and sprinted back up the path toward his truck. He ran out of breath faster than he expected to and realized he hadn't run a step in months. He heard his phone beep and knew it was a text from Cpl. Cash.

When he got to his truck, he rifled through the console for a pen. He knew he had one. When he finally found it, he jotted down the date and time of his MEPS visit on the back of Cash's card. He sat in the driver's seat and breathed deeply. This was really happening.

CHAPTER THIRTY

Beau pulled into the driveway and parked next to Ivy's car. Eli's home health nurse was coming out the front door, making her way to her own vehicle, which was parked off the side of the driveway under his mother's favorite oak tree. Beau didn't really care for the home health nurse. Something about the way she looked at him made him feel as if she was judging him, and not in a good way. Beau could almost hear her thinking "look what you did" every time she laid eyes on him.

She had never been rude to him, never said anything off-putting. She'd actually never spoken more than a few words to him, but there was something in her gaze that made his feelings of guilt more palpable and it was difficult for him to take. Every time he saw her, he would spend the rest of the day wishing he could trade places with his brother. He'd been having nightmares for months, and for some reason, they were always worse after Eli's weekly home health visits.

Beau avoided eye contact as best he could, but when the nurse, whom everyone called Ms. Tammy, passed him on the sidewalk, she said, "Good afternoon."

"Hi." Beau wasn't sure how else to respond, so he just said, "Have a good one."

He walked up the steps to the porch and took note of the fact that his mother had been working on the flowerbeds again. She hadn't touched the landscaping since before graduation, and somehow seeing her handiwork, another indication that things were slowly returning to normal, caused Beau to seethe with resentment. Why did it bother him so badly to see everyone else coping? Why was he the only one facing the reality of Eli's condition? Why was he the only one who couldn't get past that night? Why was he the only one reliving it over and over?

As he entered the house through the grand front doors, he got a whiff of something sweet. He couldn't tell if it was something cooking, or if it was those plug-in air fresheners his mom liked so much. He could hear the muffled voices of Ivy and his mother coming from the kitchen. Dinner was still hours away and he wasn't sure what to do with his time. He held the folder containing his ASVAB scores and MEPS appointment down by his side, close to his body. He paused for a moment, toying with the idea of going into the kitchen before going upstairs, but when he felt the weight of the folder in his hand, he decided to go upstairs first.

After placing his folder on the dresser in his room, he stared at himself in the mirror for a while. He no longer recognized his own face. Over the past few months, he had become so far removed from the person he used to be that somehow his reflection had morphed into a collection of unfamiliar shapes.

After a few minutes, he heard a knock at the door. When he opened it, Ivy was standing on the other side. They hadn't spoken, or so much as even looked at each other, in weeks.

"I've decided to go on a mission trip," Ivy blurted it out, Beau stood silent. "I'm only telling you this because I feel like you need to know. Not about me going necessarily, but that it's okay to keep living." She glanced around the room and then back at Beau again, "I'm trying to forgive you, I really am, and I'm trying to forgive myself for being excited about doing something that takes me away from Eli and what I thought my life was going to be. I just wanted you to know that you're not the only one dealing with stuff." She didn't show much emotion, and once she'd said her peace, she turned to walk away. Beau didn't speak a word, but he had heard every single one of hers. As she made her way to the stairs, she turned back toward him, "Your mom will need your help while I'm gone." And with that, she was gliding down the stairs, a trail of soft brown hair breezing behind her.

Beau closed the door behind her. "She's trying to forgive me," he thought to himself, "as if I expect her forgiveness. I can't forgive myself, how could anybody else forgive me?"

He walked over to the bed and lay down on his back. He threw his arms behind his head and stared at the ceiling. As he did, his eyes were drawn to the small pink stain over the bed. He allowed himself to indulge in a memory from his childhood. He and Eli were chasing each other with sticky hands they'd purchased from a vending machine with their own money. At some point, Eli started swinging his above his head like a lasso. Within under a minute, it broke and flew at lightning speed through the air before coming to a rest on the ceiling above Beau's bed with a gooey thud.

They had climbed up onto the bed and jumped in order to reach the jelly-like mass. They were finally successful, leaving behind a bright red stain. They had looked at each other in a panic. If their mother saw the stain, it was all over. They had spent the next half hour sneaking through the house to retrieve various cleaning products and a sponge from the kitchen. They used a thumb tack to attach the sponge to Beau's wooden baseball bat and then worked with all they had to scrub the red off the ceiling. Eventually, the stain had faded to a light pink and they both swore an oath of secrecy — an oath they'd both kept to this day.

If Valerie had ever seen the stain, she hadn't said a word. As Beau thought about how hard they'd laughed when the hand made a splat sound against the ceiling, he felt a burning sensation in his chest. His eyes grew wet and he was forced to acknowledge that it wasn't just guilt he was dealing with. He missed his brother — his best friend.

~

Beau woke up with a jolt. He looked over at the clock. He'd been asleep for over two hours. His dad would soon be home and then his mom would get dinner on the table. He reveled at the thought of dropping his news in his father's lap over dinner, a whole day early. He'd kept his plans secret, and he assumed his parents had been discussing how they'd handle his lack of achievement when the deadline was up. He was right, but he didn't know about the many hours of sleep Joe had lost over the situation. He was just letting his anger fuel him.

Valerie was shocked when she looked over and saw Beau setting the table. He hadn't voluntarily lifted a finger around the house in so long, she started to ask him what was wrong, but she held her tongue and instead said, "Thank you!"

As Beau put out the place settings, he slid his folder under his placemat. Valerie thought he was being helpful, but he knew his motivations were anything but noble. As he grabbed glasses from the cabinet, he had to admit that dinner smelled good. He'd gotten used to eating cold leftovers after his parents went to bed, so everything about this moment was a change of pace. He heard the door from the garage open and close, and his father walked into the kitchen through the mud room. Valerie greeted him as she always did and Beau felt his hands get sweaty. Joe immediately began to unbutton his dress shirt, but not before making eye contact with Beau. It was impossible for Joe to hide his shock at seeing Beau in the kitchen, though he clearly tried.

When dinner was on the table, Beau was the first to sit. Val and Joe exchanged a look. Valerie shrugged her shoulders. Ten minutes later, they'd said grace, everyone had food on their plates, and some in their bellies. Joe and Valerie made small talk and Beau waited impatiently for someone to bring up the next day's deadline, but nothing was said — his Mom and Dad didn't even hint at the subject. When Valerie mentioned ice cream for dessert and started to get up from the table for bowls, Beau couldn't hold it in anymore, "I joined the Marines!" The words flew out of his mouth and landed on the table with a thud, or at least it seemed that way to him. Neither Valerie nor Joe said anything. Were they in shock? Beau reached under his placemat and slid his folder across the table to his father. He braced himself for a monumental freak out.

Joe opened the folder and looked at its contents. He lifted Cpl. Cash's card and looked it over. When he flipped to the backside, he saw the MEPS appointment info. Valerie was still standing, motionless, in the kitchen. She put down her plate and closed the cabinet that contained the bowls, wiped her hands on a towel and walked back to her place at the table. Joe handed her the folder. She silently looked it over.

This was not going at all how Beau had expected. He looked back and forth between his parents when his father's voice broke the silence, "When did you make this decision?"

"On the couch, as I was talking to Kevin about the Air Force," Beau remembered exactly.

"Why the Marines? Of all the branches, why the Marines? Why not the Air Force like Kevin?" Valerie spoke next. She didn't sound emotional or upset in any way, but she did ask the one question Beau didn't want to answer. Beau saw her look at Joe, and he could tell from her glance that, though she appeared poised, she was a ball of churning emotions inside.

He shrugged and finally said, "Every time I see a Marine on a poster or by that big box in Wal-Mart at Christmas collecting toys, I think they look like they've got everything together. They look, I don't know…" He trailed off. He had no intention of telling her he joined the Marines because he was hoping to die as a hero instead of the guy he was now — the guy who put his own brother into a coma.

Joe wiped his mouth with his napkin. His heart was beating out of his chest, and though he thought the Marines might have been an impulsive decision, he considered Beau's decision to be divinely inspired. He had been praying since the first day that he'd not have to enforce the consequences of his son's failure to make the two-week deadline, and that prayer had literally been answered — not today, but a whole week ago, when Beau made his choice.

"And you've already signed?" Joe asked.

"Well, kind of. Not officially because I have to go through a physical and stuff. But, I did get good ASVAB scores and my recruiter says he's never had anyone's stuff go through as fast as mine has.

"What about your, you know, your legal stuff?" Valerie asked gently.

"I had to have a waiver for it, but even that has gone through. Cpl. Cash, that's my recruiter, he says it normally takes weeks, but mine came back in a day. He called it a miracle. He wants to meet you guys."

"I'm surprised we haven't already," Valerie gave her son an inquisitive look.

"I'm not," said Joe.

Suddenly, rubbing it in their faces seemed stupid and Beau's approach had totally backfired. His parents weren't freaking out at all. They were clearly concerned, but there were no theatrics, and they certainly didn't seem to feel guilty about making him choose a path before he was ready. "I wanted to do it on my own."

"I have so many questions. What will you be doing? Where will you be? When will you leave?" Valerie peppered him.

"I don't know any of that yet."

"But you could still change your mind if you wanted to?" Valerie added, in a tender, caring and accusing tone.

"I'm not going to, Mom," Beau retorted.

"I just meant, you still have options," she tried to clarify.

"Son, are you absolutely sure the Marines, the military in general, is the way you want to go? It's a big commitment. It will consume your whole life and you could potentially even risk your life." Joe's tone was serious, but not hostile or angry.

"I'm sure."

"Then I will support you. We both will, right Val?" Joe looked at his wife.

"Of course, but," Valerie reached for Beau's hand, "please make absolutely sure this is what you want to do. At least humor me by letting me pray about it, please?"

Beau sighed, "Fine Mom, yes. You pray, and I'll make sure it's what I really want."

With that, the news was out and Joe and Valerie had something new to discuss. But, they didn't freak out. They didn't try to talk Beau out of joining. They didn't shed tears or get angry. Beau had been completely wrong about their reactions, and yet somehow, though he'd wanted the theatrics, he was much happier with this outcome. Valerie stood to get the ice cream bowls.

"I'm going to break out the sundae stuff people, we'll call this a celebration," Valerie said. Beau could tell she was still trying to convince herself the Marines were a good choice, and he didn't stop her.

"That sounds great," Joe said. He was so taken aback by the timing, and so relieved that he'd avoided kicking his son out of their home that, for him, it felt like a lot to celebrate. He briefly wondered if his shock would eventually turn to fear, but he quickly shook the thought away. Today was a good day!

CHAPTER THIRTY-ONE

Months flew by like a shot from a gun as the holidays gave way to travel preparations for both Ivy and Beau. Everything seemed to move too quickly for Val's liking, but she decided movement was better than standing still, at least right now. It seemed like no time before Ivy's background checks were done and her official training was complete. She was taking culture classes to learn more about the people of Zimbabwe while she waited for the trip to come to fruition. So much more had been involved than she had expected.

Beau had learned that his chosen job would mean months of waiting before he would leave for boot camp. He used the time to prepare physically. He worked out all the time and ran every day. Both Joe and Val had no doubts about his ability to handle the physical training, but there again, the physical strain was the last thing on their minds. And then, just like that, all the prep was over, the ball was in motion and everything was new.

~

The phone rang at 5:47 p.m. as Valerie was prepping for dinner, at the end of what had been a very long, emotional week. Beau had been in San Diego for about two days, and officially part of the Marine Corps for around twelve hours. Ivy had been in Zimbabwe for four days and had already called three times. When Valerie saw the words *MCRD, San Diego* on the caller ID, she nearly dropped the phone trying to click the green call button.

"Hello!" She called into the receiver.

Instead of a traditional greeting, Val was forced to pull the phone away from her ear a few inches, because all she could hear was yelling. There was a drill instructor screaming "be louder" in the background as Beau simultaneously rattled off a clearly scripted statement at the top of his lungs. He said he had arrived safely at the Marine Corps Recruit Depot in San Diego, and then he rattled off some indiscernible flight information.

Valerie grabbed a pen, expecting an address, but instead she heard Beau say that he'd be sending a letter via postal mail that contained his mailing address and platoon number, he followed by shouting that his projected graduation date was November 29. He said if there were any changes, he'd immediately contact her with the details and then closed with a rapid, "I love you, bye."

Val hung up the phone and stood silently for a minute. She couldn't help but tear up. Her first contact with Beau since he'd left for boot camp was not at all what she'd expected, but she had to admit, she technically got everything she wanted. He was fine, he would write, and he loved them. The odd thing was that Beau's canned statement contained far more words than she probably would have gotten if there'd been no script.

When Joe came home, she told him all about the phone call. He asked a few questions, to which she had no answers, and then they finished preparing dinner together. As they sat to eat, they discussed how different everything had become in such a short period of time. Only this time, it wasn't a sad conversation. Instead, it was an acceptance. They had somehow managed to find peace in the midst of the chaos.

After dinner, Joe went online to find a calendar of events that takes place during Marine Corps basic training. He thought it might help his wife to have something tangible that would let her know what Beau was doing on a daily basis, even though he was out of contact. They didn't expect any additional phone calls, but Joe knew Valerie would be checking the mailbox multiple times a day during the next twelve weeks. He printed a list of boot camp events and handed it to Valerie. She read over the first few days and found some solace in the fact that the phone call she received was perfectly normal. She immediately began discussing plans for her and Joe to travel out to San Diego for graduation, acknowledging that her biggest challenge would be finding someone who would be able to stay with Eli while they were gone.

The evening came and went and Ivy did not call. Both Joe and Valerie found it a little bit odd, considering that she had already called three times in four days, and they had grown to expect a daily update. As they sat together watching a movie, they both wondered if they were equipped to handle living in a world where their children were independent.

~

Beau hadn't slept in thirty-six hours. His voice hurt from screaming "aye, sir," repeatedly. He'd been in a million lines, herded from place to place, told when to stand, when to sit, when to breathe. He'd been caught asleep on his feet at one point, and a DI had laid into him with a blistering passion. Strangely, he didn't really mind being told what to do. He felt a certain amount of relief in not relying on his own skills to choose his next move. But, despite that fact, he had no desire to suffer the wrath of a drill instructor again.

His head still felt strange with no hair on it. His ten-second shower with a group of other men had done little more than make his skin wet. He was jumpy, but exhausted at the same time. This night would be his first night of sleep since he arrived in San Diego, and, at this point, he was so tired, he was beginning to doubt his choice. As he closed his eyes, his body rigid in his bunk, as if he were somehow still at attention, he remembered a poster on the wall of the football field house back home, the poster read *Fatigue makes cowards of us all – Vince Lombardi* and, as he recalled the message, he resolved himself to pushing through this moment and to surviving the next twelve weeks.

He awakened to the deafening sound of metal on metal, after what felt like maybe two hours of sleep. A drill instructor was throwing trashcans around the room. Everyone was clamoring around, trying to get on their feet when the DI informed them they only had thirty seconds to be dressed and ready to make their beds and officially meet their senior drill instructor. At the end of the chaos and yelling, Beau was seated with his fellow recruits, cross legged, on the bright white tile floor in straight, neat rows, three deep on both sides of an isle left in the middle.

The team of drill instructors was introduced one by one, and at the end of the introductions, they recited the Drill Instructor's Pledge before the recruits were handed off to their senior DI, SSgt. Juarez. Juarez was short, intense and in what appeared to be impeccable shape, but the thing that struck Beau the most was his intensely deep and terrifying voice. The minute he began to speak, Beau could see everyone tighten up just a little. The man was formidable, and everyone knew it, before he'd even spoken ten words.

When Juarez told the men to get to their feet, without touching anyone or anything around them, Beau immediately pulled his elbow away from the footlocker it had been touching ever so lightly for the duration of the introductions. He did his best to get to his feet without making contact with anyone. The guy next to him lost his balance and almost fell over. SSgt. Juarez made short work of calling him out and Beau felt uncomfortable merely being within three feet of the man. Within moments, the day had begun and Beau would spend much of it in a classroom, learning about Marine Corp customs and traditions, and trying in vain to focus though his sleep deprivation.

~

Ivy carried water from the well across the field and poured it into the irrigation ditch her team had spent the day digging. Cheers erupted all around. There would be no planting until October, but getting the ground ready at a new site was a huge undertaking and testing the irrigation was a final step. It was a moment for celebration, because it was the first step in constructing something worthwhile and would be a building block for building a more permanent irrigation system as planting season began. She was finally to the point where all the training she'd done for her trip was coming into play. Sustainable farming would make a huge difference for the people in the villages nearby and she was excited to be part of it. The church services she'd been to were unlike anything she'd known, and the people who worshipped there approached their faith with such abandon and trust that she found herself renewed just by being around them.

There were more Christians than she had expected, and the locals seemed to have taken a liking to her, but she'd also encountered a witch doctor and a number of people who believed they were cursed and one man who always looked at her like he planned to cook and eat her, but nobody paid him any mind, so she chose to follow suit. She had also learned that time was a general guideline in Zimbabwe and not something to be set in stone. Everyone seemed to be late to everything. Still, she found herself enthralled with the culture. She had abandoned some of her creature comforts but had remained far more comfortable than she'd expected.

Now that she was getting busy, her mind stayed largely occupied, but as she carried the bucket of water across the field, alongside a few of the local farmers, she thought about how much Eli would have loved to be a part of it. She wondered how he was doing. Somehow, even though he couldn't speak to her, hold her hand, or even acknowledge her existence, she missed his company. Still, despite not being on site for very long, she couldn't believe how quickly the time had passed. She missed home, but she loved her current work and had determined that she was right where God wanted her in that moment.

While lost in her own thoughts, one of the local Shona women came to her, emphatically suggesting she join the women in preparing for the evening meal. She couldn't understand her words, but understood her gestures enough that she already knew what the woman wanted before the missionary team's translator filled her in. She looked to her team for guidance, as if to ask, "Is this okay?" She received a few smiles and one nod from her team leader who knew the people well, so she smiled at the woman and walked with her back toward the village, where other women were already gathering around large cast iron pots. She looked over her shoulder at the people she'd be working with for the next few months. They were standing in the field, no doubt discussing the drive back to their quarters and the "second supper" they'd have later in the evening as a group. As she looked around, absorbing her surroundings, she felt a sense of peace and accomplishment. She thought about how small this was in the grand scheme of the world, but how much impact it would have for the people of the surrounding villages, and she briefly indulged her own feelings of pride as she considered her role and the guts it had taken for her to make the trip in the first place.

CHAPTER THIRTY-TWO

Valerie had been reading about Combat Logistics for weeks. The minute Beau chose his operational specialty, or MOS, as he'd called it for short, she'd been on a mission to learn everything she could about it. She'd learned that there were almost too many jobs to count and after all these weeks, she was more confused than ever. But she did know that, once he graduated boot camp, he'd get some leave before going to school for at least a few weeks. She also knew that his choice of MOS meant he'd deploy, probably a lot, and she was doing her best to prepare for that reality.

She'd been writing to Beau every day since receiving that first letter. He'd written a few times, each letter extremely short and to the point, which she understood. She had been following his journey week by week using the document Joe had printed for her. She knew that Beau would never be the same, but she hoped, somehow, that he'd be better than he was when he left. When she had read that boot camp would break him down and rebuild him, she had wondered how he could possibly be any more broken down than he was when he'd kissed her goodbye. Her prayer was that they'd at least rebuild him into someone who no longer hated himself and the world he lived in.

Joe had already asked off work for graduation and Valerie had taken care of plane tickets and hotel accommodations. As Beau entered testing week, they felt confident his graduation date would not change, and he'd given them no indication to think things would go south. Joe had picked up a paperback book that explained the making of a Marine, and he'd gotten really excited as he talked about the Crucible. He began watching the news and reading every article that mentioned the Marine Corps, and he purchased a USMC garden flag for the flower bed out front. He'd found a renewed sense of pride in his son, and he managed to hide is worry well, though he confided in her that some of the men from church had agreed to pray for his ability to claim God's peace and, at the same time, pray for Beau's safety as he headed into a career that would, without a doubt, take him into dangerous territory.

Valerie had written to Beau about his father's flag out front, about the reading and his pride in his son, but she had no way of knowing whether or not he'd received the message. She was so ready for graduation, which would consist of a couple days of ceremonies, and she wanted to hug Beau's neck again. Being emotionally separated from both her boys had taken a toll on her heart.

She also missed Ivy. After just two weeks without her, Val had realized how much she loved having her around. It had been more than a week since Ivy's last call, and Valerie was beginning to worry about her. She wanted to talk to her before they left for San Diego and was holding out hope she might be back in time to travel with them, though she hadn't discussed this idea with Joe.

~

Meanwhile, in California, Beau had grown used to hearing his name called during mail call. Letters from his mother had come regularly and he largely expected more of the same. But on this day, he received a letter with an unfamiliar postmark. The last person he had expected to hear from during boot camp was Ivy Zellway.

When he opened the letter, he learned that she was nearing the end of her twelve-week mission trip to Zimbabwe. At the same time, he was nearing the end of his journey through the hellish experience known as Marine Corps Boot Camp. The irony of the timing was not lost on Beau. But his shock at having received a letter from her impacted him more, so much so that he half expected some bad news to reveal itself in the forthcoming pages.

Instead, Ivy had chosen him as a confidant. He assumed she chose him out of fear, and she knew he wouldn't tell because he had no one to tell. She led into her secret by emphasizing that her feelings for Eli had not changed, a disclaimer she apparently thought important. The letter continued to say that she was strongly considering a continuation of her mission trip.

She'd fallen in love with the people and the culture, but couldn't bring herself to tell anyone back home that she wanted to stay for a longer term. She mentioned her desire to see a full planting season, and of course, a harvest come to fruition. She talked about some of the sustainable farming efforts they had been working toward to bring food and livelihood to the region, and Beau could actually feel her passion for the project through her writing. And, by all rights, it was the most interesting letter Beau had received since arriving in San Diego. Though he appreciated the letters from his mom, every week was basically the same, there'd been no change in Eli's condition, no change around home, and the only marginally exciting experiences in her life were that Joe had once again taken up weightlifting and had decided to play on the church softball team.

As Beau read Ivy's words, it dawned on him how grown up she sounded. He felt like he was reading a letter from someone above his station in life. He skimmed the words as he endured some teasing and prodding from members of his newly formed brotherhood, but he managed to remain as stoic as ever and relatively unfazed. He shooed them off and they didn't push back too much. Beau had become known by his platoon for his bearing. He had apparently maintained the same look on his face since he boarded the bus. For Beau, it had been effortless. He simply tapped into the place in his head where he kept Eli, and it was easy.

She had finished her letter with niceties, wishing him well in his training, hoping for news of his next base, and so on. He was surprised at this, since the last time he saw her, she still seemed to hate him. When he finished reading, he sat holding the letter, wondering what, if anything, she expected him to do about it. He wasn't even sure he cared. Should he tell his parents? Why would he do that? Why, exactly, did she choose him to confide in? He looked at the postmark again. Her letter had been weeks in coming. Even if he did try to write her back, there's no way she'd get it before he was long gone. At a loss, he folded the letter and put it in his footlocker alongside the others. There was no time to dwell on it, and Beau did his best to dismiss it. His efforts were aided by SSgt Juarez, who had entered the room barking the next task of the day.

~

Little did he know how Ivy had agonized over that letter. She needed to tell someone — anyone — about her desires, but she feared breaking the news to Valerie, and especially to her mother. What would people think? Would they think she had abandoned Eli when he needed her most? On a quiet evening in Zimbabwe, she had rolled through her mental list of friends and family, wondering who she might confide in. When she remembered that Valerie had sent her Beau's address at boot camp, she settled on him as the perfect confidant. He was away from home, and he was the last person on earth who would judge her. She had started and restarted her letter several times, each time trashing it and arguing with herself over how silly she was being. Finally, she finished the letter, having convinced herself it was a stupid thing to worry over.

In the end, her letter to Beau was just a warm up, a warm up for not only choosing a long-term mission, but also for breaking the news to her parents and Valerie. Besides, it was time she made amends with Beau. How could she discuss forgiveness with the locals, some of whom had far greater things to forgive than she could ever imagine, and not attempt to forgive Beau for his mistake? She knew he hated himself for what had happened, and she decided that hating him herself was a waste of energy. Besides, if Christ can forgive everyone for everything, and His spirit lived inside of her, who was she to deny Beau that same grace?

CHAPTER THIRTY-THREE

Valerie wanted to look as proud as she felt on Family Day in San Diego. Having arrived in town the day before, she and Joe were rested and ready for what promised to be an exciting day. Despite their concern that Beau had made a rash decision, they'd spent so much time learning everything they could about the United States Marine Corps, their customs, their missions, their calling, their training and their history, that both of them had effectively become the two proudest USMC parents in the history of parenting, to themselves at least. She had been told that Family Day was a casual day, and just for the occasion, she'd purchased a gray sweatshirt with USMC emblazed across the front in pink letters, and the word "mom" written in very small, white, cursive letters across the bottom of the C. Joe wore a simple T-shirt that said "proud" across the front, the O being the globe depicted in the Marine Corps crest. He planned to carry an ordinary hoodie, just in case the fall air grew too cool.

Family Day started at eight o'clock, so, naturally, Joe and Val were up by six and downstairs for their continental breakfast forty-five minutes later. They were buzzing. They looked around, noting the number of USMC shirts and bags in the room.

"This is so exciting!" Valerie was beaming. "I have watched so many videos online, I can't stand the wait! I wish Ivy had made it back. She would have loved this, too. And Eli, oh, Eli would be so proud."

"I know. I can't stand the suspense. Maybe we should have gone to that breakfast thing after all," Joe responded. "I still think it would be a madhouse, but I'm ready to get the show on the road."

"We have an orientation first and then this 'drill instructor's brief,' whatever that means. We won't see him until the run probably." Valerie read intently from the schedule she had printed, as she chewed her bagel with strawberry cream cheese. "Tomorrow is the actual graduation ceremony."

"Well, let's hurry up and get over there. I want to be early for whatever happens. Before we go, we need to call Pete again to check on Eli. He's really come through for us, again."

"Yes, he certainly has. Now, don't you feel bad about all that mean stuff you said about him?" Valerie gave him a wink.

Joe smirked, "Not really. He's still an overgrown child. He just happens to be a child with a heart of gold and the ability to dial down his level of obnoxious when he's needed."

~

After sitting through orientation and a drill instructors briefing, Joe and Valerie were beyond ready for the motivational run. Valerie had noted that people in the crowd were calling it a Moto run, and she wondered if she and Joe would sound like idiots if they did the same. They had been told that the smartest play was to stay in one place, and that each company and each platoon would make two passes by the crowd. Joe had his video camera ready and Valerie was poised to take as many still pictures as her phone camera would hold. They found a spot right on the curb outside the Command Museum, close to the MC, because they'd been early to arrive, just as Joe had mandated. They knew that Beau was part of Bravo Company, platoon 1022, of the First Recruit Training Battalion, but the crowds were so intense, their objective was simply to get close enough to see everything clearly.

The MC was doing an amazing job getting everybody pumped up. Valerie could feel her heart beating faster and faster as she anticipated the moment the Marines would come through the archway to her right. Each company would come through as a unit, this much she knew, but she and Joe were unprepared for the impressive display of unity they were about to witness. Tensions in the crowd were thick, people were cheering and trying to get closer to the front, but, still, everyone seemed to be unified. Somehow, they were already part of something bigger than themselves, despite the fact that they were just visiting. They shared a common bond now, love for the United States Marines.

Joe and Valerie could hear the MC's voice pouring through the sound system, but they had trouble making out his words. The crowd was loud, and being outdoors didn't improve their chances for quality sound balance. Soon though, they could hear the faint sounds of a cadence in the distance. Valerie began crying immediately. As the MC announced the imminent arrival of the Marines, the crowd around Valerie and Joe began clapping and screaming in a frenzy.

Off to the right, they could see a few red shirts, and red flags, gliding in unison, leading the pack of green-clad Marines on a unified jog through the archway. They watched as Alpha Company made their way through the arch, stopped, and on command made a sharp left turn to face the audience. Joe was amused by the fact that many of the young Marines still appeared somewhat terrified. It also seemed that some of them may have received instructions not to make eye contact, or at least to avoid anything that might cause smiles or a break in bearing. With all the screaming, cheering, and people going crazy, it was easy to see why the day of celebration would require extra effort on the part of the young Marines.

When Bravo Company was announced, Val and Joe listened intently for the announcement of Platoon 1022. When they heard the numbers, they screamed their heads off with the others supporting the same group. The excitement was palpable. As Bravo Company moved forward, they came to a stop, just as Alpha Company had done before them. Joe and Valerie were thrilled that they'd somehow managed to be standing directly across from Beau's platoon.

When the company halted and made its sharp left turn to face the crowd, Joe and Valerie got their first good look at the Marine Beau had become. His jaw was chiseled, his shoulders broad, he looked lean and strong. The high and tight Marine-issue haircut suited him. Tears streamed down Valerie's face as she screamed and clapped and took pictures, alongside the other mothers, sisters and girlfriends with whom she now shared this bond. She'd snapped a quick picture of Joe, whose eyes were wet with tears of pride.

Beau stared straight ahead, they couldn't tell if he'd seen them, but they took in the shape of him and their arms ached to hug their baby boy. Soon, Bravo Company, along with Platoon 1022, made a sharp right turn on their heels and returned to their run formation. They were off again, singing cadence in perfect unison — the picture of a free nation and a future of service.

~

Every event that unfolded during the day was hemmed in emotion, each building to what Joe and Valerie now knew as liberty. Once the Marines were released for liberty, they were free to go anywhere on the Depot they chose, as long as they remained within the confines of the gates. Joe and Valerie waited with eager anticipation through the Emblem Ceremony. Though the ceremony was moving and memorable, it was difficult to remain focused during what Valerie considered one of the longest half hours of her life. She could see Beau, dressed in what she now knew was his service uniform and garrison cover, thanks to Joe and his new library of Marine Corps literature. She could hardly wait to squeeze him. Though secretly, she and Joe both wondered about his emotional state.

When the Marines were finally released for liberty, she and Joe rushed the parade deck with everyone else, weaving in and out of the crowd, seeking their prize. Joe spotted him first and pointed so Val could see. They all looked so similar in their uniforms. Beau had his back to them, he was shaking hands with a fellow graduate. He turned and began scanning the crowd with his eyes. He spotted Joe's upraised hand, and then saw Valerie's head, jumping up and disappearing, then jumping up and disappearing again, as she struggled to see over a rather robust gentleman standing in front of her. Beau smirked at the sight of his Whac-A-Mole mother and began walking toward them.

Joe wrapped his arms around his son and squeezed hard. Valerie took pictures, and then they switched, as seamlessly as they ever had during their tenure as parents. Val held Beau with a fury, longer than she had in a long time. He rested his chin on her head and, through his still-raw emotions, he could physically feel her love for him, and he allowed himself just a moment to indulge in the pure, un-angry, un-bitter feeling of his mother's embrace.

Beau walked with his parents all over the Depot, he showed them everything he could — the museum, the yellow footprints, the doors he would only pass through once, the bunk that had been impeccably made and the showers he'd shared with an entire platoon. When Joe and Val met SSgt. Juarez, he expressed genuine affection for Beau. Joe later admitted that meeting the drill instructors was his favorite part of the day and Beau used that admission as confirmation of his father's senility. "That man is horrifying, Dad," Beau had said unenthusiastically. "You're officially senile. Mom, we need to put him in a home."

He made note of their USMC attire and, though he said nothing, he felt true gratitude for parents like his, who supported him despite his failures and loved him despite his mistakes. In a way, their forgiveness only made him hate himself more, and that fact was made all the more prominent by his brother's absence.

At two thirty, they hopped the last shuttle to The Bay View Restaurant. Beau ordered a large pizza. Joe and Val laughed when the server asked, "Will that be all?" and Beau gestured to his parents, with a look that said she was crazy for assuming they'd share. After ordering, they sat together at a table, using the time as an opportunity to reconnect.

"So tomorrow, you're officially a Marine!" Val exclaimed excitedly. "We are so, so proud of you. You have no idea!"

"Seriously, son, we are so proud," Joe affirmed.

"Thanks." Beau nodded.

"So, tomorrow when you're released, you are officially on leave, right?" Valerie asked. Beau nodded as he shoved another bite of pizza into his mouth. "We'll have a whole day after lunch, our flight doesn't leave until midmorning the day after tomorrow. So, is there anything here you'd like to do or see before we head home?" The excitement in Val's voice was obvious.

Beau wiped his mouth with his napkin, being careful not to get food on his uniform. "Honestly, the first thing I'd like to do is take a shower, alone. And then I'd like to take a nap." Joe laughed out loud at his son's answer, though Beau was as straight faced as ever.

"I think we can handle that," Valerie chuckled her response.

Suddenly, something in his mother's voice jolted the memory of Ivy's letter loose in his mind. "There's something else I need to tell you about. I don't know if I'm supposed to for sure, but I think that's what she wants," Beau began cryptically.

"What?" Joe asked, confused.

"Ivy wrote me a letter. She wants to stay in Zimbabwe and she's scared to tell anyone. Something about staying until the harvest, I have no idea why she told me, but there it is." Beau blurted out the news with an absence of emotion, in a militant way that pierced Joe's heart.

"What? Why would she be scared to tell us?" Valerie asked. Beau shrugged his response.

"I guess that explains why she hasn't called lately," Joe interjected. "I wonder if her parents know."

Again, Beau shrugged. "I don't think so, but I don't know for sure," Beau added.

"Well, I guess I should put this on my list for when we get home. I can't believe she'd think we'd be mad at her for staying longer," Valerie said.

"We won't be upset, but I bet her mom will be." Joe was leaning back in his chair, his arms behind his head in a stretch.

Valerie sighed. "She was so worried Eli would wake up and she wouldn't be there. I bet she's feeling a little guilty for not wanting to hurry home."

"Well, at least now you know." Beau took a sip from his drink.

"So, tell us about training. We want to hear all about it," Joe changed the subject. Under the circumstances, he felt that Beau should be the center of attention, regardless of Ivy's inner turmoil.

~

Graduation morning was just as exciting as the prior day, but this day held a different kind of tension. Valerie chose to dress up for the occasion and chose a button down shirt and khakis for Joe. After their continental breakfast, they headed over to Shepherd Field for an array of ceremonies, which would culminate with a ten o'clock graduation. Joe and Val were captivated by every ceremony and every formality. They made an intentional effort to be present in every moment and to absorb every experience.

When graduation time came, and the Marines began marching onto the field, Valerie burst into tears again. She had cried all day, even the national anthem sent her over the edge. As Beau's platoon marched in, they strained to pick him out of the crowd.

"There he is!" Val whisper-shouted to Joe as she pointed at Beau, "He's in front, carrying the platoon flag! See? I wonder how he got that job? He's dressed differently and everything." She glanced at Joe, who was grinning ear to ear.

As the ceremony continued, they watched as Beau joined the flag bearers from other platoons at the center of the parade field. They moved sharply, precisely. It was nothing short of impressive. Drill instructors joined the soon-to-be graduates in the center of the field and they made beautifully precise work of transferring the flags. Within a minute, the MC began discussing what it meant to be an honor graduate, and Valerie began bouncing in her seat.

“He didn’t tell us! Are you kidding me? An honor graduate?” She wiped tears from her cheeks as she pointed and whispered to the lady on her left, “That’s my son.” Joe beamed, his eyes glistening. He squeezed Valerie’s hand. The ceremony continued as honor graduates were recognized, and they made their pride known with cheers and tears.

The remaining formalities brought laughter and pride, and when the graduates were dismissed by their drill instructors, in what would be the last and most welcomed command they received during their time at the Depot, freedom became theirs. Joe turned to Valerie, and through the onslaught of cheers, leaned into her ear to say, “Today is a good day.”

CHAPTER THIRTY-FOUR

When Private First Class McKnight arrived home for ten days of leave, he found his Uncle Pete waiting for him with open arms on the front porch. Inside, the house had been decked out with red, white and blue balloons and signs congratulating the new Marine. Pete had invited the whole family over, all of whom were waiting in the great room. When Beau stepped into sight, the room erupted. They'd all heard about his selection as an honor graduate, they'd all heard about the moving ceremonies and how dignified and grown up Beau had become over the last three months. And they were all eager to become part of what Valerie had described as the extended family of the USMC.

Joe placed the bags he was toting at the bottom of the stairs, and after Beau had greeted many of his guests, he excused himself to carry his bag upstairs. As he walked by, he grabbed his parents' bags and climbed the steps to the second floor. Joe and Valerie began to buzz around the room, sharing their experiences with the family and gushing about Beau's transformation. Beau dropped the bags on the second floor and made a beeline for Eli's room. When he walked into the room, nothing had changed. Eli's hair was longer, but he looked exactly the same. Somehow, Beau had expected to find something new, but he didn't. Eli just lay there in his hospital bed, sleeping.

Beau sat down next to his brother, "Well, you're not going to believe what I just did." He looked at Eli and sighed, "I don't know why I'm telling you, because you can't even hear me, but I joined the Marines. I just graduated boot camp. As of now, little brother, I am Pfc. McKnight, USMC," Beau chuckled at his own words. Even he couldn't believe that boot camp was done and he was now, officially, a Marine. Just two years before, he had told the recruiter at his high school that he'd rather wear a pink tutu to school every day of his senior year than join the military. Now, the military had become the best part of his life. He sat for a few more minutes, looking at Eli, and marveled at how much his life had changed in the course of twelve short months, and then he stood to his feet and, with one last look, made his way back downstairs to greet the family waiting for him. They wanted to celebrate his accomplishments. And though he had to admit to himself that he felt a certain sense of pride in becoming a United States Marine, he would never allow himself to feel worthy of celebration, not as long as Eli continued to suffer the consequences of his mistakes.

Downstairs again, the party continued with food, drinks and lots of hugs. Everyone talked about Beau's physique, his haircut and his chiseled jawline. His cousin challenged him to a push-up contest, which Beau won easily. After several hours, his grandparents, aunts, uncles and cousins began to leave. Once everyone was gone, Beau plopped onto the sofa and put his feet up. He fell asleep, and both Joe and Valerie decided to just let him sleep. After about an hour, Beau was startled awake when his phone began buzzing in his pocket. When he pulled it out, he saw a text message from one of his high school teammates who had heard about his triumphant return and wanted to invite him to go out that night.

Beau got up and walked into the kitchen where he told his parents about the message and asked if they had any objections to his spending some time with his old teammates that evening. Before boot camp, Joe and Valerie might've hesitated at such a request, but both of them knew for certain that Beau wouldn't do anything to risk his status as a Marine.

"Sure, I think that will be alright. We don't have anything planned for tonight," Valerie said.

"You might need to put some gas in your truck. I drove it for you a few times, just to keep the dust knocked out, but I didn't fill it up before I parked it last time." Joe's statement showed that he approved of Beau's plan for the evening.

"Thanks." Beau turned to make his way up the stairs. He wanted to freshen up.

Though her son was decidedly adult-like now, Valerie couldn't help herself. She just had to remind him, "Remember who you are and what you just went through." Beau knew exactly what she was referring to, and part of him admitted that she had every right to be concerned, because three months of boot camp would never erase all the months of torment he'd put them through beforehand. But, the other part of him was insulted that she felt she needed to mention it at all, as if he'd forgotten.

"I will." He responded flatly.

~

Beau pulled into the parking lot of the sports bar, stepped out, slid his wallet into his jeans pocket, and then ran his hand over his high and tight. He locked his truck and dropped his keys into his pocket. He walked across the parking lot and through the doors of the sports bar. At the door, the attendant was checking IDs. Beau held out his hand and signaled for the attendant to mark him as under age. Once he had a big black X on the back of his hand, he made his way into the bar, passing the tables and the stage, where a band was setting up, and headed to the back where his friends were waiting at the pool tables.

Several of his old teammates began to call out to him immediately, rubbing his head and giving him pats on the back. All of them knew what had happened, the whole town knew what had happened, but none of them had experienced love loss for Beau — he was still something of a hometown icon. He had been in hiding for so many months that coming out to celebrate felt like a big deal. When the waitress came around, Heavy, who was always in the mood for food, ordered everyone a burger, fries and Coke. He didn't even ask, but just assumed that everyone else was hungry, too.

The group played pool, cracked jokes, and talked about some of the girls in the room. Beau told stories about boot camp. He filled them in on his terrifying drill instructors and some of the funny things that had happened during his time in San Diego. When the waitress returned with their food and drinks, Smitty slyly pulled a black flask out of his back pocket and proceeded to spike his drink. He made his way around the group, pouring a shot of whiskey into every Coke. At first, Beau hesitated, fearing where the alcohol would take him. But, he gave in and held out his cup. The group of friends continued their celebration into the night.

Occasionally, Smitty would go out to his car to refill the flask. Just after midnight, though, everyone seemed to have had enough. Beau was exhausted, but he knew he needed to wait a while before trying to drive. And though he didn't believe himself to be intoxicated, fear of prior events prevented him from taking chances. Slowly, the group of friends began to dissipate, sharing hugs and congratulations with Beau as they made their way to their individual vehicles, each one assuring the others that he was okay to drive. Each one chewing gum or dipping tobacco, because someone, somewhere, had told them it would cover up alcohol on their breath.

Beau elected to stay behind and wait. He wasn't taking any chances. After he said his goodbyes, he asked the waitress for water and he made his way over to a table near the band. As the music played, Beau felt himself being watched. He couldn't shake the feeling and began to scan the room for people who might be looking in his direction. Finally, in the corner, he saw a group of girls sitting at a round table, each sipping a drink and munching on what appeared to be a giant pile of chili cheese fries in the middle of the table. One of the girls was smoking, as were about twenty other people in the bar. It had become a popular establishment for smokers, because it was one of the few places around that still allowed smoking in doors. Through the waft of smoke, Beau could see a pair of eyes looking in his direction. When he caught her, she looked away. Beau squinted into the smoke and began to notice something familiar about the girl's face. Eventually, he saw her say something to her friends, slide out of the corner chair, and make her way across the dance floor toward Beau's table.

Beau was transfixed. She was gorgeous. She looked down at the ground as she walked across the wooden floor and her long blonde hair cascaded delicately in front of her face. Beau hadn't spoken to a girl in so many months, he'd lost count. For the first time in his young adult life, he felt his heart beating faster as his nerves began to get the better of him. When the blonde beauty pushed her hair out of her face, Beau's heart almost stopped.

"Julia?" Beau stood up quickly and took a step toward the girl. He could see her friends watching from behind her.

"I thought that was you, but I wasn't sure. You've changed a little bit." Julia Snyder hadn't laid eyes on Beau McKnight since before she broke his heart.

"I could say the same about you." Beau couldn't help himself, and he looked her up and down without trying to hide it. She had grown into a tall, shapely, absolutely stunning beauty. "D-do you want to sit down?" Beau stuttered a little as he pulled out a chair, at a loss for how he should behave. Julia had destroyed him, but not a day had passed that she hadn't crossed his mind in some way or another. He had often wondered what she was doing, where she was, and who she had become. He always thought of himself as an idiot for giving her any thought at all, but his young heart had cared so deeply for her that he couldn't help but long for that feeling again. He hadn't found it with anyone else, but the moment he saw Julia's face, he was overcome with a flood of memories.

"It's been a long time. You look great!" Julia said, as she touched his forearm with her hand.

"You do too," Beau said.

"I guess we've got some catching up to do, don't we?" Julia smiled and tucked her hair behind her ear. She'd clearly had braces. The pretty girl Beau had known when they were younger had a few dental imperfections. But this girl, this girl was perfect.

Julia filled him in on what had been happening in her life since she moved away. Beau was reluctant to share much, but he relished her words as she talked about the ups and downs of her life, her plans for the future, and her uncertainty about where life was going. Before they knew it, an hour had passed and Julia's friends were approaching, no doubt to snag her for the ride home. Before they could reach the table, Beau worked up the nerve to ask Julia if she wanted to join him for a late-night snack at the infamous, "Casa de la Waffles." She laughed, smiled and nodded her yes. When her friends reached the table, she introduced them to Beau and told them that she'd known him for a long time. She also let them know that he would be taking her home. The girlfriends exchanged hugs and left Julia and Beau alone. Beau felt like he had entered an alternate universe.

After splitting a waffle and having a cup of coffee, which took an hour because they had talked nonstop, Beau drove Julia to her apartment complex. She and a group of friends had moved in together, and she was working part-time as a waitress to pay the bills while she attended community college. She told him she had come back to the area because some of her happiest memories in life had taken place there, and since she still wasn't sure where she was going in life, it made sense that she should, at least, start somewhere she'd been happy. She was jovial, infectious, so much so that Beau couldn't imagine her being anything other than happy.

Instead of going inside right away, Julia led Beau to the courtyard, where she sat on a bench, leaving room for him to sit. Eventually, as the night shifted into day, Beau began to come clean about Eli and what had happened. He watched tears fill Julia's eyes and glisten in the light when he told her the details of the story. He looked down at the ground, irrationally blaming himself for her pain, as well. Every tear that had fallen because of Eli's predicament had been his fault, it didn't matter whose eyes did the crying. Julia could see the pain in Beau's face as he relayed the story. He continued on, explaining his spiral, his father's ultimatum, and how he had just graduated from boot camp. He bared his soul, for the first time in eternity.

Eventually, the sun was rising. Beau and Julia had talked the entire night. She programmed her number into his phone and sent herself a text. "We need to do this again," she said with a smile.

"Absolutely," Beau agreed. "How about tonight?" Beau asked eagerly, smiling in her direction. He didn't want to waste time, because he didn't have much time to waste.

Julia laughed, "I'm supposed to work from five until nine tonight. But you could pick me up at the restaurant, if nine isn't too late."

"I'll see you at nine." Beau reached out his hand, and then felt like an idiot when she looked at it in confusion and, instead, moved in to hug him. He hugged her back and told her he couldn't wait to see her again. He walked her to her door and turned to head back to his truck. Before he had even unlocked the door, he felt his phone buzzing in his pocket. He pulled it out and found a text from Julia that read <SEE YOU SOON!> He put his phone back in his pocket, and with a genuine smile on his face, he got into his truck to drive home for some much-needed sleep.

CHAPTER THIRTY-FIVE

When Ivy finally worked up the courage to call home and admit her desire to stay in Zimbabwe, she found that her mother was the only one opposed to the idea. For one thing, mission trips are expensive. For another, it seemed that Mrs. Zellway was very supportive of her daughter's travels, as long as they didn't last too long. She missed her daughter immensely and had a harder time letting go than she thought she would. The idea that Ivy wouldn't be home during the holidays was almost more than she could take.

Val scolded Ivy for not calling sooner and praised her for following her heart's desire. She told Ivy that she missed her dearly, but that she was also so proud of her, and she knew just how much Ivy had probably struggled with the decision to extend her time in Africa. In truth, Val was thrilled over Ivy's happiness. Ivy had struggled so much after Eli's accident, it was good to see her moving forward, despite his condition. She assured Ivy that Eli was still in good hands. She also assured her that Eli would be thrilled for her as well and she need not worry about things back home. She promised that she was still believing that a miracle would happen and promised that Eli would wake up — someday — though every day that passed with no change made it more and more difficult for her to hang onto that belief.

Ivy explained to Valerie that her team's sustainable farming efforts wouldn't become fully recognized until harvest time. She couldn't bear the thought of not seeing it through. Valerie, of course, supported her choices. Ivy confided in Val that her mother was angry with her and wanted her to come home, but she also confessed that her mom's anger hadn't swayed her decision in the slightest, and she still felt strongly that she was following God's will for her life.

"Your mom just misses you," Val told her. "She had you under her roof for nearly two decades. It's an adjustment for sure. I cried every night for the first three weeks Beau was in boot camp."

"I promised her I would call more, video chat more, and write more. I really had avoided it for the last few weeks because I was afraid of what she'd say," Ivy responded.

"And me too, I take it?"

Ivy laughed, "Maybe just a little."

Val didn't tell Ivy that she knew about her letter to Beau, and that she'd read it. Nor did she tell her she knew about her struggle to forgive Beau for what had happened to Eli, but she did tell her about Julia. Ivy remembered Julia. They'd been friends years ago. They lost touch when Julia moved away, and for Val's benefit, she expressed her excitement for Beau. Inside though, she wondered if Julia knew about Beau's history with girls after she left. If she didn't, what would happen if she found out? She shook the thought from her mind. She had to resist the urge to build a stockpile of ammo against him, because she knew if she had the ammo, she might not be able to resist using it.

Valerie filled Ivy in on all the news, shared all her stories from Beau's graduation and agreed to email pictures. She requested pictures of Zimbabwe in return, and the conversation turned to a pleasant discussion about the people and the culture there. They discussed the beauty of the landscape, the amazing church services, the pagan histories and the immense sensation that God's influence was welcome there. As the conversation waned, Ivy felt both a great relief and, at the same time, the weight of guilt on her back. This time, her guilt stemmed not from what others might think about her, but from the fact that, though she missed Eli, she didn't feel a desire to return home. For the moment, she was right where she wanted to be, and it terrified her.

~

Beau's rekindled relationship with Julia had moved at lightning speed over the course of the last nine days. They'd become inseparable. Valerie and Joe had adored Julia as a young girl, and it was easy to pick up where they left off, adoring her again as a young woman. The romance was burning intensely, and both Beau and Julia felt they were somehow making up for lost time.

They had shared a kiss on their second night together and their desires had heated quickly from there. Beau had shared similar moments with girls before, but this time, there was something powerfully different. This time, he felt it not just physically, but in his heart. This time, he was invested — though he tried not to be.

Julia knew she shouldn't have given into his advances so easily, but she couldn't seem to help herself. She was in love. He was leaving. She wanted something that felt real and, even if misguided, she thought giving him her body was the right choice.

As he prepared to leave for the school of infantry at Camp Pendleton, he began to feel uncertain about the longevity of his rekindled romance with Julia. Despite her reassurance that she was in it for the long haul, no matter where he traveled, the scars on his heart from their first breakup felt fresh when he thought about losing her again. He did his best to keep a wall around his emotions, even with her, though her presence had provided him with a few days of reprieve from his self-imposed life sentence of guilt. He hadn't felt a sense of freedom since the day he woke up in the hospital, but in her arms, he forgot about his reality for a little while and instead focused solely on her.

The morning of his departure was difficult. He and Julia planned to spend a couple of hours together, alone, before his parents drove them to the airport. He would be gone for eight weeks this time, then it was on to Camp Lejeune. Because of his future function as a Marine, his infantry training was set to last for a full fifty-nine days, even though he'd assured his mother he wasn't technically infantry, his job would require a more robust infantry training. From there, he'd be sent to train for his MOS in North Carolina, at his first duty station. He had packed his bags two days earlier and had placed his dress uniform into a garment bag. He knew he was supposed to check in wearing his uniform, but he also knew he wasn't supposed to travel in uniform, so that garment bag would become his carry on, just in case, and he hoped beyond hopes his uniform didn't look like garbage upon his arrival. He wanted to be ready. Though he had found a new reason to miss home, he was eager to run away from his mistakes and from his brother's broken body.

The goodbyes were bittersweet. Beau spent the better part of an hour in Eli's room, touching his things, talking to him and then scoffing at his own behavior. He saw the picture he'd taken to the hospital on Eli's dresser, tucked behind the frame of the mirror, on full display. He looked at it for a while, remembering the day it was taken, when things were simple.

"You don't mind if I take this, do you?" He looked back at Eli, "Clearly, that's a 'no.'" He rolled his eyes at his own reflex to ask. He grabbed the photo and held it with both hands, looking at it. "I guess this is it for a while, Eliza. I wish you were actually here to care." He patted Eli's chest and turned to walk away. But before he left the room, he turned back and placed his forehead on top of Eli's head. "I'll be right back with some socks," he whispered.

Beau promised to call as soon as he could and Julia promised to write, call, and message him every day. He thought he might get some time at Christmas, but he wasn't sure. He wasn't sure about much, except that he was walking into his time as a boot, a moniker given to new Marines fresh out of boot camp when they begin their tours. He already knew he'd remain a boot until he deployed, and he secretly hoped that time would come quickly.

~

SOI training was intense, but far less punishing than boot camp. Beau became known for his brooding, serious approach to training, but then again, that's how he'd come to approach life in general. He displayed a confident prowess in his tactical abilities, and his leadership was genuinely impressed by him. His tragedy-forced approach to life had, so far, served him well in his tenure as a Marine. His perpetual state of bitterness somehow aided his ability to follow orders and execute commands.

His training had been extended to longer than eight weeks, because it fell during the holiday season. After four days of liberty for Thanksgiving, four days for Christmas and four days for New Years, between which he was forced to report back to Camp Pendleton, Beau had spent lots of money on airfare and was now low on funds. Joe and Valerie had offered to pay for his flights home during the holidays, but Beau was too proud to let that happen and more than ready for the ordeal to be over. During his time home, he spent every minute he could with Julia, and she had become a fixture at the McKnight home. She'd even helped out with Eli's care, and Valerie had begun to encourage her attendance at church and at the women's ministry functions, in a way only Valerie McKnight could manage without coming off as pushy.

Beau had elected not to tell his parents about their opportunity to attend graduation this time, and he knew they'd be furious if they found out. So, he did tell them he'd received commendation as an honor grad for a second time. Joe and Valerie were beyond proud. Beau had found success again, just in a way completely different than the one they had expected. Success looked good on him, even if he rarely smiled.

Joe had taken the news and run with it this time, posting and messaging everyone he knew to talk about Beau's accomplishments. He loved bragging on his boy. Eventually, a news reporter got wind of the development and soon the family learned a news report had been reported in the local paper, seemingly offering Beau some redemptive press. The headline had read, *Local Man Excels In Military Service Following*

Tragic Accident. Nearly everyone in town knew about Beau's newfound success within a matter of days.

Beau's circumstances had improved, and things were looking up, but emotionally, he refused himself the luxury of feeling any delight in his successes. Every gift Eli had received for two Christmases remained unopened, gathering dust in his room, and Beau simply couldn't deal with that reality. No matter how much time passed, his feelings of guilt never dissipated and being around his family, around Eli, took him right back to that night.

Beau's MOS training would start immediately. Once he arrived in North Carolina, that training would last about eight weeks and then he'd begin working, right there at Camp Lejeune. Joe had agreed to drive Beau's truck all the way from Texas to Camp Lejeune, and then fly back. He relished the chance to see Beau in his new environment. Valerie had already begun packing some boxes of extra clothes and things Beau might want upon arriving at his new home. Every shirt she folded prompted tears. Julia had already started talking about flying out to see him, she just didn't know when, or how she'd pull it off financially.

Valerie suspected the physical nature of their relationship. Joe had taught his sons about the sanctity of marriage and the importance of purity as soon as they were old enough to know the birds and the bees, but somehow, it hadn't sunk in where Beau was concerned. As a result, Val bit her tongue every time Julia mentioned visiting Beau in North

Carolina. She knew she should voice her opposition, but she didn't want to risk pushing Beau further away.

Caught up in a whirlwind of change, Valerie found herself struggling to imagine a life without Beau under her roof. She also ached for Eli, who seemed stuck in a time warp. Yes, she was keeping his face shaved and his hair cut, but his life was passing him by as he slept and, she had to admit, hers was passing too. Now, with Joe's drive to North Carolina only days away, she'd found herself in a strange limbo between grief and relief. On the one hand, she was relieved that his life was moving forward, on the other she grieved both his absence and the fact that Eli's life had been lost to him — at least for now.

CHAPTER THIRTY-SIX

"Why you always got that look on your face, McKnight? Always be lookin' like somebody took a dump in your Cheerios." Cpl. Johnson gave Beau a jab to his arm. Johnson was a joker. Literally, everything was a joke to him, and he had a lot of ammunition when it came to Beau.

"Yeah, McKnight, your hangdog face is hard to look at. Makes me feel like I need to call your mama." Pfc. Andrew Mack laughed through his words. Andy was lovingly called Big Mack by pretty much everyone in the platoon, and he was arguably one of the smartest guys Beau had ever met, yet he was also one of the most country.

"Hangdog? What in God's name is a hangdog?" Johnson used a few expletives when he asked the question and then followed his question with a wisecrack about Andy's accent.

"Don't bring God into this. McKnight's ugly face of shame and dejection ain't God's fault." Andy reached into his pocket and pulled out a bag of candy. “Hey, Hangdog, you want some candy?” He dangled the bag in front of Beau and looked at Johnson, “This is how we cheer my baby sister up when she’s all sad-sack. Maybe it will work on ol’ Hangdog.”

Johnson cracked up as he responded, “Ol’ Hangdog. I like it Mack.” He smacked Andy’s back and turned to a few of the other guys and announced, “Hear ye, hear ye. McKnight’s sad, sorry, ugly hind parts have been renamed. He’s now Pfc. Hangdog.”

And just like that, on an ordinary Wednesday afternoon at Camp Lejeune, Beau McKnight’s face, which, when not in motion, resembled that of a scolded puppy, earned him the nickname “Hangdog.” He had no objections to the moniker, at least it wasn’t Big Mack, and he knew that even if he had objected, it wouldn’t have mattered. Like it or not, Hangdog would stick.

~

In the few months since Beau had been at Camp Lejeune, he had finished his MOS training and had become a member of the working force. He'd endured quite an adjustment period, struggling to successfully manage his own finances and his own time. He’d also learned that alcohol could be easily acquired, if one really wanted it, and most of the single Marines got really bored, really fast. As a result, he'd fallen into a routine of working and partying, within the confines of curfew that is.

Being stateside meant Beau was allowed to have a personal vehicle, a luxury many of his fellow Marines did not have. Because of this, he quickly became the unofficial chauffeur. No matter where he went, he was toting someone. Everyone was eager to get off base as often as they could.

Big Mack wasn't a partier, but he always seemed to be in the truck. Mack was always happy, had a ruddy complexion and a huge smile. He had become Beau's roommate on his first day in the barracks. Beau found him frustrating. He literally read his Bible for hours every day and it drove Beau crazy. He wondered how, of all people, with all kinds of habits, he had ended up with Andy and his Bible. But, Mack was also very witty and outspoken, which Beau appreciated. Everyone else in the platoon loved him for his accent and his sense of humor, his work ethic, his ability to come out on top in everything he did, and his tendency to preach in a relatively dramatic fashion whenever something was going wrong.

Despite the fact that his general state of chronic happiness got under Beau's skin, he was a good roommate. He didn't interfere with Beau's conversations on the phone, he would leave the room if Beau wanted to video chat with Julia, he kept his space neat and, in general, accommodated Beau in every way. He even bought snacks for them to share and seemed genuinely interested in Beau as a person, though he never pushed when Beau said he didn't feel like talking.

It had become Beau's turn to settle into a new normal. His routine was set and his new family was a group of strangers from all over the country, who'd each taken the challenge of becoming United States Marines. But, despite his brand-new life as an adult, he spoke to Valerie every single day. In part because she called him every day, and in part because he missed home, though he'd never admit it.

~

One bright, Tuesday morning at 0900, mail call brought with it a letter for Beau. When he looked at the return address, he saw it was from Julia. At first, he felt fear. Why would she write instead of just calling? It crossed his mind that this may be a Dear John letter. But then it dawned on him that he had just spoken to Julia the night before, and everything was fine. He took the letter back to his room and fell onto his only chair. He used the end of an ink pen to loosen the edge of the envelope, which felt strangely full. When he pulled out a paper and unfolded it at its creases, he found inside a narrow, gift-wrapped package. He didn't know if he should read the letter first, or open the package. But, curiosity got the better of him and he began to peel the paper away from his gift. Inside, he found a pregnancy test — a positive pregnancy test.

Suddenly, there was a ringing in his ears. He dropped the test on the floor and grabbed the letter. He couldn't focus on the words, but he read the words "I'm pregnant," written in loopy letters penned in green ink, surrounded by hearts, Xs and Os. Beau was too stunned to experience an emotion. He didn't know if he was happy or upset. He wasn't ready to be a father. He wasn't remotely close to the vicinity of being ready. He couldn't breathe, and was nearly hyperventilating when Andy came into the room. When Beau heard the door, he snatched the pregnancy test off the floor quickly and shoved it back into the envelope. He folded the letter and walked it over to his closet, which was secured by a combination lock. He unlocked the closet, put the letter inside, and proceeded to stare out the window as all the blood drained from his face.

“Are you okay?” Andy asked. He got no response. He then snapped his fingers, “Yo, Hangdog, are you in there?”

"Yeah, I'm fine." Beau answered him, but Andy knew he was lying.

"If you say so," Andy said.

"I do." Beau glared at him. He knew he should call Julia, but he didn't know what he would say to her. He knew she would want him to be happy, but he didn't feel happy. He might have felt happy, had he been ready. He wanted kids, just not yet. He wanted kids with her even, just not now. Beau shoved his hands in his pockets as he stormed out of the dorm room and headed down the hall. Andy stuck his head out and called after him to try and find out where he was going, but Beau ignored him. He passed by half a dozen of his friends, all of whom waved at him, while some tried to strike up a conversation or find out where he was headed. Beau ignored them all, leaving them turning to each other and speculating about what was going on.

Beau slogged all the way to his truck, got in and started it up, but then he just sat there. He put his forehead on the steering wheel, gripped the wheel with his strong hands, and let out a guttural yell. It was too much. He sat in his truck until it was time to go to the chow hall with his buddies. He didn't feel like eating, but he knew if he didn't show they would grow suspicious and ask more questions. That night, everyone noticed he was quieter than usual. Everyone noticed his crinkled forehead and the deep line of worry between his eyebrows. Andy was the only one with the guts to ask what was up, but Beau made short work of ignoring him. Just before curfew, Beau could feel his phone buzzing in his pocket. He pulled it out to discover that Julia was calling. He couldn't talk to her. He ignored her call and dropped his phone back into his pocket. He needed to sleep on the news. He needed to process what was happening. He needed time, or maybe, he wanted more time — time to pretend this wasn't happening.

Beau woke the next morning in a daze. He felt no better after a night's sleep than he had when he opened the letter. Julia had tried to call again, and the voicemail she left was endearing. She didn't sound upset, she didn't sound worried. As he listened to her message and heard her voice, she sounded confident — confident in both herself and in their relationship. She seemed assured. Beau went to his closet and read the letter again. In it, Julia affirmed what a great father he would make, how adorable their baby would be, and how much she already loved the new life growing inside her.

He played the voicemail on his phone once again, and though he was running out of time to get to PT, he wanted to call her. But, as he put the phone to his ear, Cpl. Johnson arrived at the door. Andy came out of the bathroom, with his toothbrush still in his mouth. He was shirtless when he asked "What's happening?"

"Word on the street is we're headed to Afghanistan." Johnson slapped the door frame with his hand and disappeared down the hallway. He was dressed in his PT gear, but he had a bounce in his step Beau had never seen before.

"For real?" Beau asked Andy. "How does he know?" Andy shrugged and turned to spit his toothpaste into the sink. "Double-time, we're cutting it close," Beau told him. He dropped his phone back onto his desk and proceeded to head out into the hallway. Andy followed behind him, tucking in his shirt as he ran.

~

By the end of the day, all anyone could talk about was the deployment. All Beau could think about was becoming a father, and then it dawned on him that he would have to break the deployment news not only to his parents, but to Julia as well. He decided, after brooding over his choices for an hour, that he would call Julia and omit the deployment news entirely during their first conversation about becoming parents. It seemed cruel to use that conversation as an opportunity to tell her he would be spending nine months in a war zone. Crueler still was the fact that he wanted to be in a war zone. He needed to be.

As he sat at his desk dialing her phone and rubbing his face with his hands, he tried his best to sound excited about her news. He knew he was faking it, and he knew it was probably wrong to fake it, but what good would it do for him to hurt her? What would it change if she knew the truth? He held the bridge of his nose with his thumb and forefinger, thinking about the fact that, even if he wanted to die, he couldn't — not now, not with a kid on the way. He cursed himself for being a screw-up. He cursed himself that his choices were now impacting Julia and would soon be impacting their baby. He cursed himself in general. As the phone rang, he wondered how long it would take for his panic to become acceptance and if his acceptance would ever become happiness at the prospect of having a child.

"Hello?" Julia answered. Her voice was crystal clear and sounded as upbeat as always.

"Hey you," Beau greeted her in his usual fashion.

"Hey to you too," Julia said. "What have you been up to? I get the feeling you've been busy."

"I have been. I've been busy opening my mail." Beau forced himself to smile as he said the words, because his mother had always told them that people can hear a smile.

Julia immediately let out a squeal, "So you're happy then? Are you so happy?"

"I think I'm still in shock!" Beau didn't want to flat out lie, so he thought shock was a better response.

Julia laughed, "Me too, actually. I panicked at first. It took me two whole weeks to get comfortable with the idea, and then I had an ultrasound and saw that little flicker of a heartbeat, and after that, I was the happiest girl in the world."

"An ultrasound? How far along are you?" Beau’s question was delivered like an alarm bell.

"I'm already over twelve weeks, into the second trimester already."

"What?" Beau asked emphatically, almost angrily, "How could you not tell me until now?"

"Because, Beau, I didn't know for sure," Julia snapped back. "I wanted to be absolutely sure. I didn't want to get you all riled up if there was nothing to be riled up about. I think it might have happened the night before you left."

Beau sighed. She'd made the right decision. "I get it. Sorry."

The conversation quickly turned to going public with the news. Julia told Beau she wasn't showing yet, but that she was really tired and had a weak stomach, especially when she smelled meat cooking, which didn't bode well for her work at the restaurant. She admitted that she'd been spending a lot of time with Val, and that she probably suspected something. "She's a smart lady, Beau," Julia said. "And she's got me going to church. For the last few weeks, I've wondered if lighting will strike me as I sit there, pregnant out of wedlock." She laughed. Beau didn't.

They decided to forego telling anyone just yet, least of all their parents. They would wait as long as they could to come clean, maybe that would give them time to think of a less painful way to break the news. Julia didn't think her parents would be too upset. Since their divorce, they spent most of their time trying to outdo each other on being the cool parent. But, Beau knew, without a doubt, that his parents, Joe especially, would go out of his mind and may even have a heart attack when he heard the news. "He's not going to be happy. I need to be far, far away for that conversation." When he heard himself say the words, he registered the fact that he also needed a plan to break the news, which was still fresh in his mind, about his deployment. On that front, he wasn't worried about his parents, but he was worried about telling his now pregnant girlfriend he'd probably miss the birth.

At chow that night, Beau's stomach was in knots. His brow had been furrowed nonstop for two days and Andy, who had an uncanny ability to discern things other people couldn't, pulled out a roll of Tums and tossed them across the table at Beau. Beau caught them and looked at Andy, nodding his thanks.

"You're even hangdoggier than usual, so I thought you could use those," Andy said drolly. Through their laughter, Beau's other buddies thanked Big Mack and his timing, heralding his antacid gift as "literally the best thing" they'd seen all week.

Beau pushed his plate away and opened the roll of Tums, popping two into his mouth before standing to his feet and bidding farewell to his friends with the raise of a single, strategic finger, a gesture that resulted in cackling laughter all around, laughter Beau could still hear ringing in his ears as he walked out into the night and headed back toward his barracks.

CHAPTER THIRTY-SEVEN

"Ninety days, Hangdog. Ninety days and we're supposed to be on our way to Okinawa, Japan. How long does pre-deployment training even last? I hate Asian food. I'd rather eat MREs." Andy was laid back on his bed, speculating about what was to be his first deployment. "I heard we won't even really know the exact day we're leaving until the day of. You think that's true?"

Beau shrugged. "I dunno. But something tells me you'll get plenty of MREs when we finally get to Afghanistan, so I wouldn't worry too much about the food — idiot." Beau was tough on Andy. From the outside looking in, he exhibited nothing but disdain for the man, but secretly, Beau really liked him. Andy made it almost impossible for Beau to hate him. Andy practically dragged the conversation out of him. Beau joked that he talked back to Andy so he could hear something besides Andy's voice all the time. Andy Mack was unlike anyone Beau had ever met. There was something about him that was magnetic. He almost glowed. Beau thought he was wired backward. He never seemed to worry about anything and when their whole platoon was taking heat, he seemed to have virtually no stress. Everything went right for Andy, and Beau both loved and loathed that fact. Being associated with Big Mack meant things, by association, seemed to go pretty well for him too.

“I’m going to try and get a couple days leave when my parents get here. They want to spend some days at the beach. They’re bringing my sister and her family and my little brother. Are you going to take leave?”

Beau nodded, “I’m going to try and go home for a few days.” Beau didn’t elaborate, but he needed to see Julia. They had to decide how long to wait before breaking the news to everyone that they’d soon be parents. Beau still felt uneasy every time he thought about it. In his mind, he’d relive all the times he and Julia had been together and beat himself up for not thinking it through in the big picture. “You’re such a screw-up,” he’d tell himself. “Can’t you do anything without it becoming some epic, life-altering catastrophe?” Then, he’d shake himself out of it and remember the sound of Julia’s voice when she talked about the baby. Beau was lost in thought, but Andy kept on talking.

“Earth to Hangdog, come in Hangdog,” Beau finally registered Andy’s words and snapped his response.

“What, for God’s sake, what?”

"I doubt He really cares if we order pizza or not, so long as we're thankful for it, but I do care. So, I'll ask again — do you want to order pizza?" Andy drew out each word of his question in a mocking manner.

"Mack, do you ever think about anything besides food and Jesus?"

"Of course I do, but right now, I'm thanking Jesus for pizza delivery. Are you in?"

"What do you think?" Beau responded.

"Good man." Andy was dialing before the words were out of his mouth. Beau shook his head, looking at Andy, the picture of peace. He sighed and shook his head again.

~

Beau sat across the dinner table from his parents on the very night they picked him up from the airport. He didn't want to waste time, he only had four days leave. All deploying Marines had been instructed to make financial preparations and to make end-of-life decisions, just in case. He slid the standard deployment power of attorney across the table so Valerie and Joe could get a good look at it.

"I am not ready for this." Valerie responded. But she read the document anyway.

"I want you guys to take care of my bills and stuff, I don't know if or when I'll have internet access and I need things to be good when I get back. Apparently, we get in big trouble if we don't pay our bills," he laughed.

"So do we," Joe added, to lighten the mood, "but nobody makes us do pushups."

"I have this form with all my bank info. My only real bills are my cellphone and truck insurance. Y'all need to sign this power of attorney. I want to go over this will thing too."

"Oh, good Lord. A will? I mean, I know it's smart and all, but my mama heart can't take this." Valerie's right hand was on her chest.

"He has insurance now, Val. And the government pays a gratuity for people killed in action. This is all part of the deal." Joe put his arm around his wife and tried to play it cool and practical, though truthfully, the discussion was emotionally draining for him too.

Beau took a deep breath, his dad was flipping through the will, scanning the pages. He looked up at Beau, and then back toward the paper.

"What am I seeing here?" Beau remained silent, his hand over his mouth. "What does this mean, 'surviving child/children'?" He stared at Beau through big eyes.

"What? Let me see that." Val snatched the will from Joe's hand and began skimming it.

"I want my insurance money spread out. There's money for you and there's money for Julia and my unborn baby." Beau hadn't originally planned to tell his parents right away, but when he was preparing his paperwork for deployment, he realized it would be best to get it all out in the open early.

Dead silence filled the room. Joe rubbed his face. Valerie's mouth hung open.

"Are you saying, is Julia, is this what I think it is?" Valerie asked in a tone that swelled with panic.

Beau nodded his head. "It is," he said.

Joe cussed under his breath, "What are you saying, Beau? Of all the…" He took a breath and rubbed his face, hard, and then took another breath to collect himself. "Son?"

"Julia's pregnant, just over three months." His words hung in the air like a wet rag, heavy and messy.

"Are you sure?" Valerie responded. "How long have you known? Why didn't you tell us?" She raised her voice a little. "How did this happen?"

"Good Lord, Val. We know how it happened. I just want to know why it happened, when God knows Beau knew exactly how to prevent it." He was looking at Val, and talking about Beau as if he weren't right there.

"It just happened, okay. I found out two weeks ago. We haven't told anybody until right now."

"Do you know how hard it is to raise a kid, Beau?" Joe asked in earnest, as if the statement could turn back time.

"It's too late for that, Joe. It's already done." Exasperated, Valerie spoke curtly.

"Do you think I wanted this?" Beau was exasperated too. "I didn't want this. I'm not ready to be a father. I know that. I'm a screw-up. Is that what you want to hear? Eli's coma was preventable too, wasn't it, and that didn't stop me either, did it?" He was practically yelling.

"Stop!" Valerie shouted back. "Don't you dare!" She stood up and walked to Beau's side of the table. "Ready or not, this is happening, right? And," she looked at Joe, "every child is a gift. You might not have planned it, but that won't stop you, or us, from loving this baby more than anything in the world. Right, Joe?"

They all sat in silence for a while, gaining their composure and processing yet another new reality. Valerie was determined to make the most of the next four days, despite the weight of this news. Between pre-deployment training and his actual deployment, she wouldn't see her son again for at least a year, and the last thing she wanted was to leave things broken.

"I have another question." At this point, Beau thought he had nothing to lose. "I want Julia to come live here while I'm gone." He looked at his parents with pleading eyes. "She's alone over there in that apartment. All that her roommates do is party, and she doesn't feel the greatest. She's not sleeping well. I just think she'd be better off here, with you guys. Is that a possibility?"

Valerie and Joe sat in stunned silence. The past half hour had been a sensory overload all by itself, and now this. "We love Julia, we do, and I'm getting to know her. But we don't exactly know her well enough to let her live here, Beau..." Valerie responded, but left her statement open-ended.

"Then this is your chance to really get to know her." Beau looked at his mother, "She's carrying your grandchild, after all."

Valerie immediately looked to Joe. "Did you hear that, Joe? Our grandchild," She spoke the words as if she were telling herself for the first time.

"I heard," Joe responded drolly. "It's a lot to process in one day, son. Let us talk it over…"

"And pray about it," Val interjected.

"Fine," Beau's response was short, but not rude. He stood up from the table, leaving all his paperwork spread out, and retreated upstairs to call Julia. On his way to his room, he paused outside Eli's door. He peered inside and noticed how thin his brother looked. He looked around the room and noticed that his mother had hung some pictures of Ivy in Zimbabwe on the walls. He thought it was pointless, but he admired his mom's tenacity. He walked to the chair beside Eli's bed and sat down. He stared into his brother's face, pale and sunken.

"I think it's time you wrapped this whole coma thing up, okay? Because, you're going to be an uncle and I'm definitely going to need you. Okay? Please?" He put his hand on Eli's arm and rested his forehead on the middle rung of the safety rail. He felt a knot form in his stomach and he did his best to conjure a memory of Eli from their childhood, something happy. He feared forgetting who they'd been. When he thought of Eli, he wanted to remember who he used to be — not this. But, lately, when he closed his eyes, all he could see was the coma. He squeezed Eli's hand and whispered again, "Please?" As he rose to his feet and turned to leave the room, he looked back over his shoulder and almost mentioned Afghanistan, but he changed his mind and shook himself back into his fortress of bitterness and shame. "He can't hear you anyway," he told himself as he made the short walk to his own room. This day had been long, but the night would be longer as he lay awake thinking about an uncertain future.

~

Julia and Beau sat in the waiting room at the Women's Health Clinic, holding hands and discussing her pending move to his parent's house. "Are you sure they're okay with it? Is it too much?"

"I'm sure this is all too much, so this will be par for the course." Beau was only half joking.

"I could just stay where I am, I'll survive."

"I don't want you to just survive. Trust me. Nobody will be better to you than my mom." He put his arm over her shoulder. "What did your parents say?"

"Mom seems excited. Dad was, I don't know, in shock maybe. He used it as an opportunity to talk about my insurance coverage. Apparently, his insurance will cover my health care until I'm twenty-three, as long as I'm a student, but it won't pay for the pregnancy. It costs me about a hundred bucks every time I come here."

"Wow!" Beau was stunned. The cost of having a baby hadn't even crossed his mind. "I can cover today's visit. You made this appointment for my benefit anyway."

She hugged him tightly. "I wanted you to see your baby, and hear his heartbeat before you deploy." Beau could hear the tears in her voice.

He hugged her back, but said nothing.

When the nurse called Julia's name, both she and Beau made their way back to an exam room, where an ultrasound tech instructed Julia to climb onto a table. After Julia lifted her shirt to expose her stomach, the tech tucked a paper sheet into the top of Julia's pants.

"Okay you two, are you ready? I heat the gel, but it might still feel a little cold." She began pushing the ultrasound probe into Julia's abdomen, steering it around and pausing occasionally to capture an image. "We might not be able to accurately determine the sex today, of course, but that won't stop me from looking!"

"It's a boy," Julia said with total confidence. "I just know it."

The technician continued to push the probe around, and when the baby's profile showed up on the screen, Beau dropped Julia's hand and walked toward the screen, his eyes fixated on the tiny figure, wiggling and squirming before his eyes.

"Do you see that flicker?" the technician asked, as she used her finger to direct Beau's eyes to the tiny pulse of light. "That's your baby's heartbeat."

Beau felt a cold sweat break out on the back of his neck as his heartrate increased. His eyes grew wet as he watched the new life forming inside Julia's womb.

"Wow!" he whispered. As he watched the screen, Julia watched his face. She wasn't sure if it was terror or nausea written across his forehead. She knew he wasn't ready, but he valiantly played the part for her benefit. She didn't yet know how to decipher his mannerisms. Was he upset? And just as she began to agonize over his ability to handle fatherhood, he began to smile. A broad, genuine, smile spread across Beau's face. A smile she'd not seen since middle school, a smile he thought he'd forgotten how to form. "Look at that, Jules." He turned to look at her, smiling, with tears in his eyes. Julia watched him watch their baby and took note of the fact that under his angry, macho, unemotional façade beat a tender heart, and she fell in love with him all over again. Two more days together before his deployment would be two million days too few.

CHAPTER THIRTY-EIGHT

After Beau returned to Camp Lejeune, he spent just over two months preparing for his journey to Okinawa, where he and his Marine brothers would spend about a month training for deployment before heading to Afghanistan. During that two months, he'd spent at least an hour every day listening to Andy talk, sometimes more. He was beginning to feel like he knew more about Andy Mack than he knew about himself. Andy had made it his personal mission to find the human parts of Beau McKnight, but Beau had been having no trouble deflecting his efforts.

One Sunday morning, the week before they were scheduled to fly out, Beau wanted nothing more than to sleep in. He wanted a day to wallow in his guilt. He'd spoken to his mom on Saturday and learned that Eli had been diagnosed with some sort of infection and was being treated with IV antibiotics. She didn't seem alarmed, but Beau took the news like the weight of the world was on his shoulders. That same morning, Andy was up early, as usual, fruitlessly trying to be quiet.

"Mack!" Beau growled.

"Sorry, I tried to be quiet."

Beau threw a pillow at him, "You're a churchy guy, why don't you get out of here and go to chapel or something?"

"I won't go to chapel. Want to go to breakfast instead?" Andy asked in his typical, irritatingly joyful tone.

Beau sat up in bed, angrily, "No! Are you nuts? Dear God, why don't you, of all people, go to chapel?" The question had been rhetorical, but Andy ran with it.

"Because I've been to chapel and it's a waste of time. It's nothing but a doctrine of tradition. Most churches are these days, you know. Most churches teach and preach stuff that isn't even in the Bible and most Christians eat that stuff up, because Christians these days are only Christians if it's convenient. They prefer tradition to truth, because the truth holds them accountable while tradition allows them to cop out. I would rather get my revelation right from the source than get a bunch of twisted mess." Andy sounded fired up.

Beau had never heard that tone. "Whoa, Mack, I didn't know you had that in you." He was wide awake now. "So, you're saying church is crap then? We may get along after all."

"No, of course not, church can be a great thing, but there are lots of churches getting it all wrong. Instead of getting truth from the Word, they get truth from years of what other people have said is the truth. It makes me crazy how many people call themselves believers, but then they use tradition as a cop out for their own responsibility when it comes to their faith."

Beau had started to get dressed as Andy ranted on about, what he called, the fallacy of modern religion and how much of a mess many well-meaning people had made over the years.

"Such as?" Beau was curious now. What in the world could the Jesus fanatic and chronically joyful Andy "Big" Mack find wrong with the Christian majority? "You rebel, you."

"Well, how about that God puts disease on people to teach them things? That's just nuts. It totally undermines Christ. It's an old covenant, plagues mentality and it minimizes literally every work of healing Christ did. I mean, if you really believe God makes you sick to teach you lessons, then why go to the doctor and try to get well? Wouldn't that be going against God's will if He wills you to be sick? Why not just stay in God's will by staying sick? It's so twisted."

Beau actually laughed. Andy made a lot of sense. He'd heard people say that Eli's coma was serving some purpose, and it infuriated him. It was somehow cathartic to hear someone else echo the same opinion.

"The Bible says Satan comes to steal, kill and destroy and Jesus came to give life to the fullest. Not one time in Scripture did Christ make someone sick, not once. He healed. Period. And yet, modern churches all over America are teaching people that we're powerless against diseases and that they're somehow God's will and to give in to them is some kind of noble act. It's totally unbiblical. God does not want us to be sick, that's why the Word says, 'By His stripes we were healed.' Past tense, Hangdog, past tense." By the time Andy was done with his spiel, he and Beau were walking down the hall of their barracks, headed to the chow hall for breakfast. Beau had never heard Andy get serious, but he was serious about this.

"You know, most Christians don't even know this is happening. They don't see it. It's been sneaking in for centuries. We've completely killed the goodness of God and Christ's sacrifice with our unbelief. We've completely negated our role and our responsibility in the relationship. God gave man dominion over the earth, and Christ literally died to pay for every single grace and gift of God — to completely atone for us in every way, yet we just continue to beg and plead with God to do things He's already done, all because we don't have the faith to take Him at His word or the guts to take the responsibility for our own faith. If people would just read the Word, believe it, and do it, we could fix so much of what's wrong with the world, but we muddle it and turn the power God gave us into a farce. Most people don't even study the Bible for themselves, and when they do, they overcomplicate it or write their own doctrine into it."

Beau listened to Andy's spiritual rant for the better part of an hour. He watched as the man stuffed an insurmountable number of pancakes into his face, as he preached to Beau about everything that was wrong with modern religion and how Jesus was being sold short and how people were missing huge blessings because they refused the take the Bible at face value, and on and on he went.

Though Beau simply shook his head and laughed at Andy's rants, he had to admit, they made total sense. The only time he'd ever heard something similar, delivered with the same kind of clarity, was when his mom streamed a podcast of her Colorado preacher, but he didn't want to mention it and open a whole new can of worms.

~

The night before they were scheduled to fly out to Okinawa, both Beau and Andy lay awake in the darkness. Both lost in their own thoughts about the months to come. Both focused on completely different things.

The only sounds in the room were the crickets chirping outside until Beau broke the silence with an unexpected confession, "I put my twin brother into a coma on the night we graduated high school and I got my girlfriend pregnant right before I came here. She found out yesterday that it's a boy." Beau couldn't believe his own ears when he said the words. What was he thinking? His words shattered the darkness — he had blurted them out with no filter. It was almost like he couldn't help himself. Up until this moment, he'd told no one.

Andy waited in silence for a few seconds before responding. He was anticipating more info, info that didn't come. "Dude, that was… abrupt." Andy had been prying into

Beau's life for months, getting nowhere, and suddenly, he'd gotten two huge disclosures that, by all rights, he had no business knowing about.

"Just forget I said that, okay?" Beau rolled over onto his side.

"If I said okay, it would be a lie, and I don't lie. So, you might as well tell me about it." Andy was, indeed, bluntly honest.

"I'm a screw-up. That's all you need to know."

"I don't buy that. You have two awards on your desk that blow that theory out of the water and I've watched you master literally everything we've done. You're almost as good as I am," he joked.

Beau laughed a little as he spoke, "You know what, let's just call it a night."

"Alright, I guess. But I warn you, tomorrow's flight is long and the plane is enclosed. You won't be able to escape." Andy made a clicking sound with his tongue against his back teeth, as if he were a cowboy on a horse.

"Whatever you say, Big Mack," Beau's comment was thick with sarcasm as he closed his eyes against the night, willing sleep to come quickly.

~

Somewhere over the Pacific, after an exhausting layover in San Diego, Beau told Andy about Eli. He left out the details, but the story was out. He even showed Andy the picture he carried of him and Eli, looking out at the sunset, shoulder to shoulder. Then, in Okinawa, laying in the dirt during an overnight training in the field, he grudgingly opened up about Julia, his eighth grade heartache, and the son they'd have in a few short months. Training passed far more quickly than any of the Marines had expected, and by the end of it all, as much as Beau had wanted to dislike him, he and Andy had developed a true friendship. Beau continued to pretend Andy was a pest and Andy continued to scratch away at the wall Beau had built around himself.

By the time they had boots on the ground in Afghanistan, Andy knew everything there was to know about what had happened with Eli. He also knew Julia, in a manner of speaking, and he'd heard all about Beau's parents and even Ivy. It had been a long road to travel, and Andy had used every mile to pester Beau into offering details he was most reluctant to give. He'd asked question after question. Beau had wanted to punch him in the face, but at the same time, he felt better. His time in the Marines had become a double life. He played one part at home and another at work. Somehow, talking to Big Mack felt like a weight lifted off his chest.

Beau had grown to love the man. Andy had taken every word he told him in stride. He didn't judge him. He didn't behave differently toward him. He treated Beau exactly the same, but better somehow. Beau had decided during their training that he didn't want to go to his grave without someone near him knowing who he really was. Some days, Beau still wanted to die. He wanted to become someone different in the eyes of the people back home, a hero and not a screw up. He wanted his pain and his guilt to go away. He was so tired of who he'd become. Other days, he thought about Julia and the baby and making a new life with them, and he knew he had something to live for. On those days, the thought of death terrified him. He was tormented by his own conscious, and Andy Mack was the only one who knew it. Andy also kept his mouth shut. He held Beau's secrets as if they were his own and that alone earned him Beau's respect.

It became obvious after a while that Andy was the real deal. He actually practiced what he preached, a man of his word. He believed every word he said when it came to the spiritual facets of life, and he had fewer doubts than anyone Beau had ever met, and everyone else seemed to see that, too. There was a Buddhist and a Hindu in their platoon, Puri and Grover, and even they listened to Big Mack when he talked about Scripture. He was part of the group, but somehow separate from them. He was unique. On bad days, a few of the other guys would go to Andy and ask him questions about his faith. Somehow, it made them feel better and Andy saw it as an opportunity to retell, what he believed to be, the best news he could ever tell anyone. Other guys, though, mocked Andy for his faith — but Andy didn't care at all. He seemed completely unfazed by it, so much so, that he robbed his mockers of their fun without lifting a finger.

Beau still found it impossible to embrace the idea of ultimate forgiveness, let alone a God who wanted good things for him. And yet, as the days inched by, he found himself more and more drawn to Andy and his Bible thumping. One afternoon, as their platoon prepared for an upcoming convoy, Beau turned the tables on Andy.

"So, of all places, how did you end up in the Marines?" Beau finished securing a load of ammunition onto a heavy cargo truck and jumped down onto the packed dirt. When he did, a cloud of dust formed in the air around his feet.

"Believe it or not, God told me to join." Andy smiled through his response.

"Be serious," Beau demanded.

"I am. I was planning to go to trade school to become a welder, but one night, I was reading the Bible and it dawned on me that I hadn't asked God what He wanted me to do with my life. I was just choosing my own way. So, I vowed not to choose until I knew what He wanted."

"And God himself told you to join the Marine Corps?" Beau rolled his eyes.

"No, really, He did." Andy grunted his words, as he hoisted a crate onto his shoulder. Beau pulled some ratchet straps from a pile. "I was laying in bed one night, asking God to use my life where He wanted it, and as plain as I can hear your voice, I heard the Spirit say, 'You're a Marine.' I didn't know I wanted to be a Marine until I heard that, but the next day, I woke up feeling like a million bucks, one hundred percent certain that I would serve a purpose as a Marine. Crazy, huh?"

"To put it mildly," Beau replied. But, he believed Andy. There was no falseness in him.

1400, Islamic State of Afghanistan / 4:30 am, Longview Texas:

The convoy spanned about a mile and consisted of nearly a hundred vehicles, each carrying weapons, fuel, food and personnel. They'd moved at a snail's pace since 0500 two days earlier, not for lack of effort, but for lack of appropriate terrain. For Beau, the virtual lack of motion caused feelings of vulnerability. They were sitting ducks and everyone knew it. Tensions were high, especially among the first timers. It dawned on Beau that he'd been training for this experience for almost a year and somehow he still felt unprepared. Several of the trucks, each carrying fifty tons of weapons and ammo, had become bogged down in the soft earth and mobility had become nearly impossible as they slowly made their way to a recently-acquired forward operating base in the Nahri Saraj District. Beau, a gunner, manned a mounted machine gun, perched atop an MRAP. They'd all learned that combat logistics convoys carried more crew-served weapons than a whole infantry company combined, and they suspected the enemy knew the same.

1427, Islamic State of Afghanistan / 4:57 am, Longview Texas:

The convoy commander had relayed reports of insurgents moving in on the area, and as a result, all eyes were on the horizon and the entire convoy fell nearly silent. About a hundred meters to the west, a mortar smashed into the ground, propelling a cloud of dust into the air and prompting immediate action on the part of the convoy.

"We have incoming!" Beau yelled into the MRAP, to Andy, who was their driver, their dismounts and their vehicle commander. Almost as soon as the words were out of his mouth, another mortar dropped at twenty-five meters to the west, and then another at twenty. "Incoming!" Beau shouted at the top of his lungs. His heart racing, he aimed his gun toward the direction of the incoming attack. "I see movement, just over that first ridge!" The sun beat down on him as, through the dust, he could see a short line of insurgent vehicles forming a makeshift wall. "They're up to something! I can see it!" Beau yelled it out, to anyone who might be listening.

The lead vehicle had not budged, frozen in time. From inside his vehicle, Beau could hear the radio, muffled voices and commands, "What are they doing? Why aren't they moving? Push, somebody tell six to push!"

Within what felt like seconds, Beau heard the gunner in the lead MRAP yell back, "I got 'em, too!" Beau looked back toward the west where he'd first spotted the enemy, he heard small arms fire in the distance and turned to see dust rising from somewhere near the rear of the convoy. His heart was beating at a rate he didn't think possible. This was the job he'd wanted, the job he'd volunteered for, it's what he was trained to do — but training isn't enough to negate the adrenaline associated with a Marine's first deployment, his first real fight.

He heard his vehicle commander yelling, "Push, push, push through! Do not stop!" There was endless radio chatter, and an endless symphony of rat-a-tat-tat as insurgents shot in the general direction of the convoy, too far away to inflict any real harm.

Another mortar resulted in a cacophony of sound that left Beau's ears ringing, "Ten meters, if that!" Beau yelled. "Two of their vehicles are moving!"

He heard his VC yelling, "Keep your head down! Give me dismounts, three hundred meters east!" Everything was loud and fast-paced. He looked toward the rear of the convoy again and squinted into the rising dust. He couldn't tell what was happening. Was it an ambush?

"Six, for the love of God, move!" He heard the convoy commander's voice over the radio.

And then, without warning, he heard the gunner ahead of him cry out, "RPG!" The flash of light was blinding, the heat from the explosion burned his skin as he reflexively turned away from the blast.

When he turned back, all he could see was flames, smoke and carnage. It was the stuff of nightmares. He couldn't hear, he couldn't breathe. As he righted himself, he heard screams coming from the lead vehicle. "They're hit! They're hit!" Beau yelled, as though he was the only one who saw what was happening. The Marines on the ground were scrambling. The scene was surreal. Another mortar round struck the ground fifty meters to Beau's right. Through the dust, Beau could see about a dozen men progressing toward the convoy. He could hear his enemy yelling in the distance, seemingly celebrating their successful RPG attack. Out of nowhere, the pinging sound of bullets against armor alerted Beau that his target was moving closer.

Dismounts moved in on the lead vehicle, quickly removing any weapons that were still intact and checking for wounded. He heard one of the men on the ground yell, "One casualty, two wounded! They're hitting the front and the back of the convoy, they're trying to pin us in!"

1449, Islamic State of Afghanistan / 5:19 am, Longview Texas:

Beau snapped back into the present, and from inside his vehicle he heard, "Wake up, McKnight!" His vehicle commander was screaming over the chaos. "If you have positive ID, engage!" He cussed at Beau and Beau turned his weapon on the approaching insurgents, he fired in three round bursts. He saw one man fall, and then the others scattered. He heard the call for air support cracking through the radio.

Off to his right again, he heard a faint voice cry out, "Incoming!" The mortar struck no more than ten meters from

Beau's vehicle, shrapnel spread in all directions, tearing into the ground, ricocheting off armor and careening in a clamor of noise so deafening that, at first, Beau didn't notice his wounds. He moved to return to his gun, but could barely lift his right arm. As he looked down, he saw blood running down over his knuckles, and then, the pain. He cried out and fell backward off the gunner seat.

He couldn't form words, he continued to cry out in pain. His VC turned toward him and yelled out, "He's taken shrapnel!" He turned and yelled out his window, and then got on the radio. Andy turned to look at Beau, who had shards of jagged metal protruding from his neck above his collarbone, from his right shoulder and from his bicep.

"Hangdog, you still with us?" Andy yelled his question, knowing full well Beau was very much alive.

"It hurts!" Beau yelled, grabbing at his neck with both his hands.

"Don't touch it!" Andy yelled, looking over his shoulder periodically. "Air support is coming! They called medevac!" He had no idea how severe Beau's wounds were, but he knew that shrapnel in the neck likely put him at high risk for severe bleeding.

Beau cried out again, writhing in pain. His head ached from the impact, his ears were ringing. The battle raged on around him as dismounts provided cover fire and truck crews worked to move weapons and materials to other vehicles. The mission must remain intact! "I'm going to see to him," Andy yelled out and immediately climbed out of the driver's seat. They weren't moving yet anyway.

The vehicle commander was busy on the radio, but forcefully yelled, "Be ready to move!" Andy could tell that Beau was on the edge of consciousness. He didn't seem to be losing too much blood, but it was clear his pain level was at a maximum. Andy assumed he had a concussion, but couldn't tell for sure.

"Hang in there, buddy. You're going to be fine." Andy grabbed Beau's left hand, partly to comfort him, but also to keep him from making his wounds worse.

Beau looked at him, and growled through gritted teeth. "Is it bad?"

In typical Big Mack fashion, Andy tried to lighten the moment. He leaned in towards Beau and said, "Nah, your perfect dimples are still intact. And, you know, they say chicks dig scars," Andy winked at his friend. As usual, he seemed to be at peace, handling the chaos in a way no one else around him could fathom. But Beau wasn't quite cognizant enough to get the joke, and he cried out in pain once again. "Let's pray okay, do you wanna pray? I'm gonna pray." Andy's response in any crisis was prayer. He was going to pray whether Beau wanted it or not. He didn't know another way to respond.

1452, Islamic State of Afghanistan / 5:22 am, Longview Texas:

"I don't care," Beau screamed in Andy's face. "Pray, don't pray, I don't give a... he cried out again, spitting and cursing, as the VC began shouting at Andy to return to his post. Andy began to pray, even as he moved back to the driver's seat, but Beau stopped him short, using his left arm to snatch at Andy's sleeve. "My brother!" he screamed. "Don't pray for me, pray for my brother!" He grunted, gnashing his teeth in pain, his eyes rolling back into his head briefly as Andy began again.

From the driver's seat, Andy called out to God at the top of his lungs, yet he asked for nothing. There was noise coming from all directions, but Andy's voice could be heard above the chaos, thanking God for His promises, for protection, for Christ and his sacrifice that guaranteed healing, for the promise of answered prayers — and then he commanded, with force and authority, that Eli wake from his coma, that his mind be restored, that his health be as perfect as God intended. He screamed scripture, as loud as his lungs would allow, his voice was full of anger as he shouted down the influences of Satan and blanketed the convoy with the presence of the Holy Spirit. It was a prayer unlike any Beau had ever heard, though his consciousness waned for much of it. The power was palpable and obvious, even to the VC, who had never been a religious man. Andy finished his prayer with a shout, "All things in Jesus name!" Almost immediately, the mortars stopped, the gunfire ceased and the sound of choppers could be heard in the distance. The VC held the radio, awestruck and speechless for the first time in his life. "They're on their way," Andy said as he turned toward Beau, strangely calm and full of certainty, "It's going to be okay, bud." The sound of Andy's voice was muffled in Beau's ears as darkness closed in around him.

~

1453, Islamic State of Afghanistan / 5:23 am, Longview Texas:

Valerie was up early. Instead of heading straight downstairs for coffee like usual, she stopped off at Eli's room instead. She had been restless throughout the night, worried about Beau, worried about Eli, and doing her best to trust that God was still good. She looked at the clock, thinking about Beau in the middle of his workday halfway around the world. She wondered what he was doing, if he was safe, and if he'd found some peace. She sat in the chair next to Eli's bed, as she'd done so many times before, and she took his hand. She ran her thumb over the back of his hand, feeling the youth in his skin. As she held his hand in hers, her head bowed against the bedrail, she felt his fingers move.

She jumped, startled by the movement. She thought perhaps it was a fluke, a reflex, but then his fingers moved again. Val jumped to her feet, watching Eli's fingers like a hawk, as if they held the keys to her future. When his leg shifted beneath his sheet, her heart leapt inside her chest. She hadn't seen him move like that since before the accident— "That's no reflex," she told herself. She walked around the bed to his right side and put a hand on his shoulder, "Eli?" she whispered. "Eli, it's time to wake up."

His eyes opened immediately, but slowly, as if he'd just stirred from a good night's sleep. "Mom?" he spoke through dry, cracked lips, as he began shifting in his bed. Valerie ran to the door of his room and began screaming for Joe. She sprinted back to Eli's bedside. "What's going on?" he asked, clearly, smoothly, without any sign of distress. His eyes were bloodshot, and he moved his head slowly as he glanced around the room, blinking forcefully against the glow of the bedside lamp.

Joe appeared in the doorway at a dead sprint, panicked. What had happened? What was wrong with Eli? "Val, what's wrong? What's happening?" He shouted into the room. His heart was pounding in his chest like a bass drum. As his eyes adjusted to the light, Julia appeared in the doorway behind him, rubbing the sleep from her eyes in a daze, having been awakened by Val's screams. Joe rubbed his face with his hands, and when he had gathered his wits and calmed his panic enough to think, he saw Val, weeping and laughing at the same time, as she stood next to Eli, who was awake — wide awake! "Eli!" He called out as he ran to his son's bedside, touching him, rubbing his head, as tears flowed over his cheeks in a cascade of gratitude. Julia stepped into the room and covered her mouth with both hands. Tears formed in her eyes, she was frozen in place. Val was crying so hard that the sound of her voice, thanking God through her tears, was nothing more than a sob.

Val and Joe flanked Eli's bed, both weeping tears of joy, both relishing in the fact that as they hugged Eli, he was lifting his frail arms in an attempt to hug them back, responding to their love, their touch, their care for the first time in more than two years.

"You've been asleep, son." Valerie wasn't sure how to answer his question. "You've been asleep for a long, long time."

"What? Asleep? No I wasn't." Eli seemed confused, but he was all there. It was him, fully, vividly. He saw Julia at the foot of his bed and struggled to place her face. She was familiar, but not familiar enough to be standing in his bedroom. As his memory began to push her identity forward in his mind, he became aware that he was missing something. "Where's Beau?" He asked, looking around the room, as if he expected to see his brother's face. "Ivy." He spoke her name aloud, as if he was remembering her face, but he didn't ask where she was, at least not yet.

Valerie glanced at Joe, they both knew Ivy would never forgive herself for this. She looked back at Eli and said, "Don't worry about anything right now." Eli was trying to sit up in his bed, clearly shaken but achingly alive.

"How do you feel?" Joe asked, as he helped Eli sit up a little straighter in his bed.

"Hungry," Eli answered, and Val burst into laughter through an onslaught of happy tears.

The Hangdog Trilogy Continues in Book Two,

~Hangdog II— Rebirth~

AUTHOR'S NOTE

Thus far in my life, I have yet to do anything one hundred percent flawlessly. This book is no exception. I have done my best to present accuracy and continuity in every line, but if you search for mistakes, you'll likely find them.

I should also add that this is a work of fiction. Names, characters, events and incidents are either the products of my imagination or used in a fictitious manner. Any resemblance to actual persons, living or dead, or actual events is purely coincidental.

WHAT I BELIEVE

As this is a work of *Christian* fiction, I would be remiss not to share the greatest news I've ever received – Christ. I believe in the One living God, and Jesus Christ as God in the flesh. I believe Christ died on the cross at the hands of sinful man to redeem me (all of us) from our sin and to restore our perfect relationship with the Father. I believe in *every* promise of Scripture. I believe in miracles – I've lived them. I believe God wants to bless us – I walk in it. I believe He wants us to live lives full of joy. I believe He wants the best for us. And I believe loving others means sharing this news, come what may.

THE PLAN OF SALVATION

Accepting this gift is simple – Once you've chosen to trust Christ as your Savior, and you truly believe in your heart that God loves you, that He sent His son, Jesus, to die as redemption for your sins, and that Christ rose again to conquer the grave, all you have to do is confess that belief.

"[9] *If you declare with your mouth, "Jesus is Lord," and believe in your heart that God raised him from the dead, you will be saved.* [10] *For it is with your heart that you believe and are justified, and it is with your mouth that you profess your faith and are saved." Romans 10:9-10*

Once you've done these things, it's time to live as a Christ follower. It's challenging, but it's the most amazing, rewarding adventure I've ever been on. Get into the Bible, find like-minded people, and take active steps to resist sin and to grow in your faith. Once you see what God has in store for your life, you, too, will want to shout it from the rooftops – I guarantee it.

Made in the USA
Lexington, KY
06 August 2018